Dagger's Edge

Shadow unbuckled her belt and slid one of her matched dagger sheaths free. She handed the dagger in its sheath to Jael.

"That's for you," Shadow said. "Go on, draw it, but be careful."

Jael cautiously drew the blade from its sheath, then gasped involuntarily. She had never seen anything like the dagger; its strange pale metal was unaccountably light. What astonished Jael was the dagger's feeling of *rightness* in her hand, as if she grasped something alive that welcomed her touch.

"Look at the edge on that," Shadow sighed. "You could cut a sunbeam in half with that edge . . ."

Praise for
ANNE LOGSTON'S
SHADOW NOVELS:

"Entertaining . . . plenty of magic, demons, and other dangers."
—*Science Fiction Chronicle*

"Shadow is bright, cheerful and charming . . . a lass who'll steal your heart and your wallet with equal verve."
—SIMON R. GREEN, bestselling author of *Robin Hood, Prince of Thieves*

"A highly entertaining ⟨...⟩ mor. Logston has a def⟨...⟩ make medieval fantasie⟨...⟩

"Thoroughly satisfying!⟨...⟩

D1010103

Ace Books by Anne Logston

SHADOW
SHADOW HUNT
SHADOW DANCE
GREENDAUGHTER
DAGGER'S EDGE

DAGGER'S EDGE

ANNE LOGSTON

ACE BOOKS, NEW YORK

If you purchased this book without a cover, you should be aware that this book is stolen property. It was reported as "unsold and destroyed" to the publisher, and neither the author nor the publisher has received any payment for this "stripped book."

This book is an Ace original edition,
and has never been previously published.

DAGGER'S EDGE

An Ace Book/published by arrangement with the author

PRINTING HISTORY
Ace edition/April 1994

All rights reserved.
Copyright © 1994 by Anne Logston.
Cover art by John Steven Gurney.
This book may not be reproduced in whole or in part,
by mimeograph or any other means, without permission.
For information address: The Berkley Publishing Group,
200 Madison Avenue, New York, NY 10016.

ISBN: 0-441-00036-3

ACE®
Ace Books are published by
The Berkley Publishing Group,
200 Madison Avenue, New York, NY 10016.
ACE and the "A" design
are trademarks belonging to Charter Communications, Inc.

PRINTED IN THE UNITED STATES OF AMERICA

10 9 8 7 6 5 4 3 2 1

To

*Bill Ruesch, Joel Monka, Mary Cook,
and, of course, Paul Logston,
expert jump starters.*

*And very special thanks to
my agent, Richard Curtis,
and my editor, Laura Anne Gilman,
for their guidance and encouragement.*

I

● Jael pulled her knees up under her chin, pressing her back against the warm stone. This was her thinking place, a niche in the northeast parapet unreachable to anyone lacking either Jael's iron-strong fingers and toes or the inclination to creep precariously along the castle wall like a spider. In the spring, when the swamp flooded and winds wafted the swamp stench southward, her thinking place was almost unbearable, but now, in late summer, the swamp was mostly dry and the west wind was sweet. Jael felt comfortable here, surrounded on three sides by stone but able to look out over the eastern edge of the Dim Reaches where it met the forest in uneasy contest.

Right now her thinking place was the only spot in the castle where Jael could find a little peace and quiet. Today Mother and Father were meeting with the City Council, and there would be arguments and shouting; after that, Mother and Father would meet with their advisers, with more arguments and shouting. After that, if events followed their normal course, they would argue and shout at each other—or Mother would, at least; Father wasn't the shouting sort, although council meetings always left them both prickly as an angry spineback. Then, if Jael was *really* unlucky and the

1

whole council ruckus had been over her—it often was—there might be more angry words, this time directed at her.

Jael couldn't remember having done anything too terrible in the last few days. Well, there was that unfortunate incident when she had sneaked to watch Nubric, one of the castle mages, working on the bathing springs, and the water elemental had gotten out of control and flooded the cellars. But it was hardly her fault if Nubric's wards weren't properly set, and nobody had caught her, anyway.

Jael sighed and shook her head mournfully. Even if she hadn't done anything wrong, the council usually ended up talking about her anyway. If they weren't arguing over whether or not she should be declared Heir, they were complaining about her failure to find a husband, or fretting over what people in the city were saying about her.

And the people of the city had plenty to say. Most of the city folk had seen elves aplenty, but few or none as odd-looking as she. Many elves were as short and slight as Jael, but only a very few of the Hidden Folk had such long, mobile ears as she did. Some elves had eyes as large and slanted as Jael's, but theirs were brown or green or black, not the polished bronze of Jael's eyes and her hair as well, which matched neither Donya's dark brown braids or Argent's silver-white one. At least her boots covered her most unusual feature, the sixth toe on her left foot. Only a tiny number of the very oldest Hidden Folk had such extra digits.

If Jael's singular appearance had given the city's folk fuel for gossip, her single birth, almost exactly nine months after Donya and Argent's marriage, had fanned the coals into flame. Jael didn't quite understand what all the fuss was about, but she knew that the rumors got worse ten years later, when the twins, Markus and Mera, were born. There'd been nothing but trouble ever since for Jael, and it was as likely as not that today's council meeting, called on short notice, meant more trouble about her, or for her.

It seemed like the start of an abysmal day.

Out of the corner of her eye, Jael saw movement at the corner of the courtyard, where the secret gate led out of the castle grounds and out of the city as well. Just as she turned to look, a familiar small, dark-haired figure stepped out of the concealing bushes and strolled leisurely toward the castle.

Jael waved as vigorously as her somewhat cramped position would allow.

"Aunt Shadow!" she shouted delightedly.

The small figure looked up and waved back, and Jael took the shortcut down, scrambling dangerously down the ivy on the castle wall rather than climbing back up to the parapet and going down through the halls. Shadow met her at the bottom and suffered stoically through Jael's energetic hug.

"Better not let your mother catch you up there," Shadow said mildly.

"It's the only place I can go to get away from the twins," Jael sighed. "They follow me everywhere."

"How old are they now? Ten?" Shadow mused. "Yes, about the age for following an older sister around, I guess. So how's Donya and Argent?"

"Mother and Father are in council right now," Jael said, sighing again. "And after the City Council, they'll be meeting their advisers, and then—"

"And then arguing for another couple of hours over whether or not to pay attention to whatever those shriveled wheezers had to say," Shadow chuckled. "Right, I know the routine. What's the problem this time? Must be pretty dire for Doe to drag me back here."

"When did she call the signet back?" Jael asked surprisedly, following Shadow to the secret door that entered Jael's own rooms.

"Almost a month ago," Shadow said. She threw herself on Jael's bed, oblivious to the travel dirt on her clothes. "I was almost to the eastern coast. And I'm here to tell you that Fortune-be-damned ring popped off my finger at a *most* inconvenient time."

"A month." Jael shook her head. "Could be anything."

"You?" Shadow grinned at her.

"That, too." Jael flopped down on the bed beside Shadow. "Half the council wants me married and declared Heir, and the other half wants me quietly sent away somewhere so that everyone can forget about me."

Shadow sighed.

"Got any wine?"

"Uh-uh. Upsets my stomach. But there's water in that jug."

Shadow grimaced.

"Never mind," she said. "I brought my own." She rummaged through the pack and pulled out a skin of wine, drinking deeply.

"Hadn't you better join Mother and Father in the council chambers?" Jael suggested.

"Nah. I won't get an intelligent word out of them until they're done with the City Council and their advisers," Shadow said lazily. "That leaves me time for a bath and a meal, and I'll meet them in their chambers. That is, if we can avoid the servants and the twins, so nobody rushes in and pulls Doe and Argent out of council."

"The servants are no trouble," Jael said negligently. "I sneak around them all the time. As for the twins, they're lessoning in their study with either Sage Abrin or Sage Germyn until midafternoon. Then they have sword practice."

"And what about you?" Shadow chuckled. "Shouldn't you be having some lessons yourself?"

Jael sighed.

"Oh, I'm not very good at anything," she said ruefully. "I can't sit still long enough to study, and everything I try to memorize gets all mixed up in my mind. My penmanship is so clumsy that I can't read my own script. I'm not strong enough for human-style swordfighting—I can hardly lift Mother's sword, let alone use it—and I trip over my own feet when I try the elvan way. Most of my tutors have all but given up on me. They don't even bother anymore to complain to Mother and Father when I skip my lessons."

"Oh, I was the same way at your age," Shadow shrugged. "All feet and elbows. But I was surprised to see you here. Shouldn't you still be in the Heartwood? It's weeks yet before it starts getting too cold."

Jael said nothing, staring at the ceiling until Shadow raised an eyebrow.

"Well, go on, little seedling," Shadow prompted. "Let's hear the bad news."

"I didn't go this summer," Jael mumbled.

"I can see that," Shadow said patiently. "But why not?"

"Mother thought I'd better stay home this year," Jael said. She didn't add that Donya's decision had come as a considerable relief to her.

* * *

There had been quite a fuss when she was eight years old. Shadow thought, and Argent agreed, that Jael should be fostered in the forest; Donya had unexpectedly demurred, saying that Jael was too young to leave home. The balance shifted, however, only a few weeks later when Donya took Jael on her first hunt; at the moment Donya's arrow struck the stag, Jael screamed, clutched her thin chest, and fell unconscious from her horse, breaking her left arm in two places.

"She has the makings of a beast-speaker," Shadow had told Donya at Jael's bedside after the healers had gone and Jael lay there feigning sleep. "It's like her ears—as if all the old blood of the elves is coming back out in her."

"I pray that's what it is," Donya said, sighing raggedly.

"If it is, she's going to need guidance that we can't give her," Shadow said firmly. "All elves have at least a little magic in their blood, but Celene says there's the makings of a mage in her, too, buried so deep it may not come out on its own. It all amounts to the same thing—she's got to go to the forest for a teacher."

Donya was silent for a long time, and when she spoke, it was so softly that Jael held her breath to hear the answer, peering cautiously through her lashes.

"Who were you thinking of?" the High Lady said at last.

"Let me take her to Mist," Shadow said. "He'll know how to deal with the wild blood in her. For her sake he'll move closer to Inner Heart, where she can come back through the Gate whenever she needs to."

Donya laughed ruefully.

"Are you sure, Shady, you're not just trying to make him more accessible for your own purposes?"

Shadow chuckled.

"Well, I wouldn't mind that, either. But look at it this way: The more I visit Mist, the more often I can check on her."

"All right," Donya said, sighing again. "I suppose it's the best thing to do for now, at least."

"Bet on it," Shadow said firmly. And as the High Lady and her friend left the room, Shadow had glanced over her shoulder and grinned, winking deliberately at Jael.

The fostering had solved some of Jael's problems. Mist was a kind and loving foster father, wise and patient with his flighty charge. He taught her all the elvan skills he could—

tracking, recognition of plants as food, medicine, or even poison, learning to read the forest's subtle signs that warned of weather changes or danger, and as much elvan-style sword-fighting as Jael could manage (even Donya admitted that her own style of swordplay required a height and strength that her wiry but small daughter would never achieve). The elves accepted her wholeheartedly and never made Jael feel self-conscious about her appearance.

In many ways, however, her time in the forest was more difficult than living in the city. Jael could not hunt because the pain and fear of the prey sometimes sent her reeling, and the myriad small pains and deaths going on around her all the time often drove her to trembling tears. The control of a beast-speaker's gift continued to elude her, despite the best teachers Mist could find.

Mist was a far more patient and less demanding teacher than Donya, but Jael knew she disappointed him with her clumsy hands and feet and seeming inability to concentrate on anything for more than a few moments at a time. Added to that was the uncanny bad luck that seemed to follow Jael; if she and Mist were preparing new furs for trade, the quick-tanning spell would as often as not leave half the skin moist and smelly. If they met other elves and stopped to share food and fire, the soupstone would unaccountably impart a rotten flavor to the stew, or the crackproofed cooking pots would develop mysterious holes and empty themselves unnoticed. If it rained, the waterproofed tent hides would drip on them all night. Mist no longer even tried to gamble when Jael was with him.

Jael's health also suffered in the forest, despite all that the best elvan healers could do for her. When the flowers bloomed, Jael's eyes and nose ran like rivers, and in damp weather, her breath wheezed like a saw through wood. She always had to leave the forest and come home early in the autumn, before the autumn rains.

This year Donya had not sent her. The High Lady's excuse, that the unusually wet spring had aggravated Jael's raspy breathing and Donya feared for her health, seemed feeble; healers in the forest were as competent as those in the city, and even Mist's temporary woven-switch camps seemed at least as good a shelter as the drafty stone castle. Jael sus-

pected that Donya's real reason had more to do with the de-
bate raging over her heirship than it did the spring floods.

"Mmm," Shadow mused. "One more thing to talk to your
mother about. I'll slip down to the baths, and you see if you
can't sneak me down some kind of a meal, will you?"

"All right, Aunt Shadow," Jael said, grinning. "Under one
condition."

Shadow eyed Jael cautiously.

"What's the price this time?"

"The story of what you were doing when Mother called the
signet back."

Shadow laughed.

"Well, that'll expand your education, that's for certain,"
Shadow said. "All right, little sapling, it's a deal."

"—so since there was still a day before the merchant caravan was going to leave, I got to make amends for the inter-
ruption," Shadow finished. She dunked under the surface of
the water again to rinse the soap out of her hair, knuckled water out of her eyes, and reached for another fish cake.

"Really? Head of a mercantile House, and you just walked
out, just like that?" Jael was duly awed.

"Well, not 'just like that,'" Shadow chuckled. "I thought I
already established that."

"Well, didn't he mind?" Jael pressed. "I mean, you'd
stayed with him for two months!"

"Let me tell you something about men, little acorn,"
Shadow said sagely. "They're glad when you arrive, they're
glad while you're there, but they're also a little bit glad when
you leave, too."

"That doesn't make any sense," Jael said crossly.

"Well, men usually don't. But wait till you see the necklace
he gave me," Shadow grinned. "Worth a couple thousand
Suns, at least. Almost makes up for all the stuff I *didn't* steal
from him. Hey, just wait, though, till I tell you about this gem
merchant I did in Keradren—"

Jael settled herself back comfortably against the stone wall,
letting Shadow ramble on, enjoying the sound of her voice
while giving only slight attention to her story. She loved to
hear Aunt Shadow tell stories about her travels; it wasn't the

stories themselves that were so exciting, but the way Shadow's eyes sparkled and her voice scaled up and down excitedly and her hands flashed animatedly in gestures almost too rapid to follow. Sometimes Jael thought that Aunt Shadow had more life in her than there was in the whole city and forest put together.

Jael felt comfortable with Aunt Shadow, a rare sensation. Donya often called Shadow in when her unpredictable daughter became too much for her or asked uncomfortable questions. Shadow never flinched from a question, nor dissembled, nor talked around it, nor bothered overmuch with politeness and tact. Jael could speak plainly and frankly to the older elf about what bothered her and expect an equally frank answer in return, whether the subject was sex, death, Shadow's own personal life, or what the peasants were saying about her. If there was a question Shadow couldn't or wouldn't answer, she said as much, and that was that. But she never refused to listen. Shadow even took Jael along when she gambled, and if she lost, she'd shrug and grin the same familiar grin, laugh, "It's only coin," and proceed to lift the winner's purse on the way out anyway.

When Jael had first complained that she seemed to be a bone of contention to everyone in Allanmere, including her own parents, and couldn't seem to do anything to her parents' or instructors' satisfaction, Shadow had pulled out a dagger and held it out, one sharp edge upright, over the table.

"See this?" Shadow said, touching the sharp edge gingerly. "Humans on the one side, elves always on the other. You can walk the dagger's edge if your balance is good, but you're likely to cut your feet in the walking. Allanmere tries to live on the dagger's edge, and so do you, Jael. Right now you're just feeling a little sore in the feet, that's all."

It had become their private joke, Jael's sore feet.

One day Jael learned that Shadow was well over five hundred years old, and asked the elf why her hair was so much shorter than that of their mutual friend Aubry, the Guildmaster of the Guild of Thieves, who hadn't even passed his first century. Shadow had been silent for a moment, and Jael wondered if she'd asked a bad question, but Shadow had grinned the same sideways grin when she answered.

"Well, little sapling," she said, "his hair's longer because it's never been cut off. I cut my hair off not too long before you were born, and it'll take a good many years to grow out completely again."

"Why did you cut it off?" Jael asked.

"I cut it off and gave it to a god," Shadow said. "At least, I think it was a god."

"Why?"

Shadow shrugged. "To swap for a cure for the Crimson Plague. You already know about the plague, don't you?"

"But the histories say Mother and Father brought back the cure," Jael argued.

"Well, they did, they did," Shadow said amiably. "But not without help. Mist had a part in it, too, and so did I. Get your mother to tell you the story someday."

"Why don't you tell me?" Jael said practically.

Shadow chuckled.

"Sorry, sapling," she said. "I think that one is your mother's story to tell, not mine."

But Donya had only blanched and changed the subject when Jael asked for the story. Certain questions, Jael had learned, elicited that reaction from her mother—why did Jael look the way she did, how had Donya and Argent gotten married, why had Jael been born without a twin, something unheard of in human-elvan pairings.

Once she had confided in her mother that she sometimes felt so stifled in the city, as if nothing would satisfy her until she ran so far and so fast that the world fell away under her. To her dismay, Donya had gone white and hurriedly turned away, but that evening had come to Jael's room, face taut and hands trembling, and quietly walked with her daughter out to the castle lawn and dismissed every guard on the grounds.

"Go on," Donya told her, her voice hoarse. "Run as far as you can, as fast as ever you can, and then come back here to me."

Jael had been puzzled and not a little frightened by her mother's intensity, but she had obeyed, running there in the moonlight, her bare feet pounding through the grass until her breath boomed hollowly and pain stitched up her side, and when she could run no more, she staggered back to her mother, who looked tired but relieved, and Donya folded her daughter into her arms with a ragged sigh.

"Feel better now?" Donya murmured, and Jael, with no breath to spare, simply nodded.

"So do I," Donya said strangely, bending to kiss Jael's rumpled hair. "Let's go back inside now."

"So what're you daydreaming about, little acorn?" Shadow said, squeezing the last of the water out of her hair.

"I heard one of Mother's mages talking about me," Jael said. "He said they're calling me Jaellyn the Cursed in the city now. Last I heard it was just Jaellyn the Unlucky, and that was bad enough."

"I wouldn't take that too seriously," Shadow comforted her. "Lady Ria, the wife of Sharl II, they called her Ria the Fey. For a while they were calling your own mother Donya the Sharp-Edged, which you could take a couple of ways if you like. For some reason humans seem to think it's necessary to give rulers kind of doubtful nicknames."

"Maybe I *am* cursed," Jael sighed. "Everything I do seems to go wrong. And when I'm around, everything anybody else does goes wrong, too."

"Now, now, nothing's gone wrong when you were with me," Shadow chided.

"What about when you took me along to watch when you did that moneychanger and the roof fell through with you on it?" Jael countered.

"Well, that wasn't the bad luck," Shadow laughed. "The bad luck was your mother finding about it."

"*I* don't think it's funny," Jael said crossly. The one thing that sometimes troubled her about Aunt Shadow was the elf's occasionally overconsistent levity.

"Neither did Donya," Shadow admitted. "Sorry, sproutling, just trying to make you feel better. But you know, Jael, that couldn't have been your fault anyway. Lirtik just got cheap and let the waterproofing spell lapse on the roof, and the supports just rotted out." Shadow chuckled. "You know, in the confusion, I *still* got a pretty good haul out of that."

"Most of which Mother and Father made you spend paying for Lirtik's healer and a new roof," Jael reminded her. "And you got off easy. I was confined to my rooms for a month."

"That's not the point," Shadow said patiently. "The point is that you aren't single-handedly responsible for all the bad luck in Allanmere, although I admit sometimes it looks like you've got hold of Fortune's left hand and won't let go. I'd feel sorry for you, but it looks like you've got that pretty well taken care of yourself. Lend me some clean clothes, and let's go find your parents before the twins are done with their lessons."

In this, however, as usual, Jael's bad luck prevailed; as soon as Shadow wrapped a towel around herself and they stepped into the corridor, Jael and Shadow all but collided with Mera and Markus, sweaty and grimy from their sword practice but their energy unabated.

"Shadow! Shadow!" Mera shrieked, throwing her arms around the elf; Markus followed suit, enveloping Shadow in a tangle of smelly hugs. Although the twins were only ten years old, sturdy, dark-haired Mera was already as tall as Jael, and a head taller than Shadow. Markus, slender and graceful like Argent, his silver hair tucked back behind delicately pointed ears, was only a little shorter and twice as bouncy.

"Where did you go? Where have you been?" Mera cried, whirling Shadow around and around until the elf retreated to put the wall at her back.

"It's been more than a year," Markus added. "Why have you stayed away so long? Have you brought us back anything nice?"

"I've been all sorts of places," Shadow said patiently, "and I've been gone a long time because those places were so far away, mostly down around the south coast. And yes, I brought you something, but you aren't going to get it until you let me get back to my pack in Jael's room."

No sooner were the words out of Shadow's mouth than the twins all but carried her down the hall to Jael's quarters, Jael trailing exasperatedly behind.

The twins did not quite dare to pass the door—Jael had made it clear, Donya and Argent supporting her, that her room was off limits on pain of death or dismemberment—but they bounced and chattered impatiently until Shadow rummaged through her pack and produced a pouch of sweets and a pair of cunningly carved bone flutes. Mera and Markus shouted with delight and vanished down the hall, loud and mismatched notes already echoing off the stone.

"Nobody in the castle will thank you for giving them those," Jael said wryly. "They make enough racket as it is."

"I didn't think about that," Shadow admitted. "I thought if they took an interest in music it might settle them down a little. Come to think of it, I've got something in here for you, too." She rummaged through the pack and tossed a small pouch to Jael.

Jael opened the pouch and examined the contents interestedly. It contained nothing but a number of polished pieces of black volcanic glass, cut into different unusual shapes.

"It's a game," Shadow told her. "The pieces fit together in many different ways, but if you fit them together the right way, they make a perfect cube."

"I've never seen anything like it," Jael admitted, already trying to fit some of the pieces together. It was far more difficult than it had looked originally. "Where did you find it?"

"I found this in a mage's shop," Shadow said. "The mage said it was to train young initiates in patience and concentration. I was there selling a potion I'd come into possession of, and this little bauble just seemed to say, 'Buy me for Jaellyn.' So I did, and thankfully it had been a good day in the market. I thought it might cheer you up someday when you were a little"—Shadow chuckled—"sore in the feet."

"Oh, Aunt Shadow, it's a wonderful gift," Jael said, grinning to acknowledge the joke. "And maybe it'll teach me concentration and patience, too, eh?"

"For your instructors' sake, I hope so," Shadow agreed. "Now hide it away before the twins see it, and find me those clothes, will you?"

Jael's tunic and trousers were too big for Shadow, of course, but not unmanageably so, and Shadow did not look too absurd with the sleeves and trousers rolled up.

"Now I'm going to talk to your parents," Shadow said, giving Jael's shoulder a squeeze. "I don't imagine they'll want you there, so I won't take you with me. See if you can find someone to clean my clothes, will you, and when we're done, you can join us for supper and I'll have a few new stories to tell you."

"Yes, Aunt Shadow." Jael sighed and sat down on the bed. Shadow paused in the doorway, then turned back.

"And don't let your mother catch you on the walls," Shadow said sternly, belying her tone with a grin and a wink.

"Yes, Aunt Shadow," Jael said solemnly, stifling an answering grin.

As soon as Shadow was gone, Jael slipped back out the hidden door to the castle grounds. At the west end of the north wall was another hidden door, this one opening to a stairway. The stairway took Jael to the second level of the castle; another passageway took her to the uppermost walk, and Jael quickly slipped out onto the parapets.

From the upper parapets Jael could easily work her way down to the balcony of an empty room on the third floor of the castle. Jael had used that balcony many times before; she took the knotted rope from its hiding place at the bottom of a huge stone urn, tied one end to the base of that same urn for anchoring, and slid down the rope to the second-floor parapets. From there she had only to edge quietly to her listening spot, a comfortable niche outside her parents' sitting-room window. From here Jael could carefully, if rather awkwardly, twist around to peer through the ivy framing the window so that she had a reasonably full view of the room.

High Lady Donya, still robed in her surcoat for council, was fussing while she poured Shadow a mug of wine.

"Sorry you were worried, Doe," Shadow said, leaning back in her chair to put her feet up on the table. "But it takes time to find merchant caravans coming north."

"You could have taken a boat," Donya said exasperatedly. "The Brightwater joins up with the Wirrilind not far south, and that flows straight down to the south coast. You could've been back here in less than two weeks."

"Boats." Shadow grimaced. "Fortune blight the leaky things. If elves were meant to float around on the water they'd have webbed feet like a duck."

"Well, I was worried!" Donya scolded. "And I would certainly think that in an emergency you'd—"

"All right, Doe," Shadow said mildly, but Jael and Donya both knew that particular tone; it meant that Shadow wasn't in the mood to take much more.

"I'm sorry." Donya sighed raggedly. "I had a rough time in council this afternoon. Argent's still there, talking to a few

people separately." She opened her jewel box and took out a
ring, handing it to Shadow. "Here's the signet back."

Shadow shook her head as she slipped the ring back onto
one slender finger.

"Didn't realize what a lead rope I was tying around my
neck when I agreed to keep this with me," she said wryly.
"Do you know what I was doing when this thing vanished off
my finger?"

"I can imagine," Donya said, chuckling.

"So tell me," Shadow said, gulping her wine, "did I hopefully miss the crisis, or did my getting dragged out of my lover's very arms have anything to do with your nasty council
session, and maybe why you didn't send Jael to the forest this
summer?"

Donya shook her head amusedly.

"Gods, Shady, I suppose you know all about the temple,
too?"

Jael's ears twitched. That must be the Temple of Baaros;
that particular temple figured prominently in many of Mother
and Father's late-night discussions, when they didn't concern
Jael herself.

"Temple?" Shadow asked, raising her black eyebrows.
"Don't tell me the sprout's gone and joined one of those
strange new celibate sects, and the elves are so disgusted they
won't let her visit?"

"Oh, Shady, don't be ridiculous," Donya chided. "No, the
Temple of Baaros doesn't have anything to do with Jaellyn—
not directly, that is."

"Well, start from the beginning, then," Shadow said resignedly. "There's plenty of wine. But try not to make it too long;
I've had nothing but a bite or two, and I'm starving."

"The Temple of Baaros opened not long after you left last
year," Donya told her. "I didn't think anything of it at first—
just another mercantile sect, god of profitable trade, you know
the type. But it's becoming a problem. The High Priest, Ankaras, has been preaching that elves are soulless creatures, descended from the union of demons and animals."

"Now, *that's* imaginative," Shadow laughed. "That explains
the pointed ears, I guess, but could he explain why we don't
have tails?"

"It's not funny," Donya said impatiently. "Shadow, you

haven't *been* here, not enough to see what's going on. The city hasn't been the same since the Crimson Plague. You remember what happened then—humans blaming elves for the plague, riots, murders—"

"Oh, come now," Shadow protested. "There's always bound to be a fuss when something like that happens. After your wedding, when everybody was well again, things settled down again pretty quickly."

"Yes, for the year before you turned the Guild over to Aubry and flew off to see the world," Donya agreed, "it settled down. More than a third of the human population of Allanmere had died, Shady. But the resentment was still there, especially following so soon after your Guild—and consequently the elves—made such a comeback at the expense of the Council of Churches. People remembered that, Shady, especially the Council of Churches."

Shadow grimaced.

"I'd have thought that lot would have gotten over it by that time," she said. "Even old Vikram."

"Vikram died in the Crimson Plague," Donya told her. "And *that* wasn't overlooked, either. Three years after that the elves discovered that new dye process and set the Dyers' Guild back half its profits. Then five years later, when the elves discovered that gold up by North Heart and flooded the market with it so the value of the Sun dropped—"

"Oh, please," Shadow chuckled. "Most of those forest elves had never held so much as a copper in their hands in their lives. Is it any wonder they threw their new wealth around foolishly?"

"Hmmm, seems I've seen a certain city elf do a bit of that herself, and she'd certainly had plenty of time to learn better," Donya sniffed, but she had to chuckle at Shadow's wide-eyed, innocent expression.

"Well, what's this got to do with this Temple of Baaros?" Shadow asked. "And Jael, for that matter?"

"All I'm saying is that the seeds of anti-elvan sentiment were planted before Jael was even born," Donya said patiently, "and it just kept growing as one thing after the other seemed to—well, as if your Fortune had Her right hand on the elves and Her left on the humans. And then when Jaellyn was born alone, instead of twins, and the way she looks—"

"Oh, Fortune favor me," Shadow groaned. "I thought *that* mess died down a few months after Jael was born."

"Well, it did," Donya admitted. "The general consensus was that the House of Sharl had been marrying into elvan blood for so many generations that it really wasn't the same anymore as an elf-human marriage. That caused a little consternation among the humans, but at least they stopped muttering about Jaellyn. But then when Mera and Markus were born, it all started up again, worse than ever, with the anti-elvan faction shouting the loudest, of course. And of course it doesn't help that disaster seems to follow Jaellyn around like a wolf on a trail, and that she can't seem to master any useful skill."

"How bad can it be?" Shadow shrugged. "I mean, Jael's plainly got elvan blood; that's never been disputed. And there's certainly no doubt in the world she's your daughter, not when you went into labor in the middle of a Fortune-be-damned City Council meeting!"

"The city's splitting apart, Shady, and Jael's the wedge," Donya sighed. "Argent and I have been fighting this ever since the wedding, but it just gets worse. The Temple of Baaros is growing every day. Do you know, there are shops and inns and taverns all over town that have 'No elves admitted' signs over their doors despite the laws and the fines, and twice as many that unofficially make elves unwelcome. The Dyers' Guild has canceled every elvan apprentice and won't even deal with elvan merchants. Elves are starting to retaliate in their own businesses, and the forest zone patrols are getting—well, even I would call it a little brutal in dealing with poachers and trespassers. The only reason trade between the forest and the city hasn't been choked off altogether is because of Argent's contacts and influence with the other merchants."

"Jael," Shadow prompted, and Jael leaned a little closer, eager to catch every word.

"It's obvious that Jaellyn has some of the old wild blood," Donya said wearily. "One look at her shows it. The elves see it as a sign from the Mother Forest that the elvan influence in the city will grow with her as Heir. The humans see it as just another sign that their own influence is decreasing, and they want Jael bypassed as Heir and one of the twins—preferably

Mera—chosen instead. It's not without precedent; Sharl the Ninth passed over his two eldest."

"Oh, please," Shadow groaned. "He did that because he had no choice; Rulia was barren and crippled, too, and Romal the Black never took anybody but stableboys and the occasional goat to his bed. Everybody in the city knows that."

"That's not the point," Donya told her. "Half the council wants Jael declared Heir immediately, and preferably betrothed even sooner, and the other half wants me to send her quietly off to some distant city to be fostered, wait a decent interval, and *then* choose one of the twins. Either way, somebody will be very, very upset. Every day I wait, they push a little harder. I was afraid to send Jael to the forest this summer, for fear either the elves or the humans would see it as significant."

"Well, it sounds to me as if the Temple of Baaros is the bellows that fans the fire," Shadow speculated. "Don't forget that anti-elvan preachings mean Argent, and you, too, Doe. It could grow into covert or even open rebellion against the ruling line because of your elvan blood. Do something about them, first."

"What should we do?" Donya asked helplessly. "We have no precedent for interfering with any temple's doctrines when they aren't actually breaking city law, and acting against the Temple of Baaros will be seen as taking the elves' side against the humans. According to Ankaras, two days from now the Temple of Baaros will be holding their Lesser Summoning. That's when Baaros himself will appear to instruct the faithful in the signs he'll send prior to his manifestation at the Grand Summoning. It's reaching a crisis point. I've sent messengers to other cities with elvan and human populations to see if they've had any trouble with this particular temple, and how they've dealt with it. I still haven't heard from a few, but most say the temple has caused no trouble. Our problem seems unique."

"Well, I have to admit that Jael doesn't seem to have much of Argent in her," Shadow said slowly. "Doe, has it ever occurred to you that—"

"At least three times an hour," Donya said miserably. "But how can I know? Argent has some Hidden Folk ancestry; so does my mother."

"That's not exactly what I meant," Shadow said gently.

"I know." Donya reached for a goblet of wine, and Jael saw, to her amazement, that her mother's hands were shaking. "But it's impossible, Shady. Just *look* at her. Her ears, her height—"

"Her coloring," Shadow said softly. "Her foot."

Jael leaned a little closer, careful not to rustle the ivy. This *was* getting interesting. What in the world were they talking about?

"I tell you, it's not possible," Donya insisted. "I took that goldenroot potion every single day until the day of my wedding."

"But you had the plague," Shadow persisted. "I've seen severe illness make the goldenroot ineffective. Not to mention all the healing potions Argent gave you, plus the potion that cured the plague, plus all the strange magic at that temple. Any of those things could have made a difference."

"Damn all, Shady, one toe doesn't prove anything," Donya exclaimed angrily. "It could just as likely have happened at that elvan festival just a few days before."

"Have you talked to Jaellyn about any of this?" Shadow asked gently.

"No, I haven't, and I don't want you to, either," Donya said adamantly.

"Don't you think she's got a right to know?" Shadow pressed. "Doe, she's the one who's being insulted—and she knows it, too, even if she doesn't really understand."

"I said no, and I meant it," Donya said stonily. "Not a word, Shady, not a hint."

"Well, what if it turns out that Argent isn't really—"

Jael leaned a little closer, just a *little*—

—and her bracing foot slipped, and Jael teetered precariously for just a moment before she tumbled off her perch. One flailing hand barely caught the ivy, and for a few moments Jael hung there under the window, praying that just for once her luck would hold and that her mother hadn't heard the noise.

Once more her luck failed her; she could hear Donya's quick footsteps toward the window. Just in time, Jael found a toehold in the stone and slid under the projection of the window. Donya leaned out the window, but overlooked Jael's small form under the ledge in the darkness.

"What's the matter?" Shadow said, joining the High Lady at the window.

"I thought I heard something," Donya said. She leaned a little farther out, and Jael ground her teeth, wishing she could melt into the comfortable solidity of the stone wall.

"You surely did," Shadow said. "Look there. That's a good storm building up to the north. I can already hear the thunder. I'd say no more than half an hour, maybe less, till it gets here."

Donya let Shadow coax her back from the window, and Jael allowed herself a silent sigh of relief, then climbed back to her perch as quietly and carefully as she could.

"Have you asked Jael what *she* wants?" Shadow asked.

"Oh, be reasonable, Shady," Donya said irritably. "In truth, it just doesn't matter *what* the children of nobility want, does it? I wouldn't be here if it did. Jaellyn can't sit still for half an hour, she can't seem to master any of her lessons, and everything she touches either breaks or falls on her. She'd be utterly miserable as High Lady, probably even more miserable than me. Mera or Markus would be a better choice, there's no avoiding it."

Jael barely stifled a huge sigh of relief. She'd been heartily dreading the day she would be declared Heir.

"But if I pass Jaellyn over," Donya continued, "the elves will complain, and the humans who have objected to her will feel that they've forced me to choose in their favor, and where will *that* end once it starts?"

Shadow sighed exasperatedly.

"Donya, just what did you want *me* to do?"

"I don't know," Donya said, more softly. "I don't know that there's anything you can do. I just wanted your advice."

"Well, you don't want to listen when I give it," Shadow said impatiently. "Are you listening to yourself? I've heard about the Temple of Baaros, I've heard about the humans, I've heard about the elves. The city's falling apart, the world's a mess. This was all supposed to be about Jael, but you've talked to me about everything *but* her. I think you're looking at this whole thing tail end first."

"What do you mean?" Donya asked suspiciously.

"Start with the smaller problems first. I think first of all we need to get Celene to pay a visit," Shadow said. "Your mother once said she thought there was magery in Jael. Let's find out just what Jael's trouble is. With that much wild blood in her, she's more than likely barren, and then you'll *have* to pass her by; even the elves will understand that. At least it gives you a place to start."

"Well, that's sound enough," Donya admitted cautiously.

Jael ground her teeth with frustration. This wasn't what she'd been wanting to hear, not at all.

"And in the meantime," Shadow said firmly, "let's dig Argent out of council chambers, send for the children, and have supper."

"And stop thinking about it in the meantime, right?" Donya said sarcastically. "Just like pinching out a candle."

"Think about it all you like," Shadow laughed. "Just don't keep talking about it, or you'll spoil our supper."

The two women turned toward the door, and Jael scrambled quickly back to her room. It took a little longer than she liked, and she collided with the maid sent to summon her in the hall rather than meeting her at Jael's room, but the servants were used to crashing into Jael in the halls anyway. Jael took only a moment to struggle into a clean tunic and rake a comb through her short, tangled bronze curls before she raced headlong down the halls and stairs to the dining hall.

She stopped outside the dining hall and hesitated outside the door, hoping to hear something more, but at that moment the twins appeared and swept her through the door in a wave of giggles. Jael disgustedly took her seat, glowering at Markus and Mera, who blithely kept up a nonstop racket until Argent silenced them with a stern glance.

Jael usually managed to dodge post-council family suppers. Mother and Father were invariably in a terrible mood, and Markus and Mera equally invariably filled the uncomfortable silence with irritating chatter. With Shadow present, however, supper became a game, Shadow's lively stories of her adventures cheering Jael's parents and keeping the twins silently enthralled. Jael ate ravenously, content to sit quietly and listen to Aunt Shadow spin stories of faraway lands, glad to see Mother lose her worried frown and Father his air of patient resignation. Even the servants lingered to hear the stories, refilling goblets a little more frequently than was really necessary; by the time supper was over, Mother and Father had had a little too much wine and were in a far more jovial mood.

Jael, however, was feeling anything but jovial. The wine only made her feel dizzy and queasy, unlike everyone else she knew. Once more she had failed to find out exactly *what* about her so concerned her mother and the City Council, and now here she was at the dining table feeling sick and headspun while Aunt Shadow and the family enjoyed themselves.

Jael stared resolutely at the nearest light globe in its cup, the only object on the table that didn't make her feel like spewing her supper. The light globes were simple magic but infinitely useful, and Allanmere had traded for the spell as soon as it had been developed in Northreach. They could be extinguished with a word and relit with another, and unlike candles, they didn't drip wax into the food. She could feel their steady magic, quiet and unobtrusive, solid as stone. If Grandmother Celene was right and Jael had the makings of a mage, maybe one day she'd be able to create spells like the light globes. It would be pleasant to be around magic all day long; its presence started a rather pleasurable humming sensation somewhere under her breastbone—

—and the globe exploded.

Jael was under the table almost without thinking; she found Shadow there already. Argent and the twins followed quickly, Donya hesitating until Argent pulled her down. Before any of them had time to speak, however, there were six more loud pops, and glass and food rained down over the sides of the table. The six of them exchanged glances, waiting, but there was nothing further. Donya first, they peered cautiously over the tabletop.

All seven light globes had exploded, littering the tabletop with sparkling shards of glass. Donya sighed and brushed a clear path through the debris on the floor with her foot, then helped the twins through the clear path and out of the glass-strewn area. She reached for Jael, but Jael had already jumped over the circle of sharp fragments.

"Supper and entertainment," Shadow said mildly, sighing over the glass in her wine goblet. "Argent, have you been underpaying your mages?"

Argent chuckled weakly.

"Celene did all the castle globes herself," he said. "Is everyone all right?"

They all were. The servants quietly cleared the ruined food and broken glass from the table. Donya, Argent, and Shadow retired to one of the smaller halls to talk, and the twins followed, eager to hear Shadow's stories, but for once Jael had no desire to accompany them. Nothing important would be said in the twins' presence, and she felt miserably ill, both from the wine and from knowing that the light globes had exploded because of *her*. Mother and Father had been too kind to say it, but such incidents were far from rare—when Jael was there, at least.

Jael didn't need to return to her room and open the shutters to know that the storm had started; the air had already grown noticeably damper and her breathing had thickened. She threw herself onto the cushions at the window nook and peered irritably through the shutters at the lightning.

She didn't like to admit it, but she was sorry she hadn't gone to the forest this year. It wasn't precisely that she wanted to go to the forest so much; it was just that she wanted to go *somewhere* that wasn't here. She was always restless around the castle, and this summer she hadn't even had the respite of a visit to the Heartwood. Sometimes she felt she couldn't bear it another *minute*—

"Enjoy the dark that much, sapling, or just afraid to light another globe?" Shadow said cheerfully, joining Jael on the window seat. She had a flagon of wine in her hand, and she drank directly from it, not bothering with a mug.

"Isn't everybody waiting for you?" Jael said sourly.

"Actually the twins are rather tipsy and have gone to bed, and Argent thought you might need a friendly ear to fill." Shadow pulled her knees up and wrapped her arms around them. "Want to talk about it?"

"Aunt Shadow, will you be going away again soon?" Jael asked.

"Well, I don't know about 'soon,' " Shadow shrugged. Lightning silvered the edge of one pointed ear. "I don't see that there's all that much I can do here, but I'll probably stay for a few days, anyway."

"When you go, would you take me with you?" Jael said suddenly, daringly.

"I don't think Doe's going to agree to that, sapling," Shadow said gently. "And your health's a bit fragile, too. You've lived too soft for the kind of traveling I do. What's the matter, little acorn, feeling rather bloody in the feet?"

"The dagger's edge gets sharper all the time," Jael sighed. "But it'd just be easier on Mother and Father if I was gone. Then they could declare Markus or Mera Heir and be done with it, and the elves wouldn't blame them if I'd run off on my own. Mother started traveling on her own when she was only fifteen years old, five years younger than I am now. As for my health, I get sick here, too, and I can buy healing potions to take with me. And I know as much about taking care of myself as Mist could teach me."

"Hmmm." Shadow's eyes narrowed. "You look so much like a half-grown fawn, sapling, that I forget sometimes you have two decades in that skinny body. Truth to tell, Jael, surviving in the Heartwood's nothing like surviving in the human wilderness—foreign cities full of people you can't trust, people who sometimes don't even speak any language you can understand—"

"Truth to tell, I'd be a weight around your feet," Jael said bitterly. "That's what you're saying, isn't it?"

"I suppose I am." Shadow laughed ruefully. "But the other part's true, too. And your mother would never forgive me— and I do mean *never*, sapling. But I'll make you a bargain, eh?"

"What kind of bargain?" Jael said suspiciously.

"It's true that your mother set out when she was younger than you," Shadow told her. "But she wasn't Heir, she wasn't leaving her city and her family in a mess, and she *was* one Fortune-be-damned good swordswoman. She'd been taking care of herself for a good many months before I met up with her, so I didn't have to spend all my time looking out for her.

"Now, here's what I'll do. You see your mother and father through this crisis. It won't be long before they have to declare an Heir, either you or one of the twins. Behave yourself and apply yourself to your defense skills, at least. I'll come back by your next birthday—not this midwinter, but the next—and if you haven't been declared Heir and if you can prove to me that you can defend yourself, I'll take you with me on my next trip if you want, whether your parents like it or not. All right?"

Jael scowled.

"Aunt Shady, I'll make *you* a bargain. If I'm still here in the city on my birthday and you think I'm ready, I'll go with you. But I won't promise I'll be here."

"Well, I can't protect you from your own foolishness," Shadow sighed. "You're your mother's daughter, plain enough, and Fortune knows I'm no better example. Do what you want, Jaellyn. Just learn to use a sword or a dagger before you do it. A young girl—especially one who looks like a half-grown child—is an easy mark in a strange city."

Jael said nothing, but opened one shutter so she could watch the storm. She didn't tell Shadow, but it wasn't strange cities she was looking for. It was wild places she wanted to see, sweeping plains, tall mountains, maybe even the endless ocean Shadow had spoken of. She wanted to drink cold mountain water that didn't taste of sulfur from the hot springs. She wanted to breathe air that wasn't thick and wet and full of smells. Shadow, who loved busy cities with noisy taverns, soft beds, and hot supper with wine, would never understand. And Shadow was right about one thing: Jael *couldn't* defend herself; she couldn't even hunt. She could set traps and snares, but that wouldn't protect her from brigands or hungry wolves.

"So tell me," Shadow said, changing the subject adroitly, "all about this Temple of Baaros."

Jael glanced sideways at the elf.

"What makes you think I know anything about it?"

"Oh, please," Shadow grinned. "Telling you that you aren't allowed in someplace is like issuing an invitation."

Jael laughed, her bad mood vanishing. Aunt Shadow always had that effect. In fact, Jael had been inside the Temple of Baaros twice now. Consulting the castle archives, Jael had found that the Temple of Baaros and the neighboring Temple of Learon the Twisted, now empty, had once been a single building, which had been divided to make room for two separate temples. The original cellars were, however, intact, although a wooden wall had been built to divide the two areas. Jael had had no difficulty cutting a small hole in the thin wooden wall, which was easily concealed by pushing some of the storage crates and barrels that the Temple of Baaros had in its cellars in front of the opening; the only difficulty had been avoiding the beggars and other indigents who made the abandoned temple their home.

The next day Jael used her new entrance to creep into the Temple of Baaros before the morning service. She'd hidden behind a large urn in the main temple, and after watching the service, couldn't understand what all the excitement was about. It was just another wrinkly priest intoning nonsense and putting his followers to sleep—and Jael with them. She was discovered afterward by Tanis, Ankaras's fair-haired, wiry young acolyte. To the utter amazement of both of them, they became fast friends almost without reservation—almost, because both of them knew, although neither would admit, that they stood on opposite sides of something important to both of them.

Jael had met Tanis surreptitiously several times in the market, and the next time she returned to the Temple of Baaros, it was with his help. Tanis showed Jael a special hiding place, a secret passage that had once run from the wall behind the altar to the cellars but which had fallen in years before. There was still room enough, however, for Jael to settle herself comfortably inside for a perfect view of the proceedings.

This second service had been more interesting. Ankaras had gone on for quite a time on the dangers of sharing the city with elves. Those trading for elvan goods were risking contamination. Those who lay with elves were committing bestiality or worse. This interested Jael very much; she'd never heard anyone in the city utter such thinly veiled treason.

Jael had heard, too, about the Lesser Summoning to take place soon. Ankaras had encourage his followers to bring friends, relatives, neighbors—all of human blood, of course —to hear the message from Baaros's own lips. Jael had reported the whole thing to her mother, not telling Donya that she had been there herself, of course; Donya believed that Jael had a friend among the worshippers, which was true, in a sense. To Jael's disappointment, however, Donya and Argent had taken no action, only cautioning Jael that it might be best to avoid the worshippers of Baaros until more was known about the temple's aims.

* * *

"So I haven't gone back since then," Jael shrugged. "I thought Mother and Father didn't think it was very important, or they would have done something."

"Time was, your mother would have been in there with sword a-swinging," Shadow chuckled. "I guess she's picked up caution and diplomacy from your father. She surely didn't learn it from me. So are you planning on seeing this Lesser Summoning?"

"Uh-huh." Jael grinned. "I've never seen a god before. Want to sneak in with me?"

"Sunrise day after tomorrow? I'm afraid not," Shadow said regretfully. "I promised Doe I'd go through the Gate and bring Celene back with me, and I've got to stop and at least visit Mist while I'm there. I don't see how I could make it back in time. Besides, your mother's sure to have sent a few people in to watch."

Jael was silent for a moment, watching the storm.

"Aunt Shadow," she said at last, "there's something wrong with me, isn't there? Really wrong, I mean, besides my nose running all the time and getting sick when it's wet out."

"Well, nothing that's going to send you back to the Mother Forest before your time," Shadow laughed. "Not unless the temple collapses on you, which wouldn't surprise me too much. Don't fret, sapling. You worry almost as much as your mother. Want to skip the temple and come to the Heartwood with me instead?"

The thought was tempting, but Jael shook her head. Indeed, her parents would undoubtedly have people at the summoning, but Jael doubted she'd get to hear whatever they reported, and Mother and Father certainly wouldn't talk to *them* in their bedroom where Jael could conveniently eavesdrop.

"All right. Well, if you don't need to talk about anything else right now, your parents do," Shadow said, giving Jael a quick hug. "Get some sleep. I'll be leaving in the morning, but I'll be back in a couple of days with Celene."

"All right," Jael sighed. "Thanks for listening."

Shadow raised the flagon and waved it as she walked toward the door.

"For wine this good," she grinned, "I can listen a long

time." She hesitated at the door. "And by the way, remember next time not to trust the Fortune-be-damned ivy. I taught you better than that."

Jael had to laugh.

"Yes, Aunt Shadow," she said. "You surely did."

II

• The next morning Jael grimly began preparations. To the amazement of Rabin, her weapons master, Jael presented herself promptly for her lesson. Instead of practicing, however, she engaged him in a practical discussion of her physical limitations and advantages and the types of armed and unarmed combat to best accommodate both. Jael was too small for regular human-style swordfighting and too clumsy for the elvan style. Very well; Rabin would commission a much lighter sword, and they would find a style she *could* use. Meanwhile she'd train with daggers. Rabin knew of a woman from the west, a member of the Thieves' Guild, who was teaching elves a new style of unarmed combat based on leverage, highly advantageous when used against a larger opponent. Rabin would contact this woman and agree on a fee for lessons. Jael would continue to practice archery and dagger throwing, where her keen sight would serve her best.

Jael agreed, then utterly astonished Rabin by suggesting that, with her parents' permission, she would come for practice twice a day, morning and afternoon, instead of once. Donya and Argent were no less surprised than Rabin, but Jael pointed out, logically enough, that given the attitude toward

29

elves in general and Jael in specific in some parts of the city, it was more important than ever that Jael learn to defend herself. Donya agreed readily, Argent a little more reluctantly, that Jael's other studies could be postponed for a few weeks while she concentrated on her physical training.

In preparation for the Lesser Summoning at the Temple of Baaros, Jael made a small pack with some food, a skin of water, a lantern, and a blanket. As an afterthought, she tucked in a small clay pot with a tight lid that she could use as a chamber pot. It would be a good many hours to dawn.

Jael ate supper in her room, pleading a headache. She planned to make an early escape after supper, but she hadn't counted on her parents' fretting over her request for additional combat lessons; Argent arrived with her supper and a potion for her headache.

"You shouldn't have drunk the wine last night," he chided gently, nodding sternly at Jael to eat. "It always makes you sick."

"It's not that bad," Jael mumbled. "I just wanted to give the rest of you a peaceful meal after last night."

"What happened to the light globes was unfortunate," Argent said, wrapping arm comfortingly around her shoulders, "but it was hardly your fault, and we'd always rather have you join us for supper. You keep so much to yourself that we hardly see you."

"Well, that should be convenient," Jael muttered.

"How can you say that?" Argent chided.

"Almost every time I walk into the room, you and Mother stop talking," Jael said bitterly. "You think I don't know you're talking about me? Why can't you talk *to* me instead? I'm not a child. I know what they're saying about me in the city. What *are* you and Mother going to do with me? Declare me Heir or send me away? I'm too old to foster, so I guess you'd have to marry me off to some lordling somewhere for alliance's sake. Is that what you've been planning?"

She regretted the words as soon as she'd said them. As far as she had read in the history of Allanmere, the ruling family had rarely arranged marriages for any issue but the Heir, and then only if the Heir was unable to find a suitable mate.

Argent sighed wearily and rubbed his hand over his eyes.

His hands were long and slender, unlike Donya's strong, sword-callused ones.

"Jaellyn, we've been receiving betrothal offers and refusing them since you were born," he said gently. "You know that. But in some ways you *are* still a child."

"I'm twenty years old!" Jael protested hotly. "Mother was only two years older when she inherited the throne of Allanmere."

"And many of Allanmere's rulers have been younger," Argent agreed. "Jaellyn, have you ever lain with a man? Or a woman, for that matter?"

Jael flushed bright red.

"I thought not." Argent stroked the tumbled curls away from his daughter's face. "Have you ever felt the desire to do so? Has your body yet burned for another's touch?"

"Father!" Jael protested, blushing even more fiercely.

"You see?" Argent touched her red cheek gently. "Your breasts haven't grown much, either. In some ways you're a child yet. Heir or not, you will not be married until you have reached your womanhood, and as you've said, you're too old to be sent to foster. I'm hurt that you'd think your mother and I would make such plans without even discussing it with you. So your question is answered, isn't it? Now eat your supper."

"I'm sorry, Father." Jael sighed. "I just seem to be the only one in this family who doesn't fit in anywhere."

"You," Argent said firmly, "are a fortunate young woman. Remember Ria, the first High Lady of Allanmere. She was raised for decades among humans, the wild blood burning in her veins with no one to understand her. You have a loving family and friends of both races who want to help you. You spend too much time feeling sorry for yourself. Now promise to eat your supper, and I'll leave you alone."

"I promise," Jael said honestly. When Argent was gone, Jael wrapped up the roast fowl, bread and cheese, and baked tubers, and ate the rest of her supper. As soon as she was done, she locked her door and slipped out the secret passage, and from there out to the city.

Allanmere was a city that lived a double life. During the day, farmers and travelers and tradesmen and merchants flocked to the market, to the shops, to the temples and taverns and brothels. At night, after the merchants had closed their stalls and the farmers had returned to their land, a different crowd inhabited the city: bored young nobles looking for excitement, thieves who preyed on the nobles, and others with a shadier sort of business to transact.

Except for a few sects that held rituals at night, under the full moon or some such, the Temple District was largely empty of its normal population. In the nighttime it was filled with beggars looking for an empty doorway to sleep in, patrolling City Guards, and other characters of less definable interest, such as Jael herself.

Jael paused outside the Temple of Ebraris, scowling at the erotic statues as she remembered her father's words. Still a child, indeed! In an instant Jael had charged up the steps; then she stopped. The Temple of Ebraris made just about anyone welcome—very welcome indeed, from what Jael had heard—but Jael didn't have so much as a copper in her pocket for an offering, and without an offering she wouldn't be admitted. This realization caused a rush of emotion that Jael finally decided bordered between annoyance and relief. She sighed disgustedly at herself and stomped back down the steps.

Jael approached the abandoned Temple of Learon the Twisted with a little more care. Most of the beggars who made their home in the temple were harmless, but there were a few who were desperate enough to jump even the High Lord and Lady's daughter, maybe just for a rough tumble, maybe to sell to one of the child brothels or pain houses that seemed to spring up no matter how the City Guard tried to keep them out. Always best to avoid trouble.

Fortunately it was early enough that most of the temple's residents were still out wringing a few last coins from pitying passersby. The temple was dark and filthy, cluttered with trash, but Jael's elvan night sight was, it seemed, the one blessing her elvan blood had given her, and the little moonlight coming in through cracks was enough to see by. Jael picked her way quietly to the cellar, and from there to the opening she had made.

The cellar of the Temple of Baaros was dark and silent, and Jael slipped through like a wraith. Unlike the abandoned temple, this cellar was kept in good repair, and there were no cracks to let in a little moonlight. Quietly Jael lit her lantern and glanced around curiously, able for the first time to get a

good look. There was little of interest to see, however—boxes
and barrels, some apparently quite old, judging by the dust;
wooden doors that likely led to old storage areas; and an iron-
ringed trapdoor in the floor that probably led to one of the
city's many subcellars. The thick dust was making Jael's nose
run and her eyes water, and she hurried to the stairs.

In the upper temple there was light enough to see by, and
Jael quickly covered her lantern. Obviously the priests had
been preparing for the summoning; the temple was festooned
with flowers, and the old, moth-eaten tapestries and golden
statues depicting the various legends of Baaros had been aired
and rehung. The statue of Baaros, a rather placid-looking,
middle-aged man with a long beard, with gold spilling out of
his hands, had been dusted and freshly painted. The summoning runes had been sprinkled in various colored patterns
around the altar and the ceremonial candles and bowls placed
in readiness. Jael grinned at the light globes, now dark, which
had been placed around the altar, making a mental note to
stay well away from the magical lights. Seeing the gold and
other valuables decorating the temple, Jael chuckled quietly to
herself: Aunt Shadow would doubtless find other ways of
passing the time in the temple than sitting in an alcove with
a meal and a blanket. But then, Aunt Shadow would have
doubtless found a way to sneak in past the priests in the
morning, rather than having to spend an uncomfortable night
sleeping in the temple.

The concealed nook was exactly as it had been the last time
Jael had been in the temple. Jael scooted some of the debris
aside to make a reasonably flat space for herself and spread
her blanket down, then dragged one of the larger chunks of
rubble closer to the peephole to serve as a seat. Jael settled
herself on her blanket as comfortably as she could. There was
still almost eight hours to wait, and probably no better way to
spend it than sleep.

The floor was hard and lumpy, however, and Jael found
sleep elusive. Now she found herself almost wishing she *had*
gone into the Temple of Ebraris. It seemed vaguely disgrace-
ful to be twenty years old and a virgin, like a member of one
of the celibate sects. Even if she felt no real desire for a man,
if he was a skilled enough lover, did it matter?

Jael shook her head disgustedly. Was she really talking

about tumbling some man she didn't even know, just to spite
her father or out of embarrassment? She didn't need Aunt
Shadow to tell her how idiotic that notion was. But, Jael admitted to herself, that wasn't the only reason—Jael wanted
something for herself, something that didn't come from being
elf or human or the High Lord and Lady's daughter. Why else
was she here, after all?

Jael pulled the rag stuffing from the peephole and peered
out into the silent, moonlit temple. She opened the door and
stepped quietly out, walking slowly around the altar and ex-
amining the summoning runes again. She knew nothing about
priestly magic, but it certainly looked complicated. At last her
eye fell on something small enough: a tiny gold incense cup
on one of the window ledges. Jael touched the cup hesitantly,
then firmed her lips and picked it up, slipping it into her
pocket. Somehow reassured, Jael returned to her hiding place,
extinguished her lantern, and curled up to sleep the hours
away.

Voices awakened her. For a moment Jael was disoriented,
but the darkness of her hiding place and the hard floor under
her cold, stiff body reminded her quickly where she was. As
quietly as she could, Jael eased herself slowly to her feet, then
crept over to her makeshift seat to peep out the crack.

It was still dark outside, but the temple was now brightly
lit by the light globes and the ceremonial candles. Ordinarily,
from her vantage point just behind and to one side of the altar, Jael would have had a perfectly unobstructed view; however, at the moment her field of vision was occluded by the
broad backside of Ankaras, High Priest of the Temple of
Baaros. Under his direction, the two lesser priests, Tanis, and
four other acolytes were making final preparations, lighting
the ceremonial candles and the light globes, placing herbs and
fresh flowers carefully on the altar, and laying the ingredients
for the summoning spell handy in small crystal bowls and
flasks. Tanis, who was senior among the acolytes, was pouring scented oil—pungently aromatic to Jael's sensitive nose—
with exaggerated care into small gold bowls painstakingly set
at particular locations on the sprinkled designs. Ankaras
looked on, mumbling under his breath—or perhaps chanting,
Jael couldn't be sure, since she couldn't see his face.

One of the acolytes apparently did something not to the

High Priest's satisfaction, for Ankaras shook the frightened lad fiercely, berating him for some time on the necessity of doing everything *just right* in a summoning. Tanis went quietly about correcting whatever the young acolyte had done wrong while Ankaras continued his lecture, but the High Priest was interrupted anyway by the arrival of the first worshippers.

The temple filled quickly, for dawn was rapidly approaching. Tanis and the other acolytes made sure that all the worshippers were seated, while Ankaras puttered with things out of Jael's view.

At last Ankaras seemed satisfied with the preparations, and he gestured the acolytes to their places. As the first dim rays of dawn began to show through the windows, Ankaras began the chant, the acolytes taking it up. The worshippers were silent, rapt, as the rite continued.

Jael shook her head, wincing. The ritual caused a tickling ache somewhere inside her, the irritating sensation growing as the chant grew in power. Ankaras was using the carefully positioned ingredients now, making ritual passes with his rod, tracing complex designs in the air, and throwing pinches of this and that into the brazier. Jael could feel power gathering around the altar, *huge* power, and the irritating sensation within her became almost unbearable. If only he'd hurry up and finish what he was doing!

Abruptly Ankaras's hand fumbled slightly, jarring one of the bowls at the corner of the altar. Unseen, a small splash of liquid spilled out, dripping from the corner of the altar onto the edge of the powder design on the floor and breaking the smooth curve of the circle.

A rather greasy gray smoke began to flow from the brazier toward the statue of Baaros behind the altar. As the cloud of smoke grew in size, it seemed to flow over the statue as if exploring its contours. The smoke gathered again at the base of the statue, and a murmur of amazement went through the watchers as an image began to form. Ankaras, his hands shaking slightly, continued the chant and the ritual passes, and the image slowly solidified. For one brief instant, Jael thought the image blurred and shifted slightly, then settled into Baaros's placid features, although its eyes glittered with sharp intelligence.

Ankaras and his lesser priests and acolytes dropped to their knees, and the worshippers fell silent. Then Ankaras rose stiffly and turned to face the congregation.

"Lord Baaros speaks to me as he will at the Grand Summoning speak to you all," Ankaras boomed, his voice deeper and harsher than it had been before. "Three are the pillars of His temple, three are His priests, and three are the signs of His omnipotence He sends to warn the unbelievers."

Jael stifled a chuckle in her hiding place. It was a well-known fact that the reason that the Temple of Baaros had only three priests was the same reason that it now occupied only half of an aged building and that the fourth pillar on the ornate front had fallen away and never been replaced—that the Temple of Baaros was still too small and new a sect, despite its growing numbers, to afford more. Many of the worshippers were of the poorer classes and could tithe little to the temple; the rest, Jael imagined, were dissatisfied merchants who begrudged the elvan competition and felt little enough inclined to donate much of their profits.

Jael turned her attention back to the ritual, realizing she had missed a good part of what Ankaras—Baaros?—had been saying.

"—water will burn, and earth shall fall from the sky. Finally stone will open its mouth and drink back its gifts. By these signs, and by the richness of the harvest, will all know the power of Baaros in preparation for the day He once again stands among you. Until the Grand Summoning, my children, farewell."

Slowly the image faded. For a moment longer the temple was silent. Then a murmur began somewhere in the crowd of worshippers, and grew, and grew until the temple was alive with astonished conversation. Against the strong protests of Ankaras and the other priests, worshippers flowed in a wave up to the altar, to the statue, scattering the carefully arranged bowls and treading the powder designs into a shapeless smudge on the stone floor.

Secure in her hiding place, Jael smiled to herself. If she hadn't had her look around the altar before the ceremony, she might have suspected some simple trick herself. "Until the Grand Summoning, my children" indeed! Obviously Ankaras had gotten his pompous nature from studying the records of his deity.

Because of the fuss, it was some time before the temple cleared out; Jael noticed, to her amusement, that by the time the worshippers had left the altar area, several of the golden bowls and implements were missing. Ankaras and his priest stayed a little longer, excitedly discussing the summoning; at last they retired, leaving the acolytes to tidy up the mess. When they finally finished and left, however, Tanis remained, striding directly to Jael's hiding place.

"Come out," he said. "I know you're hiding in there again."

Jael abashedly opened the door.

"How did you know I was here?"

"I knew you couldn't miss the summoning," Tanis said patiently. "I'm just glad you stayed in here instead of trying to disguise yourself as a worshipper. All the acolytes were stationed at the doors to look for any elves trying to sneak in. I was looking for you under every cowl."

"I'm too short to sit in the back," Jael laughed.

"Well, you had a good view, then," Tanis said good-naturedly. "But you'd best leave before one of the priests takes it in mind to come back. Come, sneak back out the way you came in and I'll meet you outside. We'll go to the market and I'll treat for pies and ale."

This maneuver proved to be more difficult than it sounded. Creeping back out of the temple posed Jael no problem, but Tanis could not be seen with her lest someone tell Ankaras. After a furtive meeting behind the temple, Tanis decided to stop at the inn where he and the other acolytes boarded and exchange his acolyte's robes for street clothing, then meet her just south of the Temple District, where they took their usual precautions—a scarf over Jael's hair and ears, a cap on Tanis's head, and plenty of smudged dirt on both faces. *Then* they had to take an alley to the market to avoid the worshippers leaving the district.

Once in the market, Jael settled herself comfortably in a small alley plaza while Tanis took too long to buy the pies and ale. Aunt Shadow would have simply stolen them. Jael had tried once, but the hot pie had burned her hands and she'd yelped and gotten caught, and her mother had been absolutely furious. Fortunately Aunt Shadow had been out of town at the time, or Jael didn't doubt the elf would have gotten a lecture even worse than Jael's.

Tanis appeared with the pies and ale and squatted down beside Jael in the alley.

"You're going to have to stop hiding in the temple," Tanis chided gently. "What if High Priest Ankaras had found you? Besides, pardon my saying it, but with all the things that seem to go wrong around you, I think I would have been more comfortable myself if you hadn't been up there during the summoning."

"But it worked," Jael protested, wiping gravy off her chin with the back of her hand. "Baaros appeared."

"That's true," Tanis admitted. "This time you seemed to bring good luck instead of bad. We only have a summoning every seven years, you know, so I've only seen one other—to remember, that is—but from what I recall and from what Ankaras said after the ritual, Baaros never appeared that clearly before. The one time I saw Him, He was just kind of a smoke shape at the back. Ankaras said it's a good sign that He appeared so clearly, means that He will have an important message for us at the Grand Summoning."

"But all these signs," Jael said curiously, "burning water, falling earth, stone opening up. Aren't those kind of nasty things to inflict on worshippers? Not to mention the rest of the city."

"Baaros doesn't cause natural disasters to occur," Tanis said patiently. "He's a mercantile god. He was only showing us His infinite knowledge in predicting the signs that would occur between now and the Grand Summoning."

"That's not what Ankaras said during the summoning," Jael argued. "Or Baaros, or whoever it was. He said Baaros would send the signs to warn the unbelievers."

"Well, Ankaras may have been speaking metaphorically," Tanis said tolerantly. "He comes from an old, traditional branch of the temple. More modern priests teach that the signs are predicted, not caused, to instill trust, rather than fear, in both Baaros's followers and unbelievers. Unfortunately my father bound me to the temple back in Loroval just before Kiernan the Wise appointed Ankaras to start up the sect in Allanmere, and Ankaras chose me as his senior acolyte. So I ended up with the traditional branch instead of the progressives."

"Did you always want to be a priest?" Jael asked him.

"No, but my father was a worshipper and a major tea and spice merchant," Tanis said, shrugging. "He almost *had* to offer one of his children to the sect, and I had no head for figures. It's not so bad, though. Respectable, anyway, and fairly secure once a temple is established."

"Sounds like me," Jael said sourly. "I won't have much of a choice, either. At least you enjoy what you're doing with your life."

Tanis grunted sympathetically, but chewed on his pie and said nothing. There was nothing to say.

"Anyway, now I've seen a real god," Jael said at last, to break the thoughtful silence.

"You've never seen your own god?" Tanis asked surprisedly. "Which one *is* your god, anyway?"

"Oh, the House used to have a family god once," Jael said carelessly. "But we don't worship at any temple. That would be showing favoritism and giving that temple a political lever. Father makes a trip once or twice a year to the Forest Altars. Mother always says you can count on a sword, not a god."

Tanis glanced at her reproachfully but said nothing, blowing on his second pie to cool it.

"There's an illusion-master doing tricks at the center of the market," Tanis suggested when they had licked the last gravy from their fingers. "Want to go watch?"

Jael glanced up at the sun. She had the new lessons with Rabin to start, but there was still an hour or two. She skipped enough meals that no one would really miss her at breakfast.

There was quite a crowd at the fountain where the mage was performing, but Jael and Tanis were able to acquire an unobstructed view from the rooftop of a neighboring building. The illusion-master, an elderly woman, laughed as merrily as her audience as she conjured tiny, jewel-sparkling fairies to swoop over the rapt watchers, complete even to the brush of filmy wings against a cheek, the weight of a tiny body on an outstretched hand. Jael was impressed with the detail of the illusion, but she'd seen better among the forest elves, especially the Hidden Folk, and she'd been hoping for something more grandiose. She sighed and leaned forward, wishing the woman could manage something a little, well, bigger.

The woman waved her hands and the tiny fairies dived in formation, tumbling lithely through the air to melt into a single form. The mage waved her hands again, this time more frantically, an expression of concern on her elderly face, but despite her best efforts another form was taking shape from the vortex of swirling, sparkling energy.

Abruptly the energy exploded outward, a roaring dragon's head emerging from the sparkling cloud, and the crowd surged backward. A few screamed, even knowing that what they saw was illusion. A lamp merchant peddling his goods on the other side of the fountain started violently, knocking a bowl of burning oil into the fountain. Abruptly the fountain spewed flaming water, splattering blistering rain on those below.

"The sign!" someone cried. "The first sign!"

Jael leaned forward, fascinated, and Tanis snatched at the edge of her tunic to keep her from tumbling off the roof. The illusionary dragon spouted a jet of illusionary flame, then vanished; the elderly illusion-master sighed with relief. Jael sighed, too, but with disappointment—the show had just become interesting. Reluctantly she followed Tanis down from their perch, Tanis giving the bemused mage a few coppers as they passed. The old lady murmured her thanks rather distractedly, leafing through her grimoire with a puzzled expression on her aged face.

"Well, it was a good show," Jael admitted, chuckling. "But I wish she'd have finished the dragon."

"She didn't mean to do a dragon, Jaellyn, and you know it," Tanis said reprovingly. "And it isn't very nice to laugh at an old lady whose spell went wrong, either, especially when people got hurt."

"I wasn't laughing at her," Jael protested, but she realized that Tanis didn't understand. She was laughing at the people who were afraid of an illusion, laughing at herself because even a simple illusion went wrong when she was there, laughing because she would rather laugh than cry.

"Did you hear what that man said?" Tanis asked after a moment's thought. "He was one of our temple's worshippers. Burning water—the first sign Baaros spoke of."

"I hadn't thought of that," Jael admitted. "Do you think Baaros made that lamp merchant's oil spill to make the water burn?"

"Certainly not," Tanis said adamantly. "That water burned some of the people. Baaros wouldn't do anything so cruel. That could be the sign, though I wouldn't have thought it would be so soon." He fell silent.

They took alleys back to the castle. Tanis still seemed annoyed with Jael when he left, so she figured she would give him a couple of days to calm down. Anyway, she had no time to worry about it; as fast as she hurried, Rabin was always waiting for her on the practice floor. Of course, her new sword was not yet ready, but Rabin had cut down a wooden practice sword until it was light enough for her. Larissa, the woman Rabin had spoken of from the Thieves' Guild, was with him; apparently her discussions and demonstrations with Rabin had been so satisfactory that Rabin decided that he and Larissa could handle Jael's training without an additional elvan master to work with Jael in sword and dagger training.

Larissa was something of an oddity herself—she was, so far as Jael could see, entirely human, but hardly taller than Jael herself, and no heavier. Her dusty blond hair was short and curly, and while her features were just too strong and angular to be called pretty, her blue eyes twinkled merrily.

"Little minnows like us have to learn to use our size to advantage," Larissa said, chuckling as she gestured at the hulking form of Rabin. "Remember, a tiny snake can fell the largest horse."

"You're going to teach me to use poison?" Jael asked excitedly. This could certainly be interesting.

"Ho, ho!" Larissa winked at Rabin. "I don't think your parents would much care for that, little heirling. No, I'll teach you to *be* poison—quick and silent and deadly as the snake's bite. You can do that with the right sword, with daggers, or with nothing but your hands and feet."

Larissa nodded to Rabin to pick up a practice sword, and she took two wooden daggers.

"When you can use two daggers at once," Larissa said, taking a ready stance, "you can divide your opponent's attention." Nodding to Rabin, they executed a blindingly fast maneuver; in the time it took Jael to blink, Rabin was on the ground, Larissa's wooden dagger at his throat.

"Now, let's do that slower so Jael can see," Larissa told Rabin, and this time Jael was able to see how Larissa had feinted with one dagger while dropping the other, seized Rabin's wrist as he extended, let the man's own weight carry him over Larissa's carefully placed foot to overbalance and fall, and follow up with the dagger to Rabin's throat.

"The move I just showed you didn't take any special grace or skill," Larissa said, "just good balance and speed. That's what I'm going to start working on with you this morning."

To Rabin's and Jael's surprise, good balance came naturally to Jael. Larissa was gratified to learn that Mist and Shadow had already given Jael a fair grounding in how to control a fall—the numerous accidents that seemed to befall her had made this an early necessity—and Shadow had taught Jael a few nasty back-alley moves as well.

"Those moves can be countered, though, by anybody with training in dirty fighting," Larissa warned. "You can't always count on surprising your opponent with unfamiliar moves. There's no substitute for skill and real experience. In the meantime, though, a few nasty tricks might save your life, or at least buy you a few extra moments."

By noon Jael was starting to regret committing to the extra lessons. Rabin tended to take pity on Jael's small size and less burly limbs, but Larissa showed no such scruples. By the time Larissa allowed Jael to stop for dinner, Jael was bruised, sore, grimed, and sweaty, and thoroughly exhausted.

"That was a good workout," Larissa admitted. Jael was gratified to see that the woman was panting and sweaty herself. "Tomorrow morning we'll try it again."

"Tomorrow morning?" Jael repeated, relieved. Apparently she was reprieved for the afternoon.

"Larissa will only be here in the mornings," Rabin said. "In the afternoons I'll work with you on your swordplay, and see if you can't learn to throw those daggers—"

"Oh." Jael sighed miserably.

"—but not today," Rabin finished, grinning at her. "You're out of practice. Do some exercises to loosen your muscles this afternoon, and take a hot bath, and we'll see what you can do tomorrow."

Jael was too sore to do anything but take Rabin's advice. She soaked in one of the castle baths for almost an hour. She had started to doze off in the hot water when her mother entered, dressed in the ordinary tunic and trousers she favored. Father was handling the official business today, then.

"People have drowned, falling asleep in the bath," Donya said mildly, sitting down cross-legged at the edge of the bathing pool. She handed Jael a goblet.

"Thank you." The cellar-cold fruit juice felt wonderful flowing down Jael's throat.

"I was watching you out the window," Donya said. "You were working hard. You did well, too, for your first lesson in a new style under a new master. Mistress."

Jael looked up surprisedly. Her mother's praise came seldom and hard, especially in combat training.

Donya reached over and pulled one of the fur rugs to the edge of the bathing pool.

"Come on out," she said. "I'll rub your back."

Jael stretched out on the fur and tried not to wince as Donya's steel-hard fingers dug into her aching muscles.

"So why this sudden interest in combat training?" Donya asked. "Extra lessons, new techniques, and I've never seen you work so hard at it before."

"I never managed to do anything right before," Jael said wryly. "This, at least, I think I can learn. I hope."

"Mmm." Donya scooped some pungent-smelling ointment out of a clay pot and rubbed it into the skin of Jael's sore arms and shoulders. "You know, Shady's a lot better at this than I am. After a battle she used to mix up the most horrible-smelling goops to smear on me, but she could all but rub the bruises away. In the mornings it seemed like I was the only warrior who didn't wake up groaning and creaking in the joints."

"How could you have enjoyed that?" Jael asked curiously. "Risking your life, I mean, and getting all hacked up." She thought to herself that just one morning of practice fighting with wooden blades was quite damaging enough.

"Well, if you're good," Donya laughed, "you don't get 'all hacked up' as much as the one you're fighting. I don't know that I actually 'enjoyed' it in the same way I enjoy a good tumble or a ride on my horse on a fine day. But there's a kind of pride in doing something well, in proving to yourself that you have the skill. Something about gambling your life on your ability—well, it gives a kind of thrill. Not really at the moment, when all you can think about is staying alive, but later, when you think about it—I can't explain it better than that."

"I guess I've never been that good at anything," Jael said glumly. She wondered if she would ever be good enough at anything to risk her life to prove it—or if she would ever want to.

"Well, some people seem to be born knowing what they're for, or what they're good at," Donya mused, "and some people take years and years. Mother used to tell me that I played with toy swords before I learned to use a privy. Shadow, on the other hand, wandered around the Heartwood not knowing what to do with herself for over a century. So you're not too odd, Jaellyn. I'm just worried about you."

Jael sat up.

"Why?"

Donya looked her daughter squarely in the eyes.

"This sudden concern with learning to fight," Donya said slowly. "Nothing's happened, has it, to make you think you're in danger? Anything that's happened in town, maybe, that you haven't wanted to tell me, or that you've heard?"

So *that* was what this mother-to-daughter talk was about! Perversely, Jael was annoyed, and then felt guilty at her own annoyance. It was *her* her mother was worried about; her question wasn't just a way of getting news out of her daughter.

"No, nothing like that," Jael said, reaching for her clothes. "Aunt Shadow gave me a lecture, that's all."

"Well, obviously it did more good than the lectures I've given you." Donya shook her head. "Sorry. That wasn't fair. You're sure there isn't something else that you should tell me?"

Tell you that I want to leave Allanmere, creep away someday to see the world?

"No, really," Jael said. "Nobody's threatened me. Nobody's said anything—anything new, anyway. People mutter when they see me. Sometimes they scowl at me." Once someone, anonymous in the crowd, had stuck out a foot to trip her, and once Jael had been hit by a rock that she wasn't certain had been thrown up by a cart, but ... "That's all."

"All right." Donya sighed unhappily. "All right." She was silent for a long moment. At last, she said awkwardly, "Is there anything at all I can do to help?"

Jael looked up, surprised at the hesitancy in Donya's voice.

"I don't see that there's anything to be done," she said. "I mean, I just have to wait and see, don't I? See what Grandmother Celene says about whether I have some magery in me or not, see whether I can learn this new type of combat, see if I can do anything useful. There's nothing else *to* do."

"Right." Donya sighed again, then sprang to her feet decisively. "That's all, then." She turned and strode out of the room.

Jael wiped off as much of the smelly salve as she could, wondering at her mother's mood as she walked back to her room. Normally Mother was happiest on the days when Argent sat in audience.

From her favorite seat on her windowsill, Jael could hear the clashing of metal from the practice field. It was far past time for the twins' lessons, so either some of the guards were practicing, or Mother had coaxed either Rabin or one of the guard captains to practice with her. Jael skipped down the hall to one of the east windows where she had a clear view of the practice field.

To Jael's delight, it was Donya and Rabin on the practice field, and Jael happily curled up on the window ledge. She loved watching her mother practice.

Donya and Rabin were in full armor as always, because they fought with their own swords, instead of the wooden beginner's sword Jael used or the blunted, pointless practice swords the twins had advanced to. Afternoon sunlight flashed off of bright steel, and the sounds of the blades striking armor or each other was like a song. Donya and Rabin danced to that music, every step perfectly placed, every movement responsive to the other's movements, every cut or parry perfectly answered. Jael was mesmerized by their skill, thinking wishfully that she could never equal it—

Suddenly strong hands pushed her. Just as Jael, caught entirely off guard, started to tumble out the window, a second set of hands grasped her tunic, pulling her back. Even before

Jael had recovered from the surprise, the giggles behind her told her who her assailants were.

"Rabin says you can't let people sneak up on you," Markus scolded, still giggling.

"You could be assinated," Mera added somberly, her pale eyes twinkling.

"That's 'assassinated,' " Jael said irritably. "And you both are going to be assassinated if you ever do that again. Now leave me alone. I'm watching Mother practice."

"*You* should be practicing," Markus said.

"It wouldn't do any good," Mera contradicted merrily. "Jael's too stumble-footed for swordplay."

"If you two don't leave me alone," Jael warned, "I'll—"

"You'll what?" Mera crowed. "We can beat you any day, armed or unarmed."

It was true, too, and Jael hated it. She ground her teeth and slid from her window perch, stalking down the hall. To her utter disgust, the twins followed.

"Where are you going?" Markus asked. "It's almost suppertime."

"Unless you don't want to come to supper," Mera said, giggling. "Father has commissioned new light globes for the table."

"And cook says what's the point in cooking a good meal just to end up full of glass."

"Besides, Father's still talking with two members of the council. They'll probably be dining with us."

In desperation, Jael retreated to her room. The twins stood outside the closed door for a few minutes, giggling and taunting, but when they could elicit no response, they grew bored and the sounds stopped. Jael knew the twins better than to be fooled by this ploy, however, and she waited. Sure enough, a few minutes later she heard the footsteps receding down the hall as the twins abandoned their game. While she waited, she pulled out pen, ink, and parchment and scrawled a hasty note—"Mother, Father, gone to meet Aunt Shadow and Grandmother. Jaellyn."

Jael waited a few minutes longer, then inched the door open slowly. The twins were indeed gone; the footsteps she'd heard hadn't been Mera using her budding magery. Jael used one of her old eating knives to pin the note to the door and slipped through the halls, carefully avoiding the servants. She'd have to hurry before the twins returned to her room, found the note, and went tattling to Mother or Father. Jael would get in trouble enough when she got back for leaving without permission.

The door to the room where the Gate had been placed was locked, of course, but Jael had a copy of the key, and the magical lock was set to recognize her; Donya had insisted, as a condition of Jael's fostering in the Heartwood, that Jael be able to return at any time, night or day, should there be a need. Jael had never gone through the Gate alone before, though. Donya or Argent had always accompanied her, and Jael realized that they must have worried that her unusually bad luck might somehow affect even the Gate. Now that she thought about it, the idea gave Jael pause, too. Hurriedly, before she could change her mind, Jael took a deep breath and stepped forward—

"Jaellyn, what are you doing?"

Jael sighed and stopped where she was, turning. Argent stood in the doorway.

"I was just—"

"I know." Argent held up her note. "I was just coming for you and the twins. Change your clothes and come down to the dining hall. There's someone here I'd like you to meet."

"Yes, Father." Jael sighed again and trudged back to her room, hoping she had something fairly presentable to wear. Father sometimes invited influential merchants, nobility from other cities, or elves from other parts of the land to supper, and on those occasions he did insist that the whole family attend.

Jael rifled through her clothing, grimacing. She hadn't kept up much of a wardrobe of finery, and most of it had met with the disasters that seemed to follow her around town. No matter how carefully the seamstresses measured and remeasured and gathered and tucked, she always looked rumpled and disheveled in even the nicest clothes, and she flatly refused to wear gowns; she inevitably found some way to trip over them every few steps. Irritably she pulled out a tunic and trousers that were in at least fair condition and jerked them on.

Jael raked a comb through her curls, grimacing at her reflection in the mirror. Her face was flushed, her pointed ears large and obvious and twitching in her agitation, her bronze eyes strange. Maybe her tunic was a little tighter across her chest, maybe not. Probably not. Jael growled and gave her tunic one last tug as she ran down the hall.

The first thing Jael noticed was that the light globes in the dining hall had been replaced by lamps and candles. Jael tried to tell herself that the new light globes were probably not ready yet, but a bitter part of herself knew that the new light globes had not been used so that there would be no unpleasant incident with a guest at supper.

"There you are, Jaellyn." Argent took her arm, leading Jael back to where Donya, hurriedly washed and formally attired, was conversing with someone. Markus and Mera were standing by, quiet and polite for once. "Lord Urien, my eldest daughter, Jaellyn. Jaellyn, I'm honored to present Lord Urien, Senior High Priest of the Temple of Baaros in Calidwyn."

Jael swallowed her surprise and attempted a curtsy; her foot slipped and she almost fell, only to be rescued by a cool hand taking hers. Jael hurriedly regained her footing and looked up in surprise into a pair of twinkling black eyes as her rescuer salvaged the gesture by raising her hand and brushing his lips across her knuckles elegantly.

"The honor is entirely mine, High Lord Argent," Urien answered, his eyes smiling complicitly at Jael. He was pale as a sage who spent too much time in his cellar library. His face was lean and angular, delicate but not quite effeminate, narrow-lipped and vaguely exotic. Fine black hair feathered around his face in straight wisps. He wore the dark blue of the Temple of Baaros, but instead of priestly robes he was dressed in a House surcoat. Jael didn't recognize the arms—of course not, if he was from Calidwyn—but they had the general look of a mercantile house.

"Lord Urien is an administrator of the Reform Temple of Baaros in Calidwyn and a representative of the main temple in Loroval," Donya explained. "The Temple of Baaros received my messages and sent him to reform the temple here in Allanmere."

"Reform it how?" Jael blurted out the words before she thought, then flushed with embarrassment. Her embarrassment doubled when she realized that Urien was still holding her hand, but she couldn't see a polite way of pulling away from him.

"The Temple of Baaros is a small mercantile sect with temples in only a few cities," Urien said smoothly. "Interfering in local politics is beyond our scope and contrary to the very interests of the temple—recruiting worshippers from the merchant class. For our temples to prosper and grow, we need the goodwill of the cities. I assure you that Ankaras went far beyond his authority in promoting treasonous sentiments. The temple in Loroval sent me to assume leadership of the temple here and rectify the problem."

"I see the table is ready," Argent said politely. "Why don't you tell us about it over supper, Lord Urien?"

"I would be delighted." Urien bowed. "May I have the honor of escorting your lovely daughter to the table?"

Donya and Argent exchanged surprised glances, which Jael vastly enjoyed—still a child, indeed!—and Argent finally smiled a little hesitantly.

"Of course, Lord Urien."

Urien's eyes twinkled again at Jael as if they had just shared a private joke, and he tucked her hand into the crook of his arm.

"—so as far as we can tell, the whole difficulty with the elves came from the trade war in Loroval, not from actual temple doctrine," Urien said, nodding to the serving maid offering another serving of roast fowl. "Since most of the priests, including Ankaras, were Loroval merchants, you can see how that sentiment found its way into the sect. The temple's never tried very vigorously to stamp out such teachings because in many cities the elves stay aloof from the human settlement anyway, so it's never become a problem until now. But you can be assured that if Ankaras can't adjust, I'll replace him myself until such time as a new High Priest can be trained. Having a temple in such a large trade city as Allanmere is very important to us, and I'm prepared to settle here as long as is necessary to see it done properly." He turned to Jael. "More wine, Lady Jaellyn?"

"Thank you," Jael said, although inwardly she winced. She'd already had three goblets full despite the price she'd pay later; she was positively *not* going to drink fruit juice like a child with this charming lord sitting next to her!

"I'll have to locate appropriate lodging, of course," Urien said. "I have a small retinue with me, a few lesser priests and acolytes. There isn't sufficient room at the present temple, I'm told, and inns don't suit me."

"There are a few large houses in the Noble District for sale," Jael said. "I know where most of them are."

"Then perhaps if your parents can arrange a suitable escort," Urien said, bowing his head slightly to Argent and Donya, "and if they will permit, I would be very grateful if you would be so gracious as to help us."

Donya's dark brows had drawn down ominously when Jael had spoken, but her frown cleared as soon as Urien mentioned escorts.

"A few of the Castle Guard should suffice," Argent smiled, patting Donya's arm. "And in the meantime I'm sure we can provide housing for you and at least part of your retinue here."

Urien inclined his head again.

"Rumors of the graciousness of the High Lord and Lady of Allanmere have not been exaggerated," Urien said politely.

Jael downed the last swig of her wine rather defiantly. At last *that* was done.

Urien glanced at her goblet and started to raise his hand for the wine steward; then he glanced at Jael and lowered his hand. He hurriedly swallowed the last sip of his own wine and leaned slightly toward Argent at his left.

"You must pardon me," Urien said in a lowered voice. "It's rather embarrassing, but I find too much wine hinders my digestion. Might I trouble you for a digestive tea instead? My valet brought some for me."

"Gladly." Argent nodded to one of the maids, who hurried to the kitchen.

"Have you met with High Priest Ankaras yet, Lord Urien?" Donya asked interestedly.

"Not yet," Urien said, smiling ruefully. "I don't imagine he will take the news well. Since it was your message which brought me, High Lady, I thought it best to come directly to you to assure you that regardless of Ankaras's reaction to the orders I bring, you will have no further difficulties from the Temple of Baaros."

"I appreciate the generosity of the temple in sending a representative so far to help us," Argent said, "and your kindness in being willing to travel so far. Ah, your tea." The serving maid had materialized as if by magic. Argent waved her around to Urien's seat.

Urien leaned toward Jael, winking surreptitiously.

"Calidwyn black tea is renowned, Lady Jaellyn. Would you care to try some?"

Jael grinned inwardly. So this whole thing had been a maneuver to get the tea for *her*, as she had suspected. But he'd done it in a charming way, if rather obvious, to save her embarrassment.

Jael accepted a cup of the hot tea, surprised at the intense, richly fragrant flavor. After the first cup she found herself craving another, and to her surprise, her stomach settled immediately. If it weren't for the castle mages, who checked every morsel of food or drink before it passed into the castle, and again before it reached the table, Jael would have suspected that some kind of potion had been added.

"Lord Urien, why don't you dress like a priest?" Mera asked. "All the priests I've seen have given up their Houses and titles."

Donya gave her daughter a chiding look, but Urien appeared undisturbed by the question.

"First, although I have the rank of a High Priest," Urien told her, "I've served in Calidwyn primarily as an administrator of the temple for the last few years, managing its funds and dealing with city officials and other temples in any conflict. Secondly, Lady Mera, Baaros allows His priests to retain their standing in their House if there is no other heir, as is true of my family. Baaros wishes the mercantile Houses to prosper, not fail, by joining His priesthood."

"Is that trade goods you brought in the caravan?" Markus asked interestedly.

"Trade goods, supplies for the temple, and my personal belongings," Urien told him. "As I said before, I came prepared to stay for as long as necessary. There should be room at the temple to store my goods until I can make other arrangements. Tomorrow, however, I'll spend the day with Ankaras, reviewing the temple records and working out a gradual change in doctrine so we don't lose our acolytes and our base of worshippers. This business of the elves I'll change immediately, but the rest will have to be more gradual. Fortunately I heard on my way through town that the Lesser Summoning was a dramatic success. That'll help us hold our worshippers until the Grand Summoning at least, and by that time I hope to have the temple running a little more effectively."

He shook his head.

"You must pardon me. I'm addressing you like a group of acolytes to be instructed. Forgive me."

"Not at all," Jael said. "I think it's very interesting." She accepted another cup of the tea.

"Well, I'm sure we will all be interested in hearing more later," Donya said, rising from the table. "But our guest is undoubtedly tired from his long journey. Lord Urien, if you'll come with me, I'll show you to your rooms, and Argent can see what he can find for your men." She glanced briefly at Jael, Markus, and Mera. "You children are excused."

Jael's face flamed. *Children?* Jael stood numbly as Donya, Argent, and Urien walked from the room, Urien glancing back to give her an apologetic shrug.

As soon as Donya, Argent, and Urien were out of sight, Jael stormed back up to her room. She tore off the tunic and trousers and flung them in a corner, jerking her old clothes back on. *Children.* Jael flounced angrily onto the bed on her stomach. Twenty years old and dismissed as a child. Wasn't that just like High Lady Donya? When she skipped her lessons, *You're too old to act like a child, Jaellyn.* But *You children are excused* when—

—when—

All right, when handsome young lords seemed to be paying attention to her! That was the song, verse and chorus, wasn't it! Someone new and interesting had come to Allanmere, and High Lady Donya and High Lord Argent didn't like the fact that this stranger was paying attention to their *child*.

Too angry to sleep, Jael slipped outside and up the walls to her thinking place, dragging along a fur to keep her warm. She curled up in the stone niche, somehow more comfortable here than in her room, warm in the fur. She stared out at the edge of the Heartwood, wishing that somehow Aunt Shadow would materialize again. Aunt Shadow never called her a *child*. Grandma Celene, too, would never condescend in such a way. But there was no use; Aunt Shadow and Celene wouldn't be back until tomorrow morning at least, probably later.

It would have been nice if she could have made it through the Gate before Father had come in. Still, it was almost worth it, meeting Lord Urien. With any luck he'd be at breakfast tomorrow. He'd be at the temple all day as he said, but perhaps he'd be back for supper.

Jael took out the puzzle Shadow had given her and examined the small, neat pieces in the moonlight. The smooth volcanic glass felt good in her hand and sparkled prettily in the moonlight, and she liked the neat way in which the pieces fit together. With almost disappointing ease, Jael found the way to fit the pieces together to form a cube. Reluctant to put the game aside, Jael experimented and found that by assembling the pieces in another manner, she could form a pyramid, then an oblong box, instead of a cube. Delighted with her unexpected success, Jael played with the pieces late into the night. As Shadow had told her, it was concentrated work; at last, Jael drifted off to sleep, the pieces still clutched comfortingly in her hand.

Jael snuggled more cozily into her comfortable nook, wishing the stone were a little softer, yawning.

Perhaps soon she'd show them all that she was no *child*.

III

● Jael yawned and stretched as best she could in the cramped space. For a moment she was disoriented; then the early morning light in her eyes reminded her that she had spent the night in her thinking place. For having spent a night on cold, hard stone with only a fur, Jael was less stiff and cramped than she would have expected; she hadn't remembered the stone fitting her so neatly, a nicely curved hollow cradling her back and another conforming perfectly to the shape of her buttocks. Even her head had fallen sideways into a pillowlike nook in the stone.

It was still early; with luck, Jael would have time for a bath before breakfast. She didn't want Lord Urien seeing her grubby and disheveled.

Fortunately it was too early even for the twins, and Jael managed an uninterrupted bath. Back in her room, however, Jael nearly groaned aloud. The only fairly attractive and intact clothing she owned was wrinkled from being flung in the corner the night before. Jael disgustedly laid the clothing out on the bed for the maids to clean and dragged out her second-best finery. Wearing her good clothing at breakfast meant she'd have to dash back to her rooms and change again before her lessons with Rabin and Larissa, but so be it.

To Jael's utter dismay, however, Lord Urien was not at breakfast; neither were Donya or Argent, having convened an early session with the City Council to discuss what Urien had told them the night before. The twins were there, and they teased Jael unmercifully about her clothing. As a result, Jael bolted her porridge and added a burned mouth to her list of complaints for the day, then had to hurry back to change clothes before she could meet Rabin and Larissa.

Today's lesson was even more strenuous than the day before, but Jael found it fascinating. Between the two masters, Jael was beginning to get some clumsy sense of what to do with her cut-down practice sword, but more interesting were Larissa's lessons. Larissa could snatch up anything from a stick to a handful of horse dung and make a weapon of it; she was just as deadly with nothing at all. By noon Jael was battered and exhausted, but satisfied; for once she felt she was actually accomplishing something and pleasing her instructors.

At noon Markus and Mera arrived, and Jael was further annoyed by the twins sitting on the wall and watching, offering unsolicited (and unwanted) advice and critiques, and giggling whenever the instructors got a strike past Jael's guard. It made every fall and bruise twice as humiliating. When Rabin and Larissa called a halt to the lesson, however, Jael discovered that the twins actually had a purpose in their visit.

"Jael's supposed to change her clothes, wash up, and meet Mother in Grandma Celene's old lab," Mera recited.

"And Mother says she may not be back for afternoon lesson," Markus added. "Mother said not to wait for her."

Jael ground her teeth. Obviously this meant that Aunt Shadow and Grandma Celene were back, but of course the twins had to sit around and taunt her rather than delivering the message immediately. Jael managed to thank Rabin and Larissa politely, then stalked back to her room to change.

As she had anticipated, Shadow and Celene were with Donya in the old laboratory. Celene had left most of her books and equipment here, and the maids had kept it clean, but the room still had the air of one that had not been used for a long time. Someone had cleared enough space to lay a simple dinner on one of the tables, and Jael was grateful; her lesson had left her with a ravenous appetite.

Aunt Shadow was almost unbearably cheerful, causing Jael to speculate that the elf had probably spent a goodly amount of time with Mist, who had come back through the Gate to visit with Aubry at the Thieves' Guild. Celene was quietly happy to enjoy her daughter's company, content to let Shadow ramble on about how many new huts there were in Inner Heart and how excellent the latest batch of moondrop wine looked to be. Jael hadn't seen Grandmother Celene for almost two years, but the former High Lady was as ageless and serenely lovely as ever.

When Jael had finished eating, Celene laid out her books and instruments and cast a few preliminary scrying spells. By the time Celene had Jael take off her shirt and began painting runes in green ink over Jael's bare back, Jael began to have the disturbing feeling that Celene wasn't any closer to finding an answer than anyone else had come.

"All right, we'll try this another way," Celene said grimly. "This is too simple to fail." She took Jael's hands in her own and muttered a short incantation, paused puzzledly, then chanted another. The second time she snatched her hands away abruptly, muttering a curse in Olvenic.

"By the Mother Forest, that hurt," Celene murmured, blowing on the fingertips of her left hand to cool them.

"What's the matter?" Jael asked. She hadn't felt a thing.

"Backlashed on me," Celene said absently. She took Jael's hands and tried another incantation with the same response.

"That's interesting," Celene said at last. "Magic won't pass through her. I can make the power go into her, but it warps somehow, twists, and won't come back out."

"But how is that possible?" Donya said. "You said there was the mage-gift in her. How can magic *not* come out of her?"

"That's not how it works," Celene said, shaking her head. "Mages don't strictly use power from inside themselves, or no one could cast anything but the simplest of spells. Mages attract magical energy to them from outside sources and use their own power to shape and channel it. Mages in control of their power, that is."

"So if Jael isn't in control of her magery," Shadow speculated, "she could be drawing power to her but she can't do anything with it?"

Celene nodded.

"During the Black Wars, the barbarian mages used to love to kill uninitiated mages, ours and their own," she said. "An uncontrolled mage usually has a great deal of power stored but unused, and killing them releases that power in one large burst. Uninitiated mages can often be recognized by involuntary release of that magic—objects fly around the room or break, and so on."

"Like the light globes," Shadow said, nodding.

"Possibly," Celene said cautiously. "I'm not positive that Jael actually is releasing any magical energy at all. If I can't even pass magic through her, I don't see how she can pass it through herself. Frankly I don't think she's absorbing magic and then releasing it; I think she's acting on the magic around her and warping it somehow."

"How is that possible if she can't use magic herself?" Donya asked, her brow wrinkling. "I thought you just said that the only way you could influence magical energy was *with* magic."

"Frankly, I don't know *how* she's doing it," Celene admitted. "I can sense the magery in her, but it's got a feel I'm not familiar with. And it's obstructed somehow. I get a sense of— well—a gap that her magic can't cross, just as cattle won't cross a bridge if you take a board or two off the middle. It's the same with her Gift—she has some of the makings of a beast-speaker, but it just won't come through."

"A gap," Donya repeated disgustedly. "Cattle and bridges. Mother, can't you tell me anything more useful than that?"

"Well, as I said, I can't tell you how she does it," Celene said, shaking her head. "But I think I can tell you *why*."

"Then tell me that," Donya said impatiently.

"The magic confused me," Celene said thoughtfully. "If I'd looked at the other problems first I might have guessed it sooner."

"Other problems?" Jael said, bristling slightly.

"Your restlessness, shortness of attention, clumsiness, extremes of emotion, and slow growth," Celene said gently, tugging Jael's short curls affectionately. "It's really quite simple —so simple I overlooked it."

"Soul-sick," Shadow said.

Celene nodded. "You saw it, too," she said.

"You both seem to know all about this, but I've never heard of it," Donya said impatiently. "What does that mean, 'soul-sick'?"

"It's not exclusively an elvan ailment, but humans don't seem to understand it," Shadow said. "Most humans go through a period of it between childhood and adulthood. It usually comes around their first sexual awakening, around the first bleeding time in a woman. It's a time when their bodies don't seem to work right, their emotions go north one minute, south the next."

"Not all elves go through it, and less now than used to," Celene said. "Elves who are Gifted, who have a larger share of the old wild blood, often do, and it's more serious for them. It's a time when the growth of their spirit hasn't caught up with their bodies and is working against them rather than with them. Their senses go awry, as do their Gifts or their magery. It's a miserable time. As Shadow said, soul-sickness is often associated with the first ripening, or with sexual awakening, as well as with an elf's Gifts or magery, as these forces all draw on similar spiritual energies. The first half-breeds had more trouble, as Jael is having, because the human half of their souls and the elvan half don't mix easily."

"Well, that's very helpful," Donya scowled. "Most important, what's to be done about it?"

"Humans simply grow out of it in time," Celene said gently. "Even you did, despite your elvan blood. If this had come on Jael sooner, I might have advised you to simply let her grow through it as the humans do. But coming so late in her years and so severely, and being linked with her Gift or her magery, I think it a more elvan soul-sickness, and the elves have learned to deal with it. Most elvan clans used to have coming-of-age rituals to take them through soul-sickness. The Hidden Folk still do."

"What kind of rituals?" Jael asked interestedly. Uncle Mist was of Hidden Folk blood, and he'd never spoken to her of such a thing.

"Oh, there's plenty of chanting and ceremony," Celene smiled, "but I think that's just the flower petals in the wine cup. What it amounts to is two days' fasting, a pilgrimage to the Forest Altars, taking a potion, and praying to the Mother Forest to heal their spirits."

"That doesn't sound very helpful," Donya scowled. "Isn't there something a little more solid to try than this, well, this religious ritual?"

"This 'religious ritual' has been working for as long as there have been elves in the Heartwood," Celene said gently. "Although I've never gone through it myself—have you, Shady?"

Shadow shook her head, grinning.

"The only cure for my spirit was the open road," she said. "But, then, I wasn't Gifted, nor a mage, nor a half-blood. Doe, I don't see how it can hurt. What do you say, little acorn?"

"How long will all this take?" Jael asked warily.

"Well, as I say, I'm not familiar with the ritual myself," Celene sighed. "With the whole business, purifications and chants and such, I would suppose at least a week, probably more."

"A week?" Jael exploded. "But I promised—"

Celene raised a hand.

"That doesn't matter. So far as I know, none of the Hidden Folk would do the ritual anyway, not for a half-blood. They let Jael into their villages, but that doesn't mean they accept her as one of their own."

"I don't want Jael in the woods that long, anyway," Donya said firmly. "It's time for the autumn rains, and when they start, her chest always sounds like a door with rusty hinges."

"What about Mist?" Shadow suggested. "He's Hidden, or used to be, and he's no farther away than the Guild. He could come here and see Jael through the preliminaries, then just take her through the Gate to the altars for the final part. Celene could temporarily move the other end of the Gate; that would save Jael any traveling at all. She couldn't be in better hands."

Donya sighed, shaking her head.

"I still don't see what good this can possibly do," she said, "but if Jael wants to try it—as you said, Shady, what harm can it do?" She turned to Jael and raised her eyebrows inquiringly.

"All right," Jael said eagerly, thinking that actually the

whole thing sounded interesting. Two days' fasting held no attraction, but still, if it could make her a mage or a beast-speaker—

"All right," Jael said again. "I'd like to try."

"Then tomorrow morning I'll fetch Mist back here," Shadow said, patting Jael on the shoulder. "Meanwhile, let's let Celene and Donya have a chance to exchange their news. Why don't you show me some of this new combat style you're learning?"

"Larissa's left by now," Jael protested, but she let Shadow lead her from the room.

Larissa had indeed already left, so Shadow gave her a lesson in dagger throwing, encouraging Jael cheerfully when her daggers flew far astray.

"You're not as bad as you think," Shadow told her. "And you're fortunate being two-handed from the start. I spent years training my off hand to throw straight. You need to build your wrist strength, but your sword training will do that anyway. Let's go get ready for supper. I want to meet this young lord from Calidwyn who's supposedly going to set the Temple of Baaros back on the proper trail."

"He may not be here for supper," Jael warned. "He had business at the temple all day." For some reason the idea of Aunt Shadow—who probably knew every possible trick for luring a man to her bed—meeting Lord Urien made Jael uneasy.

"Then I'll take supper with Mist and Aubry and enjoy seeing the city again," Shadow shrugged. Then she grinned. "I want to find one of those taverns that don't admit elves."

"And do what?" Jael asked eagerly.

"Oh, I don't know," Shadow speculated. "Under the Compact, no business in the city can exclude elves. So since the place is acting against the law anyway, do you think the law might turn a blind eye if the tavern misplaced the night's takings?"

"Well, the City Guard might or might not," Jael admitted. "If it was just up to Father, you could burn the place down. Mother would probably light the torch for you. But Mother and Father aren't the magistrates. So you'd best not get caught, and then it doesn't matter, does it?"

"There's that," Shadow laughed. "Want to come along for the fun, little acorn?"

The offer was tempting, but Urien *might* be at supper; besides, a brief image occurred to Jael of the tavern indeed burning down—with Shadow and Jael in it. Or perhaps the leakproofing spell on every cask in the place might fail at once, wine and ale mingling in brown and purple streams on the floor—

"Sorry, Aunt Shadow," Jael chuckled. "Grandmother Celene is seldom ever here. Mother will be disappointed if I don't stay for supper, especially after she came here on my account."

"I see you're learning politics already," Shadow said ruefully. "All right. Your mother would be furious if I took you out drinking, anyway, even with Mist and Aubry."

To Jael's delight, Lord Urien was back for supper. Again, he escorted Jael to the table. Jael, who was still rather angry at Mother and Father over their treatment of her the night before, could hardly keep a triumphant grin from her face as the lord sat beside her.

"I spoke with High Priest Ankaras at some length today," Urien told them with a sigh. "He was not receptive to the changes of doctrine suggested. I was forced to chastise him and remove him from his station, which means more responsibilities for me and the priests I brought with me. I'll have to completely assume leadership of the temple until Ankaras can accept the changes, or until a new High Priest can be trained. He's so angry now that he will be of no use at all to me during the transition, and his lesser priests are equally uncooperative. That's unfortunate, because worshippers are more accepting of doctrinal changes presented by their own priests. Ankaras may even attempt to obstruct my efforts."

"I wish there was some way we could help," Donya said regretfully. "But unless Ankaras is violating some city law, we can't interfere—especially in this case."

"I quite understand," Urien said graciously. "In fact, it has concerned me that you may be exposing yourselves to rumors of bias simply by allowing me to stay here, especially when I assume a position as High Priest of the temple. If I can't find suitable lodging tomorrow, I think it will be best that I stay at an inn until permanent lodging can be found."

"Surely that's not necessary," Argent protested.

"With respect, you and your lady are not the only ones who could be accused of bias," Urien told him politely. "Ankaras and his priests, and those worshippers who are resistant to the change, might bring a similar charge if I were to remain here, that the High Lord and Lady were privately exerting their influence on me to change temple doctrine to suit them."

"Of course, you're right," Donya said firmly. "I don't want anything to endanger your authority over the temple."

Jael fought down a sigh of disappointment. Although she was looking forward to helping Lord Urien with his search for a home, she had hoped that he would be staying at the castle for at least a few days, maybe longer.

Urien turned to Jael.

"I hope you haven't regretted your offer to help me find lodging," he said. "I hadn't intended to avail myself of that offer so soon."

"A friend from the Heartwood is coming to see Jael tomorrow morning—" Donya began.

"—but I can be ready to go at midmorning," Jael finished hurriedly, ignoring Donya's frown.

"You have no idea how I appreciate this assistance," Urien said to Donya and Argent, giving Jael a smile of thanks. "By the way, if you will pardon my boldness, I instructed my footman to bring samples of several of my family's trade goods for you to examine. If the quality meets with your approval, I will attempt to market these goods in the city. I donate a good part of my profits to the temple, of course, and the temple here is small enough that the funds are desperately needed, especially as we will doubtless lose some worshippers with the change in doctrine."

"Probably more than some," Argent told him regretfully. "The temple didn't start the anti-elvan sentiment in Allanmere, only fostered it. Mercantile sects are popular in a city such as this, of course, but I'm afraid that the hostility toward elves came first, and Ankaras's teachings simply attracted those people to the Temple of Baaros."

"In a trade city the size of Allanmere, I am certain the

Temple of Baaros can flourish without the necessity of alienating the elvan citizens and flaunting disrespect for the city's laws," Urien said smoothly. "As I said, I expect us to lose some worshippers at first, but I have no doubt the temple will benefit in the long view." He smiled. "But let me return to my efforts to shamelessly forward my trade goods."

He raised one hand, and several of his servants came forward bearing trays. There were small cups of liquors and wine, samples of fine pottery and swatches of cloth, tiny bowls of spices, and cunning metalwork, including some jewelry. Jael was quite impressed by the latter items, intricately whorled gold work set with deep purple-red stones.

"Especially when dealing with trade in a new city, my family deals primarily in items desired by the nobility," Urien said, almost apologetically. "I selected expensive, high-profit items to maximize the benefit of a small shipment."

"There are a number of shops that deal almost exclusively within the Noble District," Donya told him, fingering the cloth samples. "Goods of this quality always sell well, and new liquors and spices are constantly in demand. We have a number of fine jewelers in the city, so that's more competitive, but I've never seen anything quite like this work."

"It's wonderful stuff," Mera announced, her mouth full of the sweets she was plucking from the platter.

"Don't eat so fast," Markus muttered, jabbing his sister in the ribs. He had taken just as many sweets, but was busily stuffing them into his pockets.

"Markus! Mera!" Donya said embarrassedly. "Gods, you're more trouble than"—her eyes flickered involuntarily to Jael, but she recovered hurriedly—"than Ankaras."

Jael flushed furiously. Gods, did any member of her family *ever* miss a chance to humiliate her?

"Oh, please let the young lord and lady have what they like, I beg you," Urien said graciously. "I intended these samples as gifts—oh, I wouldn't dare call them that, it might be misconstrued by some as bribery—but if my goods meet with such approval, what can I be but flattered?"

"I don't see any of the tea you were drinking among these samples," Argent said curiously, sipping the wine from a small crystal cup.

"I beg your forgiveness, High Lord Argent," Urien said, dismayed. "I would have had to bring a large shipment of the black tea in order to make a suitable profit. I brought only a small private stock for myself, so it didn't occur to me to bring a sample for you. But I would be more than happy to share—"

"Oh, no, no," Argent said hurriedly. He smiled, taking a bite of cheese before sampling another liquor. "As you may know, Lord Urien, I used to run an herbal shop in town with my sister Elaria, who now manages it alone. To be quite honest, I've tasted so many teas in my years in the shop that I'm afraid they've lost all attraction for me. I can't even enjoy a good pipe of dreamweed these days—I find myself evaluating the resin content and speculating on the rainfall in the harvest year."

Urien laughed.

"Do you know, I find the same thing happening every time I try a new wine," he said. "High Lady Donya, you don't want to drink that out of the cup. It's Bluebright essence, quite potent. Take one of the lumps of sugar on the saucer beside the cup, and pour a drop or two on the sugar, then eat it."

"Bluebright?" Donya hesitated. "I've never heard of it."

Urien waved the tray over and took a sugar lump for himself, dripped a little of the liquid from the tiny spoon in the bowl, and popped the lump of sugar into his mouth.

"I wouldn't like to joust afterward," he smiled, "but it's quite safe. Bluebright has become something of a fashion in Calidwyn."

Urien was interrupted as Markus, fumbling through the goods on one of the trays, knocked over several of the small cups and bowls. Donya flushed, muttering apologies as she tried to clean up the mess. Urien gallantly dismissed the incident.

While Donya's attention was on Markus, Jael surreptitiously took a lump of sugar, dipped a corner in the liquid, and shoved it into her mouth. A furious heat burst through her mouth, melting into a delightful mintlike coolness; Jael sucked in her breath sharply and, glancing up, met Urien's eyes. Urien gave her an engaging grin and a wink that promised he could keep her secret, then turned back to Donya, who had laid her sugar down on her plate.

"If you don't object, I'd like to have my herbalists examine this first," Donya said apologetically. "I'm always a little cautious about a new intoxicant in town."

"Of course, of course," Urien said easily. "Your caution for your people does you honor. I won't attempt to market the Bluebright until you give me permission. And now, if you'll excuse me—"

"Of course," Argent said. "Thank you for showing us the samples, Lord Urien, and for your news of the temple."

Urien stood, bowing over Jael's hand.

"I will meet you and your escort at midmorning, Lady Jaellyn," he said. "Good evening."

"Good evening," Jael said, blushing again, but this time not with embarrassment.

Donya and Argent again walked with Urien through the hall, but this time Jael was glad for the opportunity to sneak away to her room while the twins still hovered over Urien's samples. She had started to feel quite strange—light and floating, warm inside, but her skin was deliciously cool. Her every movement seemed wonderfully drawn out and slow, as if she moved under water. A little unsteadily, Jael made her way to her room, sighing with relief as she latched the door behind her.

To Jaellyn's surprise, there was a wooden box lying on her pillow. An apology from her parents? Jaellyn scowled. They had plenty to apologize for, no doubt of that. But forthright Donya would have simply apologized, and that would be that; quiet and thoughtful Argent might have given her a gift, but he would have given it to her himself.

Jael reached for the box. It seemed to take hundreds of tiny motions before she grasped it. The design on the lid was strange; then Jael recognized it as the coat of arms that Lord Urien had worn on his surcoat. A gift from Lord Urien! Jael smiled delightedly as a familiar scent reached her nose—the black tea from Lord Urien's own private stock.

Jael opened the box. The tea was in small blocks, each block stamped with Lord Urien's coat of arms and wrapped in thin parchment. The sweet, heady fragrance made Jael's mouth water, and she lifted the small blocks out, admiring their precise edges. To her surprise, however, under the first layer of blocks of tea, at the center of the box, was a small pouch. Jael opened it, then gasped.

What spilled from the pouch was a small pendant of the exquisite whorled gold work Jael had seen in the dining hall, in an unusual glyphlike shape. At the center of the pendant was one of the purple-red stones, this one as large as the nail on her first finger. Little flashes of bloodred light shone from the gem. The pendant hung on a long, breath-fine gold chain.

The pendant had to be worth a small fortune. Jael smiled as she realized why Urien had hidden the pouch in the box of tea; Mother and Father, who worried when the lord paid attention to their *child*, would no doubt have made a positively *legendary* outcry if Lord Urien had given their daughter such a gift. Jael hurriedly lifted the chain over her neck, slipping the pendant into the front of her shirt and grinning to herself. *Two* special gifts, and in just a few days! It almost made up for the way Mother and Father had been treating her.

Jael lay back on her bed, enjoying the floating feeling in her head. Quite a fashion in Calidwyn, eh? Hopefully it would become a fashion here, too.

She poured herself a mug of water and lay sipping it.

Perhaps she'd just stay up all night enjoying this wonderful watery looseness in her muscles, the feeling that her mind would drift right up through the ceiling. Yes, she'd just stay up all night and—

Jael blinked as sunlight dazzled her eyes.

"Huh?" she muttered.

"I said, Mist is here," Donya said irritably from the doorway. "Really, Jaellyn, you're old enough to take your finery off yourself before you go to sleep. Change your clothes and come down to the dining hall."

Jael groaned and crawled out of bed, stumbling to the washbasin. The water in the pitcher was icy cold and shocked her face, and Jael realized that she was chilled through; sometime during the night the fire had died, and she hadn't even roused enough to crawl under the covers. Her nose was already running.

Something fell from the bed to the floor, and Jael picked it up, scowling puzzledly at the half-melted, twisted mass of metal in her hand. Surely it couldn't be the mug she'd been drinking from. Had she gotten up and somehow dropped it in the fire, then later raked it out? Well, no time to wonder now. Shivering, Jael pulled on clean clothes and trotted down the halls. Fortunately, the fires in the dining hall had been lit long before, banishing the last of the chill from the huge room.

Mist was sitting with Shadow and Celene, chatting animatedly over bread, cheese, and fruit. Jael smiled to herself. Apparently Aubry had been indulging his forest cousin's vanity in the market; Mist was garbed handsomely in new pale green silks that contrasted beautifully with his pale skin and hair. Mist grinned proudly as he saw Jael noticing his clothes, but he rose and came to embrace her warmly.

"Good morn, little fawn," Mist murmured into her hair. "I missed you in the forest this summer."

Jael sighed and leaned her head on Mist's shoulder, for a brief moment at peace.

"I missed the forest, foster father," she said. "But I missed you more."

Donya, looking profoundly uncomfortable, cleared her throat awkwardly. Argent chuckled and patted her arm as Mist followed Jaellyn back to the table.

"When Celene told me that Jael was soul-sick, I was ashamed not to have seen it sooner," Mist said, grinning wryly. "And I knew better than any of you the full extent of the old wild blood in her. Unfortunately, like you, I saw what was happening around her instead of watching Jael herself. It hardly excuses me to say that since I left my own clan, I haven't seen a case of soul-sickness in decades."

"I still don't understand what this—this ritual is supposed to do," Donya muttered.

"There are many possible answers," Mist told her. "Most of the Hidden Folk would say that the Mother Forest uses the ritual as a gateway to heal the troubled soul. Some potions, such as the one used in the ritual, can temporarily heal soul-sickness by placing body and spirit in balance, and some believe that once that balance is achieved, the dreamer can then learn how to maintain it. Others believe, though, that the dreaming potion simply allows the one taking it to explore the hidden places in their own soul, and that the altars simply provide a safe haven and the proper atmosphere for doing it. There's no doubt, though, that the altars are conducive to certain magical operations."

"That's true," Celene said, nodding. "The altars are a node that attracts and focuses certain natural energies in the forest. Scryings, for example, are much clearer there, and healing magic is more potent and focused."

"All right, but what about the rest of it?" Donya pressed.

"Well, I agree with Celene that most of the trappings are probably unnecessary," Mist admitted. "The spirit journey is used as a kind of adulthood ritual in some of the hidden clans. The two days' fasting simply purifies the blood and makes the potion more effective, just as wine affects us more strongly if we haven't eaten."

"I don't know that I like Jael missing her meals," Donya said worriedly. "She's so thin already. And just what's in this potion?"

"Why, I don't know," Mist said, frowning. "I never made it, nor have I ever drunk it."

"Elaria and I made the potion many times, before we moved to the city," Argent said, taking Donya's hand. "The shop has all the necessary ingredients. Dreamweed tincture, of course; a few other herbs and berries, roots and the like that you've probably never heard of, in a base of moondrop wine. A few of the ingredients are also dream-producing, like the dreamweed; others are sleep-inducing. The only ingredient of any real concern is dried and powdered snake-eye mushrooms. In large enough quantities the mushrooms are poisonous, even deadly, but only a tiny dose is used for the potion. Elaria and I can make the potion ourselves, to be certain it's properly prepared and safe." He turned to Jael. "If you still want to do this, of course."

Suddenly, with the five of them sitting there looking at her so soberly, Jael was unsure. Then Shadow winked at her, and abruptly Jael wanted to laugh. Other than two days' food, what did she have to lose? At worst, she'd have an uncomfortable nap at the altars and a few bad dreams. At best, maybe she could sit at a table without finding bits of broken light globes in her food.

"Of course," Jael said, shrugging. "After all this trouble you've all already gone through, I've got to try, at least."

"Then you can begin your fast after breakfast," Mist told her. "During your fast you may drink water, tea, or vegetable broth, and you may eat raw or plain boiled potherbs, but nothing else. As you're so thin, I believe honey for your tea should be acceptable."

Shadow grimaced.

"Fortune favor us, Mist, she'll be pissing green by the time she's done," she said disgustedly. "No wine?"

"It's only for two days," Jael said practically. "Besides, wine makes me sick anyway." She shrugged and glanced over the table. "Since this is my last meal, pass me some of that sausage, will you? And the cheese, and the bread and honey, and the potatoes."

"Donya tells us you're helping the new priest of the Temple of Baaros find a house," Shadow grinned. "That should distract you from your growling stomach. Say, when do I meet this champion of Allanmere's elves?"

"He should be at supper tonight," Donya said quickly. "Supper will be early, because afterward Argent is meeting with some members of the Council of Churches. Why don't you all come?"

"I do thank you for the invitation, daughter," Celene said gently. "But if I am going to move the other side of the Gate nearer to the altars, I'll need to confer with several other mages, both here and in the forest. Two days will barely give me enough time for preparation and casting the spell."

Mist, who rarely came into town, had heard only a little of the news of the Temple of Baaros; he was vitally interested in the whole story and relieved to learn of Lord Urien's purpose in coming. While Donya and Argent told him all that had occurred, Jael stuffed herself with as much food as she could hold. Fortunately last night's experiment with Bluebright had had none of the ill effects Jael experienced when she drank wine or other liquors. Jael swallowed one last honey-smeared bun and sighed as she pushed away from the table.

"Time to start starving," she said regretfully. "If everyone will excuse me, I want to wash up before I meet Lord Urien."

There was just time enough for a brief splash in the bathing pool before Jael had to run for the main hall. Lord Urien was there with four guards—two of his own, and two of the Castle Guard, apparently Jael's "escorts."

"I had thought to bring a few more servants with us," Urien apologized. "It's so cold, though, I thought a small carriage would be more comfortable and more private. However, if you would rather walk—"

"Oh, no, a carriage sounds perfect," Jael said hurriedly, realizing what that meant—Lord Urien and herself alone in the carriage, with the guards riding outside.

Urien apparently had not brought his own carriage to town, for Jael recognized the waiting vehicle as a hired carriage from one of the local businesses. It was luxuriously comfortable, however, with a weatherproofing spell to warm the interior. Jael was unaccustomed to the lord's politeness in extending a hand to help her in first, but she grinned quietly to herself when he sat down beside her, instead of taking the opposite seat.

"There're three houses I know of that should still be available," Jael told him. "Two are on North Street and one is on River Road, but the one on River Road may be too far south."

"Then let's look at that one first," Urien said gaily. "In this weather, the farther south, the better."

Jael stuck her head outside long enough to give directions to the driver and make sure that none of the guards would be able to hear the conversation inside the carriage. She ducked back inside, shivering, and Urien gallantly took off his furlined cloak, wrapping it around her.

"Thank you," Jael said, smiling. "And thanks for the tea, too."

"I'm glad you liked the tea," Urien smiled back, his eyes twinkling.

"I liked this, too." Jael fished the pendant out of her shirt. "I've never seen anything so beautiful. It must be very valuable."

"It looks beautiful on you," Urien said. He grinned sheepishly. "But I should confess that that piece was made by a cousin of mine, so I got rather a good bargain on it. Nonetheless, I was afraid the High Lord and Lady might disapprove."

"Disapprove? Mother would chew coal and breathe fire," Jael said wryly.

Urien laughed.

"I would think your parents would be accustomed to such

attentions by now," he said gently. "Surely your suitors have given you many gifts."

"Suitors?" Jael wiped the blank expression off her face as quickly as she could. Of course Urien would expect her to have had suitors; most daughters of noble birth would have been long married by now. "Well—"

Urien raised his eyebrows.

"Surely a lovely young noblewoman like yourself has had many suitors," he said inquiringly.

"Well, you heard Mother," Jael said awkwardly. "As she sees it, I'm just one of the children."

"Ah." Urien took her hand, stroking it sympathetically. "How frustrating that must be for you."

"It surely is," Jael said sourly. Urien's hands were cool, and Jael realized uncomfortably that she was still wearing his cloak. "I'm warmer now, if you want this back," Jael said hesitantly.

"We'll share it." Urien moved a little closer, draping the spacious cloak around both of them—and his arm around Jael's shoulders in the process. Jael was not fooled by this maneuver—a quiet, unobtrusive observer around town could watch almost every possible technique of flirting—but when Urien attempted nothing more intimate, Jael smiled rather triumphantly to herself and settled comfortably against his side.

When Jael had cautioned that the house on River Road might be too far south, she had not been referring to climate. Southern Noble District bordered on Rivertown, not a desirable neighborhood. The house Jael had seen was indeed still available, but it fronted on a tavern and a brothel, and there were beggars in the alleys on both sides. Urien insisted on seeing the house anyway, and Jael found the excursion interesting; Jael had never seen the large stone buildings empty, and the rooms seemed icy cold and echoingly large.

"Well, it is a fine house," Urien said regretfully several hours later, when they had made their way from the upper rooms to the cellar. "Unfortunately I must agree that the neighborhood isn't suitable."

"I told you that before we ever got inside," Jael laughed as they settled into the coach.

"Ah, but then I would have had to take you back to the castle that much sooner," Urien smiled back. "Shall we dine in the market?"

Jael sighed.

"I can't eat," she said. "I have to fast for two days for this elvan ritual. It's supposed to unblock my magic and make me stop tripping over my own feet."

"A miraculous ritual indeed," Urien chuckled. "But are you a mage, then?"

"Not yet," Jael said ruefully. "Grandmother Celene says I've got it, but I can't use it. Mother doesn't think the ritual is going to work, either. So I'm probably starving for two days for nothing."

"What a pity," Urien sighed. "I heard there was a man selling dragon in the plaza."

Jael had thought that after her hearty breakfast, she wouldn't want food for hours and hours; at the mention of dragon, however, her mouth watered.

"There's no reason you shouldn't eat, just because I can't," Jael said, trying valiantly not to look hungry.

"Eat while you go hungry? Certainly not," Urien said indignantly. "Is there nothing you can have?"

"Boiled potherbs and vegetable broth," Jael said miserably, wishing she had simply said she was not hungry. "Tea."

"Then we will find an obliging inn." Urien leaned out the carriage window and spoke to the driver; Jael, utterly amazed, was escorted grandly into the Silver Scepter, where other nobles looked on rather dubiously as Jael and Urien were served plates of plain boiled greens and cups of steaming tea from Urien's stock.

Urien raised an eyebrow at the potherbs, but smiled at Jael and raised his cup of tea in a congenial toast.

"Very healthful, I'm sure, and balancing to the body's humors," he chuckled. "Well calculated to reduce an overgenerous waist."

Jael, who had never cared for boiled potherbs, found the food abysmal, but the tea was even more delicious than Jael remembered it, and that made the greens more tolerable. Jael was even more embarrassed when she realized that Urien was being charged two Suns for the miserable meal, but Urien simply laughed, joking that on the caravan to Allanmere, his servants had gathered whole pans full of fresh potherbs and cooked them up for not so much as a copper, and with the added flavoring of meat. He asked the maid to brew another pot of tea and pour it into a heat-spelled pot for the afternoon, and paid yet another Sun for that; Jael started to protest, then realized that to a merchant who could afford to give her a pendant worth doubtless hundreds of Suns, three Suns for a meal was likely nothing new to him.

They looked at one of the houses on North Street, but the other was closed and locked, although a peep in at the windows showed it to be empty.

"That wouldn't stop Aunt Shadow for a minute," Jael said, sighing. "I suppose we'll just have to contact the owner and come back tomorrow."

"How terrible," Urien chuckled, and Jael grinned at him.

"Did you arrange for this house to be closed up?" she asked.

"No, I didn't even know where it was. How could I?" Urien protested, but he was smiling. "But it'll have to be day after tomorrow, Lady Jaellyn. I can't neglect the temple."

"I can't go then," Jael said disappointedly. "I've got to go to that elvan ritual I mentioned, and I don't know for certain how long it'll take." Jael bit back a sigh, stifling her disappointment. She could scarcely expect the lord to spend all his time with her; he had, after all, come to Allanmere to deal with the Temple of Baaros, not to visit her.

"If you don't mind, then, I'll wait to see the other house when you can come with me," Urien said. "I still must contact the owner, and tramping through cold, dusty, empty houses is much more interesting with a pleasant companion."

Urien reached for the clay pot of tea; however, to his disgust, the pot had cracked, leaking the tea over the floor of the carriage.

"I see it's a matter of pride not to use a sealing spell on pottery locally," he said wryly. "I'm sorry. Next time I'll bring a metal pot."

Jael said nothing, squirming inwardly. She'd be willing to bet that there *had* been a sealing spell on the pot—before it was placed in the carriage with Jael. No, there was no chance that she was going to tell Lord Urien about *that* unfortunate problem; besides, if luck was with her for once, in a couple of days it wouldn't matter.

When they reached the castle, Urien escorted Jael to her room after dismissing the guards.

"I must change before supper, and be sure that my people have moved the rest of my belongings to the inn," he said regretfully. He bowed over her hand and kissed it, his lips cool against her knuckles. "But perhaps you would care to walk with me in the gardens after supper. High Lord Argent told me that supper would be early tonight. It's a little chill, but the changing colors of the leaves are beautiful in the sunset."

Jael was amazed to realize she was blushing.

"I'd like that very much," she said, forcing her voice to firmness. She'd be boiled in oil before she would simper like some tittering, idiotic maiden. She hooked one finger through the gold chain of the pendant, pulling the chain up a little so Urien could see it. "Thank you again for your gift. It's lovely."

"Then perhaps it is worthy of its wearer," Urien said smoothly. "Until supper, then."

Jael stood watching after him for a few moments, then sighed and closed her door, wondering dismally what she could possibly wear to supper. Maybe it was time to call in Mother's seamstresses and see what they could make up new for her. Maybe—

Jael shook her head, flopping onto her bed. Mooning over finery and blushing! Soon she'd be dropping handkerchiefs and giggling and darkening her eyelashes. What in the Mother Forest's name did she think she was doing with Urien anyway? Certainly she was enjoying the attention, but what was she hoping for? Even if she wanted to marry him and become the lady of a large merchant family—an abysmal thought—there was no chance at all that her parents would ever permit her to marry a merchant and priest who would, in all probability, soon be returning to another city. Not marriage, then.

A few nights' passion with a handsome, romantic nobleman from a far city? Jael sighed disgustedly at the idea. Did she really want Urien in her bed, or was she merely that desperate to prove that she *wasn't* a child? And prove it to whom, Urien or herself? Her mind might be curious, but her body wouldn't care if she waited twenty more years for her first tumble.

"Jael!"

The whispered voice came from Jael's window, and Jael was surprised at the face peeping in.

"Tanis?" Jael hurried over. "What are you doing here?"

"I sneaked away from the temple," Tanis admitted. "They dismissed all the acolytes, anyway, while the priests are all locked in rooms arguing. I wanted to come and apologize for scolding you like an old grandmother in the market. It's not your fault that—well—"

"—that everything goes wrong all around me," Jael finished. "Well, it is my fault in a way, even though I don't mean to do it. That's all right, Tanis. I seem to sour everybody's milk at some time or other. I'm just glad you're not still angry with me. I don't have many friends. Don't you want to come in?"

"No, I've got to hurry back to the temple before I'm missed," Tanis said with a sigh. "And tomorrow High Priest Urien is going to be looking through all the temple records, so I'll be busy all day carrying scrolls back and forth. But do you want to go to the market tomorrow evening?"

"All right," Jael said eagerly. An evening of Tanis's lively, undemanding company was just what she needed. Then she remembered and sighed. "I probably can't. I've got to go to the Heartwood the next morning for this elvan ritual, and Mist will likely have me meditating all evening or something. Can we go when I get back?"

"Of course," Tanis said. "Any evening that High Priest Urien doesn't have me digging through the temple archives."

"What do you think of Lord—High Priest Urien, anyway?" Jael asked him.

"I don't know." Tanis frowned. "I was almost relieved when he came. I was worrying that the temple would be thrown out of the city, I suppose. And he knows everything about how to run a temple, I think. But he's—I don't know. Somehow I don't like him."

"Why not?" Jael pressed, surprised to find herself bristling a little.

"I don't know," Tanis said, shrugging. "It's like when you bite into a meat pie and the meat's spoiled, but the spices hide the flavor. At first you don't notice anything, and then you can't figure out why the pie doesn't taste right. And the next thing you know, you're spewing your guts out in the privy."

Jael had to laugh at that.

"I don't think Mother quite likes him either," Jael confessed. "I don't know why. I think he's been very friendly and polite."

"He certainly wasn't polite with Ankaras," Tanis said wryly. "He got so angry I thought he'd lock us all up in the cellar. He has all of us doing menial work now, while he and his priests do all the rituals and make the decisions."

"Well, he's Ankaras's superior, isn't he?" Jael asked. "Doesn't Ankaras have to obey him?"

"We all do," Tanis said with a sigh. "Well, I'll meet with you when you get back, then."

"All right," Jael said, wondering a little at Tanis's attitude. From what she'd seen at the temple, Ankaras had seemed a very harsh master indeed. She couldn't imagine Urien, however angry, being so severe.

Because the early autumn weather often necessitated Jael drinking potions and herbal teas, Jael always kept a kettle and water near the fireplace in her room. Now she filled the kettle and heated the water, shaving some of Urien's tea into the water to brew, sniffing pleasurably at the aroma as the heat of the fire warmed her through.

There was time for a leisurely bath before supper, and by the time Jael had found something suitable to wear from her scanty wardrobe, only her growling stomach marred her mood. A last cup of hot, sweet tea somewhat soothed her hunger, and for once she did not have to rush down to supper.

Shadow and Mist were already there, as were Mother and Father, chatting with Lord Urien. Urien appeared completely at his ease, despite being the only full-blood human in the room. He smiled delightedly when Jael entered the room.

"Good evening, Lady Jaellyn," he said, taking Jael's hand and turning so that his back was to the others. "I was thanking your parents again for allowing you to help me find a house. It is most kind of them, and of you, it being such a tedious job in this weather." He grinned and winked deliberately.

"Oh, I don't mind," Jael said, grinning back and joining in the game. "I'd rather look at houses than go to fighting practice, at least."

There were still candles at the table instead of light globes, and now Jael was sure that Mother and Father had delayed replacing the light globes because of her. To Jael's relief, however, no place had been set for Markus or Mera, probably because of their behavior the night before.

"So you didn't find anything suitable?" Shadow asked. "What about the two houses on North Street I saw yesterday?"

"We saw one of them," Urien said. "It might suffice, but I'd prefer to see the other before I make my choice."

"Who owns the western house, the one with the blue glass windows?" Jael asked her parents. "You know, the one with that awful gargoyle statue on the roof."

Shadow laughed.

"That used to belong to Numan, the merchant who sold statuary to the temples," she said. "I once heard he put that gargoyle on the roof because he couldn't sell it. I was in that house once. It's a fairly comfortable place, and there's a nice hidden cache behind a stone in the hearth for your valuables."

"And how did you manage to learn that?" Mist asked Shadow, grinning.

"Well, why do you think I was there?" Shadow joked back. "To tumble that snag-toothed old corpse?"

"Aunt Shadow used to be Guildmistress of the Guild of Thieves," Jael explained to Urien.

"Oh, my." Urien bowed. "I am honored, Guildmistress."

"Retired," Shadow corrected. "Aubry's the one you have to deal with now. Although he's got more respect for the Temple District than I ever did, I admit."

"Then I will in turn admit that what you say is a relief," Urien chuckled. "My poor temple has little enough wealth to sustain it that I'm afraid we can afford few 'donations' to the Guild."

"Isn't that a little odd, an improverished temple to a mercantile god?" Mist asked confusedly.

"Baaros's blessings are meant for His worshippers, not for the luxury and comfort of His priests," Urien said patiently.

"Most priests, being from mercantile houses themselves, have some private wealth to use for their personal comfort, but the temples themselves are funded by the offerings of the worshippers."

"An interesting system," Shadow said thoughtfully. "Most temples supposedly don't allow their priests to keep personal wealth, but feed and keep them out of temple funds."

Urien smiled, but his explanation of temple economics was interrupted by the arrival of the servants bearing platters of food. Urien escorted Jael to the table, and when Jael was served a plate of plain boiled greens, she was afraid that Urien would request the same for himself out of misplaced gallantry; fortunately, Urien hesitated, but finally helped himself to the venison roast.

Shadow had heard most of the news about the Temple of Baaros from Donya and Argent (and likely from Aubry as well), but she didn't seem to mind hearing it again from Urien. Jael toyed with her greens—only two meals and already she was heartily sick of the taste—and ground her teeth. At least Aunt Shadow wasn't actively flirting with Urien. Jael was privately of the opinion that there was probably no man in Allanmere who could withstand so formidable an assault. Jael glanced down surreptitiously at her still almost-flat chest, wiry legs, and rumpled tunic, and sighed disgustedly.

As Urien sipped a last goblet of wine after the meal, however, he said casually, "With your permission, of course, High Lord Argent, High Lady Donya, I asked Lady Jaellyn if she might be so kind as to show me the castle gardens after supper. I had only the barest glance through the window of my room, but it seemed to me that the colors of the leaves at this time of year must be truly beautiful."

Donya frowned, the beginnings of a scowl lining her forehead, and even Argent looked doubtful; Jael was starting to fume when Shadow laughed merrily.

"So tell me, Doe, when did you and Argent decide to become jailers instead of rulers? For Fortune's sake, Jael's old enough to decide for herself to go for a walk in the garden with a handsome fellow. If you frown one more time, I'll tell everyone here at the table about our first night in Fernwold, when you and that—"

"All right. All right," Donya said hastily, her cheeks flaming.

"A shame," Argent added, patting Donya's arm and smiling at her, "it would have made interesting listening. Nonetheless, Lord Urien, Shadow is right. Thank you for your courtesy, but Jaellyn is quite old enough to answer for herself. I might add that there is a lovely view of the sunset on the west walk. Come, my dear, I'd like to consult with Mist about Jaellyn's potion."

Jael hadn't really expected that Urien would make it known to everyone that they were going to go walking; it made her feel a little shy as she took Urien's arm and showed him which corridors to take to reach the garden door at the north side of the castle. They were fortunate that supper had been early; it being early autumn, there was little daylight left so late in the afternoon.

Jael had always loved the castle gardens. Exquisitely carved statues had been commissioned for it, and exotic trees and flowers had been brought in by merchants from distant countries, planted and trimmed artistically, and, where necessary, individually tended with selective weatherproofing spells. Several of Allanmere's underground springs had been magically tapped and directed to feed several stone fountains. Mother had told her that some parts of the garden were centuries old, dating back to the reign of Ria the Fey. Most of the garden had been destroyed during the Black Wars, and later rulers had neglected it, but High Lord Adren, Jael's great-great-grandfather, had restored it, and Grandmother Celene had made it her special hobby.

The garden fairly sparkled with magic, and Jael was always careful to touch nothing but the stone benches and bowers where those visiting the garden could take their rest.

Ordinarily the trees would still be green this early in the autumn, but the past few days had been unseasonably cold, and many of the trees displayed a rainbow of brilliant color.

"This is lovely," Urien said. "Where is this west walk that your father mentioned?"

Jael had known immediately what Argent meant when he recommended the west walk. A small stand of trees had been planted on a slight rise so that the sun seemed to set into the trees, not the city wall. A small bower overgrown with moondrop vines had been placed for just this purpose, and the view included one of the sparkling fountains.

"What a pleasant place," Urien said, smiling and motioning to Jael to sit beside him in the bower.

"Father built it for Mother before I was born," Jael said, sitting down. She grinned. "I think it was so she'd spend more time sitting in the garden instead of practice fighting with the guard captains while she was pregnant."

"And are you a warrior like your mother?" Urien took Jael's hand, turned it palm up, and traced a finger gently across her palm. "You don't have the sword calluses."

"Me, a warrior?" Jael laughed at the idea. "I'm studying, of course, but I doubt that I'll ever be any good at it. If my weapons master doesn't give me something to trip over, my own feet serve just fine."

"Not a warrior, not yet a mage, neither elf nor human," Urien said sympathetically. "How frustrating that must be for you."

"Aunt Shadow would say I have sore feet from walking the dagger's edge," Jael said wryly. "But that's common in Allanmere these days."

"There is nothing common about you, Lady Jaellyn," Urien corrected gently. He raised her hand and deliberately kissed her fingertips, sending shivers down Jael's spine.

"You—uh—don't have to call me 'lady,' " she said. "Most of my friends just call me Jael."

"Jael is a child's name," Urien murmured. He brushed his lips over her fingertips again. "You are a lovely young woman, not a child . . . Jaellyn."

He leaned forward slowly, his eyes on hers, giving Jael plenty of time to draw back if she wished to. Jael did not draw back, although her heart was beating fast and she shivered slightly as his cool lips touched hers. She waited for her heart to sing, her body to come alive—

Nothing.

Urien did not press her beyond that first kiss, and a faint frown troubled his eyes as he took her other hand, holding them between his own.

"Have I offended you?" he asked softly.

"No, oh, no," Jael said hurriedly, searching her mind for some plausible excuse. *No, it's just that I've never been kissed before.* Not that one. *No, it's just that nothing happens when you kiss me.* Uh-*uh.* "No, I guess I just keep expecting Mother to coming running down the path to see what I'm doing."

"Of course." His smile was so understanding that Jael was horribly embarrassed, sure that he could see right through her feeble pretense. "And we must not alarm your parents, or they might not allow me to see you again. Come, there's little light left. We'll go back now, and your mother will be pleased."

Jael walked back silently, thoroughly disgusted with herself. Gods, what was *wrong* with her? Maybe it was the fasting. *And maybe some wicked sorcerer put a curse on me the day I was born.*

Urien escorted her back to the main hall, where a rather surprised Donya met them. Urien thanked her again for the hospitality of the castle and bowed over Jael's hand formally before he left.

"Well?" Donya demanded when Urien had gone. "What happened?"

"Nothing! Nothing happened!" Jael's sudden anger surprised her. "We walked in the garden, we looked at the trees, we watched the sun go down. What did you think, that he was going to tumble me on the ground with guards looking down from the parapets? That I'd let him?"

"No!" Donya flushed. "No. I didn't mean—no, that's wrong. I suppose I did." She took a deep breath and laid a callused hand on Jael's shoulder. "I'm sorry. By the time I was your age, I was no maiden, as you've probably gathered from Shadow's stories. At your age, if I'd been in a beautiful garden at sunset with a charming and handsome young fellow, I probably *would* have tumbled him. And the only thing that would have concerned my mother would be if he was the husband of some other city's High Lady, or if I hadn't been taking my goldenroot potion. So."

Donya took another deep breath and shook her head.

"Do what you want, Jaellyn. Just be wise and please don't get your heart broken by a lord we know nothing about." She squeezed Jael's shoulder roughly. "And if Shadow isn't here and you need someone to talk to—well, I'll do the best I can.

I've always been better with swords than words." She turned away.

"Mother—" Jael hesitated a moment too long; Donya was gone.

Jael sighed and climbed the stairs toward her room, realizing that all too often words were not enough.

Perhaps they never were.

IV

"I don't understand why I have to go under a sleep spell," Jael complained. "I've walked through the Gate before."

"Fasting not only purifies the blood, but also intensifies magical energies in the body," Mist explained patiently. "You have already seen the effects that your uncontrolled energies can cause on even simple magics, and that effect is stronger now than when you were younger. Would you wish to see what will happen if a Gate goes awry with us passing through it?"

"It's a simple spell," Celene reassured her. "I'll release it as soon as we are safely through the Gate."

"And if Fortune favors us," Shadow added, "you can walk back through on your own feet."

"Are you coming, Aunt Shadow?" Jael asked with relief.

"Your mother suggested it," Shadow said with a grin. "Be flattered. It's some time since I've *volunteered* to spend the night sleeping on the ground. But it might cause problems if some of the people in town heard that the High Lord and High Lady were involved in elvan rituals, so I said I'd come along. Besides, this way I can enjoy Mist's company while you're napping."

"Is that all that happens?" Donya asked warily. "You give her this potion and she lies there and dreams?"

"I will ask the Mother Forest to guide her," Mist said. "But the true journey is Jael's alone to make."

"And how long does she just lie there sleeping?" Donya asked.

"We begin the ritual at sunset, so we will arrive a little early," Mist said. "She should return from her journey at sunrise, perhaps a little later. We'll come back through the Gate as soon as the effects of the potion are completely gone."

"She will be perfectly safe," Argent assured Donya, stroking her hair. "Elaria checked each ingredient in the potion and I blended it myself. Mist has plenty of blankets and furs to keep Jael warm while she sleeps. Shadow and Mist will be nearby if Jael needs them, and there is no place in the forest more protected than the Forest Altars."

"Of course, you're right," Donya said hastily. She tousled Jael's hair, kissing the top of her head in a rare gesture of affection. "Mage or not, Jaellyn, come back safe and at peace with yourself and I'll be happy."

"Not as happy as I'll be," Jael said wryly. "Right now I'd be happy just to eat something—other than boiled greens, that is."

"Well, when you come home tomorrow," Donya said comfortingly, "we'll have a feast ready and you can stuff yourself till you're sick, if you like."

Argent pulled Jael close.

"Remember how much we love you," he murmured. "I will ask the Mother Forest to protect and guide you."

Jael said nothing, but hugged back hard. His long, pale hair smelled of herbs, a familiar, comforting scent.

"Fortune favor us, she's not going to her death, Argent," Shadow said good-naturedly. "One night napping in the forest hardly warrants this fuss. Come along, little sapling, and let's get this done with. Celene, do you want to cast the spell at the Gate, so Mist won't have to carry her through the halls? She's almost as tall as he is."

"I'll carry her," Donya said quickly.

"Better cast the spell here," Celene agreed. "Jael might be able to affect the Gate merely by being near it. Jael, better to sit down so you won't fall."

Jael sighed and sat, uncomfortable with all the attention. As Aunt Shadow said, what was the fuss about a few missed meals and an uncomfortable night sleeping in the forest? Her nose would run and she'd wake up stiff, and likely nothing much would come of it.

Celene gave her an encouraging smile, chanted a few words, and leaned over to touch Jael's eyelids gently. Jael had just time to think, *I wonder how this is going to feel—*

Jael opened her eyes, surprised to see leaves instead of stone overhead. Celene patted her cheek comfortingly.

"All finished, granddaughter," she said. "I was almost surprised that the spell worked on you. I half expected you to turn into a bird instead, or some such."

"I wish you'd told me that *before* you cast it," Jael grumbled, scrambling to her feet. "I'd rather have ridden into the Heartwood on horses."

"Jaellyn, the sleep spell is so simple that there was no risk worth mentioning," Celene said gently. "I was only jesting. Now come along, and tomorrow we will see how great a mage you've become."

"No doubt I'll become such a great mage that I can break every light globe in the castle, instead of just in the one room," Jael chuckled.

It was forbidden to cast a Gate spell within the area of the Forest Altars, but the altars were less than a mile from the Gate. Celene, Mist, Shadow, and Jael arrived with plenty of sunlight left.

"What do I do now?" Jael asked, when they had cleared the offerings from one of the altars and laid a few warm furs over it.

"You can help us set up our camp," Mist said. "We will be close, but not so close that our fire or our voices might distract you."

"Besides, I will *not* camp without a fire, as well as something to cook over it," Shadow said firmly. "And that means we have to leave the area of the altars to hunt. But we'll still be near enough to hear you if you should need us."

They made a camp at one of the already cleared sites just outside the stones defining the area of the altars, and Shadow excused herself, saying that she would hunt something for supper while Mist helped Jael prepare.

There was little enough, however, to prepare. Mist drew a clay flask from his pack and followed Jael back to the chosen altar, bringing several furs and blankets with him.

"It's been a little chill these past few nights," Mist said. "I will stay until you are asleep, then see that you are well covered. You take chill too easily, little fawn." He glanced up at the setting sun, then pulled the stopper out of the flask. "This will taste terrible, but I brought some water for you to drink with it."

Jael took the flask. It felt heavy, and the smell of the potion was unpleasantly sweet and pungent.

"All of it?" she asked dubiously.

"Every drop," Mist said firmly. "If you drink it down quickly, you'll taste it less."

Jael took a deep breath and tipped up the flask. The liquid was thick and syrupy, obviously sweetened heavily with honey, but the liquid burned its way down her throat anyway. Jael grimaced and sipped water from the skin that Mist offered.

"Lie down," Mist said. "The potion will start to take effect in a few moments."

Jael climbed awkwardly onto the altar, making herself as comfortable as she could on the fur-covered stone. Mist folded a fur to cushion her head, then laid several blankets and furs over her.

"You'll start feeling heavy and warm," Mist said. He clasped her hand warmly. "After a time your thoughts will begin to drift. When that starts to happen, focus your thoughts inward, downward. Send your thoughts down through yourself and into the earth, down to the roots of the trees. Think of those roots as your own roots, and follow them down as far as you can go."

Jael sighed and squirmed a little. The fur was ticklish under her, annoying. She wanted to push it aside. She was too hot; she wanted to feel the cool of the stone against her back.

"When you've gone down as far as you can go, you will find a peaceful place there, like a still forest pool," Mist said, his voice smooth and soothing. "This place exists at the center of yourself. Your magic is in that place, your soul is in that place, your wholeness is there in that peaceful place. Go there and find it and bring it back with you."

"Uh-huh." Jael heard her own voice as if from a great distance. She felt far too hot and vaguely sick, but the heat and the nausea were far away, too. Her muscles were still a little sore, too, from the previous day's exertions; she had spent the whole day training with Rabin and Larissa, having nothing better to pass the time.

Mist's voice faded out, but she could still feel the pressure of his hand. Then that was gone, too, and somehow Jael was glad; she wanted to be alone. She squirmed around on the stone until she managed to push the fur out from under her, and the weathered stone was smooth and delightful against her cheek.

There was no focusing her thoughts downward; she was pulled down like iron shavings to a lodestone. Earth was around her, warm and moist and musky with leaf mold, tunneled by worms, laced with roots. There were thoughts around her, too—worm-thoughts and beetle-thoughts and other noisy pulses of hunger, of fear, of pain and birth and death. There was nothing soothing or peaceful here; it was too alive, too moving and varied of texture and confusing.

Under the forest soil was denser earth, more roots, finer and longer and pale from the dark, squirming things that had never seen the sun, blind, writhing life even more confused and confusing than that above. There was nothing to be found at the end of the roots but their pale, searching tips. How could she think of them as her roots, these frail, blind things? Jael knew a moment of panic—how could she find peace, how could she find herself here in this writhing chaos of life?

Almost instinctively she sank deeper. Under the earth was water—not a still pool as Mist had described, but water pushing up hot and sulfurous from the earth, bubbling and frothing toward the surface. Then down under the water—

Stone.

Jael sank into stone as she might sink into a soft bed after a rigorous combat lesson, gratefully, every muscle in her body sighing its surrender. Stone surrounded her, smooth and firm and solid, and yet it was alive, too, holding in its heart a memory of liquid fire. The fire called to her, like a distant memory, vague and indistinct but beckoning, a pleasurable tinge like the sight of home after a long journey, but when she reached for it, it was always just beyond her grasp. Desperately she followed that vein of fire deeper, farther, but it seemed to retreat even as she approached, growing ever more distant even as the world receded far behind her. Just a little farther and she could reach it—almost—almost—

Something seized her, as if a warm, strong hand had grasped the back of her shirt, pulling her back, back through stone, through water, through earth, back up. Jael howled with disappointment, reaching desperately for the stone, but the force pulling her back was too strong, and the red thread of fire melted slowly into darkness.

Jael was warm and comfortable, cradled smoothly and comfortingly. Slowly sound intruded—early morning sounds of birds and insects. Sunlight trickled through her eyelashes like water; reluctantly, Jael yawned and rubbed her eyes. To her surprise, she felt neither stiff nor groggy; rather, she was utterly relaxed and as refreshed as after a swim in the river on a hot day. Jael tried to stretch, only to find that she had somehow wedged herself into a rather cramped, if comfortable, space.

"Good morning, little acorn," Shadow said cheerily from somewhere out of sight. "Are you ready for us to pry you out of there?"

"Uh—" Jael squirmed and found her quarters even more cramped than she had originally thought. She looked upward through what appeared to be the entrance to a den or burrow. Had she found some animal's lair and crawled in? "What happened?"

"That's a good question." Shadow's face appeared in the opening, her mischievous black eyes sparkling with laughter. "Maybe you can tell us."

"Where am I?" Jael asked confusedly.

"You're still on the altar," Shadow said. She paused. "Or rather *in* the altar. It seems to have—ah—caved in with you. Can you wriggle around so we can grab either your arms or your legs?"

Jael tried, but her stone womb made every movement difficult. Gradually she worked one arm loose, then the other, by bending her back into a screaming angle. Shadow locked both her hands around one wrist, Mist around the other, and they pulled, with several protests from Jael and worried instructions from Celene. Gradually Jael squirmed painfully free, scraping her hips, knees, and elbows unmercifully in the process.

When she at last wriggled out of the tight space, Jael turned and gaped at the place she had recently occupied. "Caved in" was not the phrase Jael would have used; rather, a Jael-sized hole seemed to have been melted half a man-height into the stone, almost enclosing her.

"Fortune favor us, that's some trick, little acorn," Shadow chuckled. Mist walked around the altar, shaking his head at the sight.

"Well, I will end the suspense," Celene smiled. She took Jael's hands. Jael held her breath, but nothing happened; after a moment, Celene shook her head sadly and released Jael's hands.

"I'm sorry, Jaellyn," she said gently. "Nothing has changed."

"Something has changed here," Mist said, looking at something at the far side of the altar. "Shadow, have you seen this?"

Jael and Celene followed Shadow around the altar. There was a simple drawing in the dirt, scratched with a stick, of a circle divided into three parts. The sword twined with the vine, symbol of Allanmere's ruling house, had been drawn in one section, and a single green leaf had been laid on the second. The arc of the third section had been rubbed out, leaving a gap, but a short distance outside the circle lay a scrap of leather bearing a symbol Jael had never seen—a highly stylized eye.

"What's this?" Jael asked, picking up the bit of leather. "What's it mean?"

"It means about what I expected," Shadow said, sighing.

"The forest sprite must have left the drawing," Mist said. He shook his head. "But how could she know that—"

"Shhh." Celene laid one hand on Mist's arm. "It's not yours to tell, Mist."

"The forest sprite?" Jael asked eagerly. "You mean Chyrie? Oh, I wish I'd seen her!"

"Well, you were fast asleep, little fawn," Mist comforted. "I don't understand this drawing, though."

"I may," Shadow said cautiously. "Mist, Celene, are you coming back through the Gate?"

"I must sleep-spell Jael again, so I will come through to awaken her," Celene said. She shook her head. "But then I will return through the Gate. This is one difficulty, I'm afraid, that Donya will have to face herself."

"I think I will stay in the forest," Mist agreed. "I think my presence would only further embarrass the High Lady."

"What are you talking about?" Jael said, a little annoyed. *She* was the one who had starved for two days and gone through the ritual for nothing, not her mother.

"We're going to have a talk with your mother," Shadow said grimly. "But first I'm going to take you to see an expert."

"An expert on what?" Jael asked warily.

"On souls," Shadow replied, shaking her head at Mist and Celene. "No, don't ask me who it is, because I can't tell you. Let's just go back through the Gate and see if we can sneak out of the castle before anyone sees us and starts asking questions."

Curiosity almost overcame Jael's disappointment at the failure of the ritual. Once they had struck camp and walked back to the Gate, Jael sat down for Celene to sleep-spell her again; at least this way she wouldn't have to wait and chafe through Shadow and Mist's rather prolonged farewell.

When Jael awakened, she was back at the castle. Jael had worried that perhaps Donya and Argent would be waiting in the room that held the Gate, but fortunately that was not the case. Celene stayed just long enough for a comforting hug, and reminded Jael to tell Donya that Celene would move the far end of the Gate back to Inner Heart as soon as she reached the other elvan mages.

Creeping quietly in and out of the castle was nothing new to Jael, and sneaking was second nature to Shadow; they easily slipped out without being observed.

"Can't we at least get some breakfast first?" Jael asked plaintively. "It's been three days now since I've eaten."

"I need to talk to someone first," Shadow told her. "After that we'll likely have time to get some food. Be patient just a little longer."

To Jael's disgust, Shadow dragged her all the way to the south end of the market. Once there, however, she simply handed Jael a few coins and told her to go buy some food,

obviously eager to have Jael out of the way. Jael bought a few
meat pies and half a roast fowl, but took care not to get too
far away, ostensibly watching a mage boring a new well while
sneaking glances at Aunt Shadow. All she saw, however, was
Aunt Shadow conversing with a flower vendor. They appeared to argue briefly, and Aunt Shadow handed over a
pouch, but the vendor gave her nothing in return. At last
Shadow joined Jael and accepted a pie.

"Was that who you brought me to see?" Jael asked skeptically. "A flower vendor?"

"No, the flower vendor is just a messenger," Shadow said.
She nodded in the direction of where the flower vendor had
been, and Jael was surprised to see that the little man was
gone already. "He's setting up the meeting."

"Who did you pay to meet with us?" Jael asked. "It looked
like a large pouch."

"It was, and that was just to pay the flower vendor to deliver the message," Shadow said ruefully. "Fortune alone
knows what we might be asked in exchange for our—ah—
consultation. After we eat I'll go buy a bottle of Dragon's
Blood and hope that's enough."

"What kind of expert gets paid in illegal liquor?" Jael
asked curiously. This was sounding interesting.

"As I told you before, an expert in souls," Shadow told her.
"Listen, Jaellyn—" Jael sat up straight; Shadow rarely called
her by her name unless she had something important to say.
"This is our secret, yours and mine," Shadow said slowly. "I
don't want to tell your mother I'm taking you to this—
expert—unless I have to. She'd skin me with a dull knife and
roast me over a slow fire."

"All right, I won't tell anyone at all," Jael promised eagerly. "I swear. But who is it?"

Shadow glanced around, then bit into her pie.

"It's Blade," she said. "The assassin."

Jael was stunned to silence; realizing that her mouth was
hanging open, she quickly closed it.

"Oh," she said weakly. "You—uh—you know *Blade*?" An
instant later she felt like a fool; what an idiotic question! If
Aunt Shadow didn't know Blade, they would scarcely be going to meet her.

"Actually she's almost a friend," Shadow grinned. "Almost. She tried to kill me once, and we saved each other's life a couple of times."

"You never told me those stories," Jael accused.

"No, because I promised her I'd never tell anyone the things I've learned about her," Shadow told her. "And you remember that you've promised that, too, my girl. Blade is one person you don't want angry with you."

Jael gulped. She'd heard many stories of the lethal assassin—that she had killed Gajik, a mage-noble of some renown, in a room warded by magic and guarded by at least fifteen men, and none had seen her enter or leave; that Denara, the city's greatest courtesan, had paid fifteen mages to locate Blade so that Denara could have a rival killed, that the mages had cast their greatest divinations and found nothing, and that Denara had been found dead apparently of terror in her apartment shortly thereafter. There were other stories—many other stories, some quite gruesome.

"Why is she an expert on souls?" Jael asked hesitantly. She could imagine one reason—because Blade had probably sent plenty of them to whatever afterlife they were bound for.

"Because she's read a lot of books on the subject," Shadow chuckled. "Listen, little sapling, the fewer questions you ask, the better you'll sleep tonight, bet on it."

They watched the mage continue his water-seeking spell for a little longer, but Shadow was so nervous that Jael could not enjoy the spectacle.

"The vendor's back," Jael said, pointing. The grizzled little man was, in fact, beckoning to them.

"Already!" Shadow said, surprised. "I didn't even have time to buy the Dragon's Blood. Well, we'll just have to see."

Shadow dragged Jael over, and the flower vendor passed Shadow a slip of parchment. Shadow read the paper, sighed, and nodded.

"Not a very good neighborhood to be taking the Heir into," Shadow grumbled, towing Jael into Rivertown. "Still, on this short notice, I have to take a meeting where I can get one."

Even on her most daring excursions, Jael had never set foot in Rivertown; it was far too dangerous a place to go alone, and Jael was almost always alone in her wanderings. Beggars and stuporous—or possibly dead—indigents were the most innocent and harmless-seeming residents of this district. Less reputable-looking inhabitants lounged in doorways or alleys, eyeing Shadow and Jael narrowly as they passed. A few openly fondled knives or swords.

"This way," Shadow said, pulling Jael into an alleyway. Jael grimaced and stepped around puddles of what smelled like urine, following Shadow through a back doorway and up a flight of stairs into a dimly lit, windowless room. In this room, a black-dressed figure sat alone at a wooden table.

"So you have returned to Allanmere, ex-Guildmistress of the Guild of Thieves," the woman said in a voice as cold and colorless as ice. "You still think you can summon me like a servant; that much has not changed."

The woman rose, and Jael was surprised; somehow she had thought the legendary Blade would be—well—larger. The woman was tall, although not as tall as Donya, but she was bonelessly lean, moving with the grace of a serpent. Her straight, chin-length hair was as midnight-black as her tunic and trousers, and her eyes were black without reflection, so black that they swallowed the light. Jael shivered and looked away from those eyes. Blade's skin was very pale, as pale as Urien's.

"Well, I was going to buy you a bottle of Dragon's Blood," Shadow apologized. "But your messenger came back too soon, and I couldn't decide which would make you more angry—to come empty-handed or to keep you waiting. I'll owe you the bottle, if you like."

"You pay your debts, I grant you," Blade said smoothly. "But I wonder what game you are playing now, bringing the High Lord's own daughter to me."

"Hmmm." Shadow glanced at Jael. "Wait here a moment, little acorn. I need to talk to Blade privately."

Shadow and Blade stepped to a dark corner of the room. Jael strained her keen ears, but the two spoke so quietly that she caught only an occasional word. At last they stepped back to the wooden table and sat down, Shadow motioning for Jael to join them.

"Show me what was drawn in the dirt," Blade told Shadow. Shadow scratched the signs into the tabletop with her dagger tip, pulling out the scrap of leather to show Blade.

"You are likely right in your suspicions," Blade said, shaking her head. "But I can confirm that." She turned those uncanny eyes on Jael. "And what price will you pay, little heirling, to know precisely who and what you are? And be sure you wish to know before you answer me. Some answers are . . . uncomfortable to know."

"I can't go through my life breaking light globes and melting altars," Jael said timidly. "I don't know how anything you could tell me could be much worse. I have some money, but not with me. Aunt Shadow didn't tell me I'd need to pay any—"

"This is my favor, not hers," Shadow interrupted. "If there's any payment, I should be the one to do it."

"Be silent," Blade said mildly, but her eyes narrowed. "My bargain is with the Heir, or there is none."

"I'm not really the Heir," Jael admitted. "I think it's as likely as not that Mother and Father will pass me by in favor of Markus or Mera. But my family pays its own debts, and I'll pay you, if you'll tell me how many Suns you want."

"I have no need for your coin, little mixed-blood," Blade said silkily. She glanced at Shadow. "And I doubt there is a corner of the world in which I could hide—or you either, my friend, for that matter—if I took from the High Lady's daughter the payment I would normally ask." Her eyes bored into Jael's. "We will leave it that you owe me a favor, High Lord's daughter, and that one day I will come to you for a favor in kind, if you will agree."

Shadow started to protest, but a glance from Blade silenced her. Jael shrugged. Aside from wreaking havoc on any magic in the area, there was little enough she could give. What harm could it do? Still, the legends she had heard—

"All right," Jael said at last. "I'll owe you a favor. As long as the favor won't harm any of my family or friends, or break the laws of Allanmere."

Blade half smiled.

"Agreed," she said. She drew a black dagger from its sheath at her hip and extended one black-gloved hand. "Give me your hand."

"Wait, now," Shadow said, alarmed. "What are you doing?"

"Do you think I can wave my hands and conjure an answer like a mage?" Blade said impatiently. "The answer is in her blood and in her soul, and there is where I will find it. Be calm. I will do her no harm."

"It's all right, Aunt Shadow," Jael said, trying to keep her voice from quivering. "If she was going to kill me, she wouldn't have bargained with me for payment." Quickly, before she lost her courage, Jael held out her hand.

"A sensible child," Blade said, taking Jael's extended hand. She nudged the edge of Jael's sleeve up a bit with the tip of the black dagger. "Be still until I am done. Attempting to jerk away could be—dangerous."

Jael bit her lip and nodded, wanting to close her eyes but too frightened to do so.

Blade touched the point of the black dagger to the skin of Jael's wrist, drawing a thin line with the sharp tip. The dagger was so sharp that Jael barely noticed the scratch until she saw a few drops of blood well up; what she felt, however, was a sudden icy chill that seemed to sweep through her like a blast of winter wind. Jael shuddered involuntarily, but she ground her teeth and did not move her arm until Blade took the dagger away. Blade raised the dagger and delicately licked the few drops of blood from the tip, and Jael shivered again.

"What you suspected is correct," Blade said, turning to Shadow. "She is not of two bloods, but three—elf and human on the one side, and you know what is the other. The bloods have mixed oddly, bringing out old and hidden traits, but there is nothing awry there. The flaw is in her soul. Her blood is of three peoples, but her soul only of two, elf and human, with the third part missing. There is an empty place in her soul where that part should dwell, and it is this emptiness in her soul which troubles her."

"Elf and human and *what*?" Jael demanded. "*What* three bloods? I don't understand."

"You will," Shadow said grimly. "All right, Blade. You have your favor, and we have our answer. And I'll still send you the bottle of Dragon's Blood, as soon as I can buy one. Come on, little acorn, and let's go back to the castle. Your mother has a story to tell you."

"Uh-*uh*," Jael said firmly. Finally, a chance to get some plain answers. "My bargain, my question. Elf and human and what?"

The faintest hint of a smile twitched the corners of Blade's lips.

"Well said, Lady Jaellyn," Blade said coolly. " 'Kresh' is the name of your father's people."

"That's not right," Jael protested. "My father's an elf. Everyone knows that."

"Your mother's husband is elf, little by-blow," Blade corrected, her lips twitching again. "And yes, that is what everyone knows. I much doubt High Lady Donya would care for the truth to be told, though rumors have been whispered nonetheless."

Jael's hands were shaking; she quickly clasped them and squeezed them hard. She understood what Blade was saying, but—

But that—

Jael glanced quickly at Shadow for support, but Shadow only sighed and patted Jael's arm.

"I'm sorry, little acorn," she said gently. "I wish you could have waited to hear that a bit more kindly put, not that your mother wouldn't have been as blunt. Satisfied now?"

Jael took a deep breath, trying to slow the thudding of her heart.

"Yes, I guess I am," she said, hating the slight quiver in her voice. She turned to Blade. "Thank you for your trouble. I don't know where to buy Dragon's Blood, but I'll give Shadow the money for it. I won't tell anyone about you, and I won't forget the favor I owe you." She held out her hand, glad that it had stopped shaking.

"Indeed you will not," Blade said coolly, ignoring the extended hand. "And you may be assured that I, in turn, will keep my silence." She raised one eyebrow. "Even though I have not been paid for it." She turned, and in the time it took Jael to blink, had vanished from the room as if by magic.

"Well, I hope you feel privileged," Shadow muttered, dragging Jael out the door and back down the stairs. "Only a double handful of people in Allanmere ever speak to her personally and walk away alive afterward."

"She must be lonely, then," Jael said. Now that she was out of that horrible, dim little room, she felt less quivery inside and wondered exactly what it was about Blade that had so frightened her.

Shadow stopped abruptly and glanced back at Jael.

"Yes, I think she is," Shadow said quietly. "Terribly lonely. But being lonely doesn't make her any less dangerous, Jaellyn, and you can't help her. The smartest thing you can do is hope you never see her again, although that's a vain hope. I don't like you owing her anything, either, especially an un-named favor."

"She's like me, isn't she?" Jael asked. "Bloody feet from walking the dagger's edge."

"More than you know," Shadow muttered. She steered Jael firmly through the market. "But that doesn't mean she'd hes-itate to stick that dagger into you if someone offered her enough Suns. Remember that."

The excitement of meeting Allanmere's most legendary as-sassin had almost taken Jael's mind off the purpose of the visit, but not entirely.

"Aunt Shadow, if Mother's elf and human and fa—"

"Not here in the middle of the market crowds," Shadow said quickly. "Listen, little sapling, you're making me walk a slippery log. Your mother made me promise I'd never speak to you about this, and one thing I don't do is break my prom-ises. Be patient just a little longer, and if Donya won't give you all the answers, I'll see that *someone* does. All right?"

"All right," Jael agreed grudgingly. After twenty years of wondering, she wanted to know *now*. "But I'm still hungry."

"Your mother promised you a feast, and I've never known Donya to break *her* word," Shadow assured her. "Wait until then. I want to get back to the Gate before your parents real-ize we took a side trip through the city."

"They won't be waiting for us now," Jael said crossly. "It's midmorning. The City Council will be in session until noon, and since it's midweek, Mother and Father will both be there."

"Well, why didn't you tell me that before I ran through the market like a doe with a wolf on her scent?" Shadow asked exasperatedly, slowing to a walk.

"Well, if you'd *explained* why you were hurrying, instead of pulling my arm out of its socket dragging me," Jael re-torted, "I *would* have told you."

"All right, all right," Shadow sighed. "I'm sorry."

They walked more leisurely through the market after that,

arriving back at the castle only a little before midday. Because
dinner preparations were under way, there was no difficulty in
avoiding the servants as Shadow and Jael slipped back to the
room holding the Gate. Once they arrived there, Jael made a
show of calling for one of the maids and asking that her parents be told that she and Shadow had returned. By the time
Jael and Shadow reached the dining hall, Donya and Argent
were already there, still dressed in their formal surcoats for
council.

"It didn't work," Jael said flatly as Donya and Argent hurried to embrace her. Blade's news had made her feel unaccountably awkward with her parents, and she endured, rather
than welcomed, their affection. "I'm still the same."

Somehow the statement tasted like a lie in her mouth. Her
elvan gifts and her magic were no closer than they ever had
been, but Jael felt that somehow she *had* changed—changed
greatly.

"Never mind," Donya said with a sigh, ruffling Jael's hair.
"You're safe and well, and nothing else really matters. What
did happen? Just a night of strange dreams?"

"Hardly that," Shadow said wryly. "Let's let this poor, hungry girl have some food and I'll tell you the story."

Halfway through the story, Donya quietly dismissed the
servants. When Shadow finished, the dining hall was absolutely silent except for the crackling of the fire. Donya stared
down at the scrap of leather bearing the eye design. Quietly
Argent reached out and folded Donya into his arms, and
Donya let him, leaning her forehead wearily on his shoulder.

As shocked as Jael had been by the news of her ancestry,
her mother's behavior shocked her more. Suddenly she
wished she had never agreed to go through the ritual, never
dreamed of fire and stone, and, most of all, *never* gone with
Shadow to see Blade to find out awkward things about her
family. This, then, was what Blade had meant, that some answers were uncomfortable to know—but Jael had thought that
the answers would be uncomfortable for *her*. She had never
thought that it might hurt her mother instead.

"All right," Donya said at last, tiredly. "All right." She
raised her head, and Jael was relieved to see that her mother's
eyes were dry. She didn't know what she would have done if

High Lady Donya, likely the greatest warrior in Allanmere, had wept.

"Maybe I should talk to Jael for you," Shadow suggested gently. "If you'd rather—"

"No." Donya straightened and took a deep breath. "What's the elvan saying? I shot the arrow, and I'll carry the kill. Jaellyn, I hope you don't mind another walk in the garden." She turned to Argent. "Do you mind if—"

"I understand." Argent clasped Donya's hand, pressing her large knuckles against his pale cheek. "Shadow and I will be in the study. She was kind enough to bring me a bottle of brandy all the way from Chernon, and I think this is a good time to open it."

Donya walked silently beside Jael through the corridors and out into the garden. Jael did not break the silence; she felt oddly as though she were walking beside a stranger.

Donya took Jael to the west walk and gestured to Jael to sit down in the bower. Donya did not sit, however, instead pacing back and forth. At last she stopped, standing braced as if for combat.

"About twenty-one years ago Aspen asked me to come to the Heartwood to see a trespasser they'd caught," Donya said slowly. "They'd never seen anyone like him before. He wasn't elf or human, but something else completely. He was sick, too. None of us realized he was carrying plague."

"The Crimson Plague?" Jael asked.

Donya nodded.

"The Crimson Plague. He'd come south to find a place where some of his people used to live in the hope of finding a cure. He didn't know about Allanmere, and he didn't know about the elves in the Heartwood, either, because it had been centuries and more since his own people had left. He didn't mean to bring plague among us—the plague wasn't even fatal to his own folk."

"I thought the elves brought the Crimson Plague into town," Jael ventured hesitantly.

"Well, they did," Donya admitted. "The elves carried the plague into town, although they couldn't catch it themselves. But it was Farryn who actually brought the plague into the forest."

"Farryn," Jael repeated, rolling the word in her mouth. "What did he look like?"

"He was almost as tall as me," Donya said with a sigh. "Slender, though. His skin was as brown as leaves in autumn, and his hair and eyes—" Donya glanced at Jael, then smiled a little as she reached out to touch Jael's polished-bronze curls. "You favor him in many ways. He had six fingers on each hand, too, and six toes on each foot."

Jael glanced down at her boots, the left boot slightly wider to accommodate the sixth toe there.

"And he melted holes in stone?" Jael asked.

"No." Donya smiled distantly. "No, Farryn could run like the wind, even over water. But another clan of the Kresh could mold stone and metal with their will, and Farryn told us that once they had lived together like one people. We saw some of their dwellings, stone shaped by their minds just as we might shape a piece of clay. Farryn must have had a little of their blood in his ancestry, a long way back, just as I have a little Hidden Folk blood in me if you go back far enough. But I was telling you about the plague.

"Farryn recovered quickly enough," Donya continued, gazing out into the garden. "He insisted that there was a cure for the Crimson Plague to be found where his people had once lived. That place was deep in the Reaches, though. Five of us went to find that cure—Farryn, Argent, Mist, Shadow, and myself."

"Mist was there?" Jael asked, surprised. "He's never said anything, not in all the summers I've spent in the Heartwood."

"He wouldn't have," Donya smiled wryly. "That was kind of him. That time in the swamp has always been a painful memory for me. I was sick at the time, and we were all miserable—it was a terrible journey, and worse for knowing that every day we were gone, more people were dying in the city. Do you remember hearing a story about a giant daggertooth?"

"They still tell that story in the market sometimes," Jael laughed. "That you killed a daggertooth bigger than a house. Nobody believes it, not really."

"That's one story that actually was true," Donya chuckled a little. "I didn't kill the daggertooth alone, but I'd like to think I had a good hand in it. And it *was* bigger than a house; I know, because it was sitting on one. One of the ruined houses of Farryn's people, that is. We hollowed that daggertooth out and used it as a boat. The boat rotted, of course; we didn't have time to cure it properly. But, you know, I still have one of its teeth."

"A boat?" Jael asked skeptically.

"A boat," Donya smiled. "Ask Shadow about that boat sometime. But Farryn was quite a warrior. Watching him with that sword—it was like a dance. I'd never seen anything like it. He moved like lightning, like the wind, and the lightning flashing off his armor and his sword . . ."

Donya was silent for a moment, and Jael wisely said nothing, although the look in her mother's eyes somehow made her uncomfortable. Donya glanced at her and sighed.

"Well." Donya shook her head. "You know what happens between men and women. I spent that night with Farryn."

"With Father right there?" Jael asked amazedly.

"I—didn't think of Argent in that way then," Donya said slowly. "Jaellyn, sometimes love comes suddenly, like an autumn whirlwind, tearing away every obstacle in its path, so powerful that there's no stopping it. It was like that with Farryn—huge and powerful, and then—and then suddenly you're left with nothing but the debris left behind after the storm."

"I suppose I'm part of the debris," Jael said, a little bitterly.

"I suppose I earned that," Donya said quietly. "Shadow's right. I should have told you a long time ago. But I wasn't certain, I swear to you. Farryn had to go back to his people, and I had to return to Allanmere. I learned that my father had died while I was gone, and for a while all I could think of was the grief. With my father dead, I had to marry immediately, and to produce an heir as soon as I could. I married Argent, and nine months later you were born."

Jael was silent for a moment, thinking about what Donya had told her. The sadness in her mother's voice, the longing—that was real.

"Did you love my fa—Argent?" Jael asked at last. "I mean, you married him only a little after—well, you know."

"Love isn't always an autumn whirlwind," Donya said after a moment's thought. "Sometimes it's like those acorns you bring back from the elvan spring festival—just a little seed in your hand, and it grows so slowly, but in the end you have a tree that towers over the forest, with roots that dig deep and strong into the earth. I love Argent, and I love you, Jaellyn. Don't ever doubt that. But I want to know what you feel." Her shoulders tensed, as if she expected an attack.

Jael was silent again. What *did* she feel? She was sorry her mother had been hurt by the revelation, but that regret was tempered with a little anger and, yes, a little resentment—why *hadn't* she been told? It was her life, after all, and look what her mother's whirlwind night had done to it!

But was that really what Jael was feeling hurt and angry about now? Did it matter, really, whether her mother had had one lover more or less, or that her lover had been a stranger from a distant land? Would Argent indeed have been hurt to know that Donya was in another's arms only a short distance away? Jealousy was a human concept, so far as Jael had seen, and elves never bothered overmuch about privacy; none of the elves in the Heartwood had ever been disturbed when Jael accidentally intruded on their trysts. Even Mother and Father—Argent, that is—had never evidenced more than a mild impatience and eagerness for Jael to go on about her business so they could get on with *theirs*.

"I don't know," Jael sighed. "I'm angry, but I suppose it's just—you know—twenty years, and everybody in the city whispering about me, and then they stop talking when I walk into the room, and all this time I never knew what they were whispering about, and I hated it. It was as if there were a joke in town that everyone was laughing at but me. But nobody in the city knows, do they? So they're just whispering because I'm odd. They never knew anything I didn't, after all."

"No one but some of the forest elves ever saw Farryn," Donya said quietly. "So the people in the city never knew anything, no. And there's certainly no joke."

"It doesn't help much, though, does it?" Jael said bitterly. "I mean, we all know now, don't we, but what good does it do?"

Donya pulled the scrap of leather out of her pocket and traced the eye design with a callused fingertip.

"Farryn wore a medallion with this design on it," she said. "He told us that it was a receptacle for his soul." Her brow furrowed in concentration. "He said that his people weren't born with their souls, that their souls were given to them when they reached a certain age, and they kept them in these—well, soul keepers is what he called them. So that's what the drawing meant, Jaellyn. Your elvan and human blood comes from me, but the Kresh elements of your soul are missing, because the Kresh aren't born with them at all."

"How can anyone not have a soul?" Jael asked, amazed. "And how can anyone *give* you one?"

"I don't know," Donya said, sighing. "Shadow might have been curious enough to ask, but I never thought it was important. Even when I bore you alone instead of twins, and I started to—to wonder, it never occurred to me that there might be an effect to your soul."

"Ankaras says that elves have no souls," Jael said slowly.

"Ankaras says that to sway his followers," Donya said distantly. "Anyone with a little sense knows that's ridiculous. No creature without a soul can work magic, and the elves have more mages than we do, although elvan magic is of a different sort than human—more linked to natural forces. Maybe that's why half-bloods like myself are rarely mages—that having both human and elvan elements in our souls, we don't have quite enough of one or the other for either human or elvan magic. I don't think anyone knows much about how souls and magic work together."

"Well, I'll have to *find* someone who knows," Jael said flatly. "That, or spend the rest of my years avoiding mages, and light globes, and leakproofed pottery, and heat-spelled crocks, and soupstones, and Gates—"

"I know what you're thinking." Donya turned swiftly to face Jael, her jaw set, her eyes hard. "I know just what you're thinking. And that, Jaellyn, is why I never told you. You're *not* going looking for him, Jaellyn. You're *not*. You've got responsibilities here. Even if you could go, even if you could keep yourself alive long enough to get there, you'd never find him. His people lived so far to the north that no one but a few nomad traders had ever met them, and they're not even there now. Farryn told me they were going to go hunting the rest of their people, and that was over twenty years ago. So there's no use to even think about it."

Jael ground her teeth, silent for fear of what she might say if she spoke. Twenty years of whispers and wondering and "You're *not* going." Twenty years of rumors and jeers and "You're *not* going." Jael clenched her shaking hands so hard that her nails bit into her palms, suddenly furious.

"Well, what do you suggest, Mother?" Jael said bitterly. "What about some of the High Lady's wisdom for her own daughter? After all, it was *your* 'autumn whirlwind' that made me this way."

"All right! It's my fault!" Donya snapped, her dark eyes blazing. "Is that what you want me to say? It's my fault. Do you think I haven't been paying for it all twenty years?"

"Not like I have," Jael retorted. "And if you have your way I'll be paying for it the rest of my life, too. Be honest, Mother—how much of it was that you didn't know, and how much of it was that you just didn't want to know?"

This time the hurt in Donya's eyes didn't bother Jael at all. She was glad when her mother made no reply, but turned away, staring out into the garden. When Donya turned back, however, her face was calm again.

"Give me one more year," Donya said quietly. "That year may see these conflicts in the city resolved so that Argent and I can decide which of you children will make the most suitable Heir. Work with your combat masters, and study the accounts of the lands outside Allanmere. I'll consult with the finest sages to see what can be done for you, and I'll send messengers north and west to learn what they can. At the end of that year, if we haven't found an answer, then whatever you decide to do, I won't oppose it."

Jael scowled. First Shadow, and now her mother! Well, at least a year was less time than Shadow wanted.

"All right," Jael said cautiously. "One year from now, or until you tell me I can go, whichever comes first. But on two conditions."

"What conditions?" Donya returned, just as cautiously.

"First, you've got to really try to find an answer for me, like you said, sending people north and west and talking to sages and so on," Jael said firmly. "If you stop trying, the bargain's canceled."

"That's fair," Donya said, nodding. "And the other?"

"That you don't treat me like a child anymore," Jael said wryly. "Even if I look like one."

"Sometimes you act like one, too," Donya said, holding up a hand to stall Jael's protest. She half smiled. "But I'll try if you will." She glanced around, then spit into her right hand like any street merchant and held it out. "Bargain?"

Jael laughed and made a show of spitting into her own hand before she clasped her mother's warm, rough fingers.

"Bargain," she said.

Donya's smile quivered, and she pulled Jael close, her embrace almost painful in its ferocity.

"You drive a tough bargain, too," Donya said at last, her voice hoarse. "You've learned a lot from Shadow."

"Nah, I think I got that from you," Jael chuckled, knuckling tears out of her eyes. "I used to hide in the meeting hall so I could watch you in council. You could be pretty tough yourself."

"I never thought of myself as much of an example," Donya said, chuckling a little, too. "Come on, let's go back inside."

Shadow and Argent were in the study as promised, sipping brandy and staring at the fire in silence.

"Are we interrupting your cheerful conversation?" Donya asked sarcastically.

"No, we were just speculating on how much brandy each of you would need, so we could drink the rest," Shadow said, chuckling. "We only left a little." She indicated two goblets on a table.

Argent rose and took Jael's hands, looking into her eyes.

"And what do you think now, Jaellyn?"

Jael knew what he meant. She grinned gamely at him.

"I think I'm more elf than human . . . Father."

Argent kissed the top of her head.

"I can't say that I'm sorry . . . daughter."

"Oh, please," Shadow groaned. "If you're all going to get weepy on me, I'm leaving." She grinned. "In fact, I'm leaving anyway."

"Don't go, Shadow, we'll stop," Donya laughed, sniffing a little. "I'll even bring out more wine."

"No, no," Shadow said quickly. "That wasn't what I meant. I think I'm ready to catch a caravan out of town."

"Oh, but, Aunt Shadow, you just arrived," Jael protested.

"Well, I didn't exactly 'arrive' as much as I got dragged back," Shadow chuckled. "But it looks like the situation with the Temple of Baaros is taken care of, and, Jael, everything I can do to help you, I've already done. Argent says there's a spice merchant sending some wagons out tomorrow morning, and I think I can talk him into hauling one more not-too-heavy elf along."

"Isn't there any way we can persuade you to stay a little longer?" Donya asked unhappily.

"Oh, I'll be back before too long," Shadow assured her. "And you can always let me know when you need me. But please," she added, "the next time you call that Fortune-be-damned signet back, I hope the timing is a little less awkward."

"Surely you won't leave today," Argent said. "The caravan doesn't leave until tomorrow."

"I need to bargain the wagon master into letting me come along," Shadow reminded him. "I want to tell Aubry good-bye, and if you don't mind me saying it, I need to hit the market one more time to pick up a few Suns for the road."

"Oh, Shadow." Donya sighed. "I'll pretend I didn't hear that." She reached for Shadow, but Shadow danced back, laughing.

"Not another round of tears and hugs," Shadow said with mock sternness. "I don't think I can stand it twice in one day. Jael, you can walk me out of the castle."

Donya insisted on loading Shadow with so many gifts that Shadow protested she would have to take a carriage to the Guild, although Jael privately thought that the bottles of wine, the heaviest items in the load, were the one gift Shadow had no objection to. Argent quietly pressed a pouch into Shadow's hand; Shadow pretended to be outraged, but she took the pouch.

"I hate saying good-bye," Shadow grumbled as she walked with Jael down the castle corridors. "But your mother flays me up and down every time I sneak away. Besides"—she hefted the pouch—"it isn't all bad." She glanced sideways at Jael. "So are you going to tell me what your mother said?"

Jael wondered why—Aunt Shadow undoubtedly knew everything already, didn't she?—but told Shadow anyway. When she was done, Shadow sat down on the castle steps, shaking her head.

"Doe's many fine things, little acorn, but she never was

much of a storyteller," she said. "Truth told, I wanted to know
what she *didn't* tell you."

"What didn't she tell me?" Jael asked quickly.

"I don't think she left much out but the festival in the
Heartwood," Shadow mused. "And that's none of your concern, anyway. But I'll tell you something Donya didn't know.
Farryn once said that the Kresh were given their souls by
their Enlightened Ones—kind of a mage-priest—at a passage
ceremony. As Donya said, none of us were curious enough to
find out more."

"Mother said that if I wait a year, I can go looking for
him," Jael said dismally. "That means another year of breaking light globes, I suppose."

"Well, then I suppose I'll just have to come back in a year,
instead of waiting for your birthday," Shadow grinned.
"That's well enough, anyway; can't say I fancied a journey
back at midwinter. But as I'll miss this birthday, I suppose I'll
give you something to make up for a year's worth of light
globes and soupstones."

Shadow unbuckled her belt and slid one of her matched
dagger sheaths free. She handed the dagger in its sheath to
Jael.

"That's for you," Shadow said. "Go on, draw it, but be
careful."

Jael cautiously drew the blade from its sheath, then gasped
involuntarily. She had never seen anything like the dagger; its
strange pale metal was unaccountably light. What astonished
Jael was the dagger's feeling of *rightness* in her hand, as if
she grasped something alive that welcomed her touch.

"Look at the edge on that," Shadow sighed. "Do you know,
in the twenty years I've had it, I've never had to use a whetstone on it—not that any whetstone I've ever seen could grind
that metal. Farryn gave me that."

"It's a wonderful dagger," Jael said wonderingly. She loved
the feel of it. The lightness of it seemed perfect to her, made
her want to handle it, to use it. "But you are sure you want
to give me this?" She forced the words out reluctantly.

"That's all right, I've got another," Shadow said cheerfully,
patting the dagger's twin on the other side of her belt. "But
I think Farryn would have wanted you to have one. Now, I
warn you, the thing's far too light in the blade for throwing,

but you could cut a sunbeam in half with that edge. You practice with it—not against live folks, mind—and we'll see what you can do next autumn." She patted Jael's shoulder. "How are you progressing on that game with all the little stone pieces?"

"Oh, I solved that right away," Jael said proudly.

Shadow grimaced.

"Do you know, I tinkered with that thing for *weeks* and couldn't get ten pieces to fit together. Hmmmph. You and stone, I suppose, make a good pair."

Jael sighed.

"Where are you going, Aunt Shadow?"

"Oh, I don't know." Shadow grinned at Jael, then winked. "I was thinking maybe north. Then west."

"Oh, Aunt Shadow, really?" The relief that flooded through Jael was like the first ray of warm sunlight after a long, cold winter. If there was anyone in the world who could find her father's people—or word of them—it was Shadow.

"Really, little sapling," Shadow chuckled. "And that's why I need to leave now, so I can get some road behind me while it's still warm enough for easy traveling, especially going north. I'll winter in Ramant or Issel, and when the northern merchants come into the city to winter, I can see what they know."

"I wish I could go with you," Jael said, sighing again. "It's hard staying here and wondering."

"Well, you've been wondering for most of your twenty years, so I don't know that much has changed," Shadow said practically. "One year more isn't going to do you any great harm. Keep working on your combat skills, just as you've been doing, and some geography wouldn't be amiss, either. All right?"

"I don't have much choice," Jael said dismally.

"There's every hope that Donya will find some doddering old sage with all the answers," Shadow said encouragingly. "Besides, you'll likely have other things to think about, with that young Lord Urien coming around to court you."

"Well, there's that," Jael admitted, brightening. In all that had happened, she had almost forgotten Lord Urien.

"Your young lord's a smooth character," Shadow said, shaking her head. "Be careful of yourself. A handsome young rogue like that's fine for a night's tumble in the furs, but don't go hanging your heart on him. Those young lordlings have only two speeds—a roll in the furs that means less to them than the cost of a goblet of wine, or an alliance marriage— and I doubt either one is really what you want. Listen to your heart—or at least to your loins—and be sure you get what you want, not just what he wants. Understand?"

"Yes, Aunt Shadow," Jael said, sighing again. If she listened to her loins, she'd never do *anything*. But Aunt Shadow knew everything there was to know about men, probably.

"Then you'll likely be the one with a few stories to tell next time I'm in town," Shadow chuckled. "Well, I can bear one more hug before I go, I suppose."

Jael buried her face in Shadow's shoulder. When Shadow left, her warm, familiar smells were what Jael always remembered the most clearly—the musky herbal essence Shadow used on her hair, the tobacco odor that clung to her clothes from the taverns she frequented, and, of course, the fragrance of wine.

It seemed wrong, somehow, to see Shadow walk out through the castle gates like any visitor might, instead of out the secret passage from the garden, so Jael turned away. Aunt Shadow wouldn't look back; she never did. One day, Jael vowed, she would walk out of Allanmere like that—whistling cheerfully, her steps light and sure, and without a backward glance.

Despite what had seemed a very long day, there was still daylight left, and Jael had no desire to return to the castle. Better to let Mother and Father alone for a while, anyway; she'd been the one to stir up this bees' nest, and best to let it settle without her.

She thought briefly of seeking out Lord Urien, but that would be awkward. What could she say? "Well, I just happened to be wandering around the Temple District and thought I'd pay a call." Uh-*uh*. But that made her think of Tanis, and Tanis would think nothing awry if the High Lord's daughter came looking for him.

That meant sneaking into the temple again; certainly the High Lord's daughter, so elflike in appearance, couldn't simply walk into the Temple of Baaros without being recognized, even wearing her usual scarf and smudges. Besides, then Urien would see her and think she had come to see him.

As it was still daylight, there was no one in the empty building adjoining the temple, and Jael was easily able to gain entry to the Temple of Baaros's cellar. Once there, however, Jael found herself uneasy. Something had changed about the cellar, something more than just the additional boxes and casks that had been stacked there. Somehow the cellar seemed colder and darker than it had been, and Jael could hear a distant rustling—were there rats here?—and a muffled sound as if something heavy stirred. Jael shivered, but did not retreat; likely there were vermin in the subcellars.

Jael had at first thought to wait in the cellar for a while to see if Tanis would come down; the rustling, however, made her decide that she would rather take the chance of being discovered than the risk of being rat-bitten. Jael crept cautiously up the cellar steps, peering out before she ventured farther.

Thanks to the additional priests and acolytes Urien had brought with him, the upper temple was much busier than it had been before, and it was some time before Jael found an opportunity to dart out of the stairwell and hide herself in her usual nook, where she could wait more safely for Tanis to appear. It was nearly an hour before the young acolyte appeared, but fortunately he was alone. When Jael whispered to him, Tanis glanced about him and quickly ducked into Jael's hiding place.

"What are you doing here?" he whispered. "Everyone's here, even High Priest Urien." Tanis's eyes narrowed. "Unless you came to see him."

"No, I came to see if you wanted to go to the market, like you said before," Jael whispered back. "I couldn't very well send a messenger, could I? Can you go?"

Tanis nodded.

"High Priest Urien just dismissed me," he said. "I was waiting to see if Thuvik would be dismissed, too, to go with me to the market. But I'd rather go with you. Let me walk out first, and I'll wave if there's no one coming."

With Tanis watching the hall, it was simple for Jael to dart to the cellar steps and make her escape through the empty temple. Tanis met her at the edge of the Temple District.

"Have you heard the news?" he said excitedly. "The second and third signs of Baaros's prophecy have happened, and just today, too!"

"What, earth flying in the air and stone opening up and swallowing something down?" Jael asked surprisedly. "All today? I didn't see anything of the sort."

"There was a mage in the market this morning boring a well," Tanis told her. "Suddenly there was a good-sized explosion, and bits of dirt and rock were hurled all over the market—earth falling from the sky. A few people were hurt, too." He frowned briefly. "But the curious part is that the explosion broke into one of the underground springs and must've ruptured a good-sized cavern down there. Three of the market wells just drained right down into the hole."

"But that wasn't anything divine, just an accident," Jael protested. She wondered uncomfortably when the explosion had happened in relation to when she had been watching that very mage.

"High Priest Urien says the sign was real," Tanis told her. "But anyway, we don't have to sneak around in the back roads now. High Priest Urien announced the change in temple doctrine at the ritual this noon, when he informed the worshippers that all the signs had occurred. High Priest Urien said he hoped to encourage the elvan merchants to join the temple, too. There was quite an uproar, I'll tell you that for nothing, and half the worshippers walked out of the temple right there even after the signs, but we expected that. Most of those who left weren't merchants anyway."

"What difference does that make?" Jael asked curiously.

"Merchants are the worshippers we want to attract," Tanis shrugged rather apologetically. "Baaros *is*, after all, the god of profitable trade. Merchants make generous offerings once they're established in the temple, and they also spread the sect to other cities. I suppose that's one reason the main temple sent High Priest Urien to put Ankaras back in line. Other cities won't welcome our temples if they have a reputation for making trouble for the ruling families."

"That's what Lord Urien told Mother and Father," Jael agreed.

"So what about this elvan ritual you mentioned?" Tanis said, changing the subject. "I didn't know you were a worshipper of—uh—what was it?"

"The Mother Forest," Jael told him. "I'm not. It wasn't really that kind of ritual. It was a kind of adulthood ritual, supposed to make me stop fouling up other people's magic."

"Supposed to?" Tanis asked, glancing at Jael sideways. "Didn't it work?"

"Nah, I guess I fouled that one up, too," Jael said sourly.

"I'm just glad you didn't ruin the Lesser Summoning," Tanis grinned. "But High Priest Urien and his lesser priests have been casting private rituals every night to commune with Baaros, and all the signs have been true, so He must be pleased with us."

Jael found, to her disgust, that she had left the castle so quickly that she had not thought to bring any money, so Tanis treated for balls of a light dough that had been fried in hot fat, then dipped in honey and cinnamon. They nibbled on the sweets and watched a troupe of jugglers perform at the center of the market. Apparently these were honest jugglers, using no magic to aid in their tricks, because nothing dropped or broke during their performance. Jael was so relieved by this blessing that at the end of the performance, she begged Tanis to give the jugglers a whole Sun, promising to reimburse him as soon as she could get her pocket money from the castle.

After the honey cakes and the jugglers, Jael took Tanis to the city wall and talked the guards into letting them up to watch the moonrise. Tanis had never been on the wall and was duly impressed with the view to the west—the width of the Brightwater River and, beyond it, the vast expanses of gently rolling farmlands.

"They'll be threshing soon," Jael mused. "As soon as we get enough sunny days in a row."

"Does Allanmere have a harvest festival?" Tanis asked. "Most cities do, but we came here after the harvest last year."

"There's one here and one in the Heartwood," Jael told him. "Different times, of course, so the elves who live or trade in town can go to both." She chuckled. "Can't cheat an elf out of a festival. The elvan festival, the Fruiting of the Vine, will be right after the last of the moondrop berries have ripened and been pressed and the wine kegged. The city's harvest festival will be sooner, as soon as the grain's brought in. A week or two, probably."

"I went to a couple of harvest festivals in Loroval," Tanis said. He hesitated for a moment. "Would you want to go to the festival with me?"

Now it was Jael's turn to hesitate. Harvest fest would be delightful with Tanis, a thrilling adventure—but what if Lord Urien later invited her? It wouldn't be fair to Tanis to accept and then cancel.

"I'd like to," she said slowly, "but I don't know if I can promise yet. Sometimes my parents expect me to show myself with them. But the festival will run for three days; surely I'll have a little free time somewhere in there."

"I'd like that," Tanis said, rather shyly. "Especially now that neither of us will be in trouble for being seen together."

"Wasn't there someone selling dragon here a day or two ago?" Jael asked suddenly, remembering when she and Urien had driven through the market. "Are they still here?"

"I think so," Tanis said, catching Jael's eagerness. "Let's find out."

Most of the dragon had already sold, but fortunately there was a little left, still fresh due to its preservation spell; Tanis had barely enough money left to pay for two slabs of the strong-flavored meat, well basted with spicy sauce, and mugs of dark beer, the only possible beverage to drink with dragon. Jael reminded herself sternly to give Tanis back some money; temple acolytes couldn't have much coin to spend in the market, and dragon was expensive.

Roast dragon and beer combined in one inevitable effect, and Tanis and Jael walked back north laughing as one or the other belched resoundingly.

"I suppose you've made up for two days of fasting," Tanis laughed.

"I suppose I have," Jael admitted, belching so loudly that passersby turned to stare with mild reproof.

"Is that a new dagger?" Tanis asked, pointing to the sheath on Jael's hip. "I've never seen you wear it before."

"Aunt Shadow gave it to me before she left this afternoon." Jael drew the dagger and handed it to Tanis. "Watch out, it's very sharp."

"By Baaros's eyes, it certainly is!" Tanis said, staring at the thin line of blood on his thumb; Jael's warning had come a bit too late. "But it's so light. I've never seen one like it. Where did it come from?"

"Uh—" Jael wondered whether to tell Tanis the whole story; after all, he was her best—and only—friend. But most humans had strange ideas about paternity, and Mother doubtless would ask her not to tell anyone. "You know, I don't think Aunt Shadow knew exactly where this was made or what it's made of." Which was true, in a way.

"I've never seen you carry anything but your eating dagger," Tanis said, carefully sheathing the dagger. "There hasn't been any trouble, has there?"

"No, it was just a gift," Jael said quickly. "But it's unusual."

"Like you," Tanis quipped. He grinned to take the sting out of his joke. "I'll stop by when I have some free time again. High Priest Urien doesn't have much use for Ankaras and the rest of us since he settled into the leadership of the temple."

To Jael's surprise, however, a message had arrived for her while she was gone; even more amazing, however, was that the parchment had been left, still sealed with Lord Urien's mark, in her room. Donya was keeping her promise, then; Jael would have expected her parents to open the scroll.

The message was simply a polite note asking Jael if she would consent to join Urien on the morrow at midmorning—with appropriate escort, of course—to look at the last house on North Street, and if she might honor him by dining with him afterward. Jael stuck the parchment through her belt and went skipping down to supper; for once she was the first, not the last, to come to table. To her surprise, new light globes had been placed.

"Well, there you are," Argent said mildly, squeezing Jael's shoulder on his way to the head of the table. "We wondered where you'd gone."

"There was dragon in the market," Jael said with a grin. "Now that I can eat real food, I wanted to get some. But I think I can eat again."

Markus and Mera followed Donya into the dining hall, but broke ranks to assault Jael from both sides.

"You went off to the forest without even telling us," Markus scowled.

"And we hardly got to see Aunt Shadow, and she left without even saying good-bye," Mera accused.

"Even Father and Mother haven't had any time at all for us," Markus said. "It must be your fault."

"It's *always* your fault," Mera added.

"Well, it's my fault again," Jael said irritably.

"Markus, Mera, that's enough," Donya said sternly. "If you haven't yet learned your lesson about behavior at the supper table, you'll have to eat in your rooms for another three days. Now sit down."

"Light globes?" Jael asked Donya and Argent, raising her eyebrow.

"I talked to Nubric and Jermyn after Shadow left this afternoon," Argent told her. "Nubric would like to try some tests. But in the meantime we'll just continue as we always have."

"Lord Urien sent me a message," Jael said, pulling the parchment from her belt and handing it to Donya. "If you don't object, and if I can take a couple of guards tomorrow morning, I'd like to go." *Now* let Donya say she was acting like a child.

"All right," Donya said, glancing at Jael before she read the parchment. "But stay away from Rivertown, Jaellyn. Last night two elves were found there with their hearts cut out."

Jael's mouth dropped open, and even Markus and Mera were silent.

"I think Lord Urien's announcement at the Temple of Baaros has only inflamed some of the anti-elvan factions in the city," Argent said gently. "This may be the work of some of those who left the Temple of Baaros because of the change of doctrine, as the two elves were minor merchants—elvan perfumes and the like. Until it's been investigated further, however, we're stationing extra guards in Rivertown, and it would be best for you to avoid the entire area."

"No doubt of that," Jael said, shivering. "I've never heard

of even an assassin cutting out hearts." She thought briefly of Blade.

"Were they very bloody?" Markus asked curiously.

"Or were the hearts gone? Did someone eat them?" Mera chimed in.

"By the Mother Forest, what a gruesome subject for supper," Argent said, shaking his head. "Markus, Mera, when we know more, you'll be told. Now, please, let's say no more about it."

Jael would have liked to ask more about the incident, but that would get Markus and Mera started again and upset Father, so she ate a little dinner, more for politeness' sake than out of hunger, and excused herself.

Back in her room, Jael saw the box of tea, and remembering its pleasant, fragrant taste, she made herself a kettleful and sipped it slowly, contemplating the pendant Urien had given her. She had never seen the like of the rich purple-red stones before, or the delicate gold work. Perhaps it had been made magically, but at least it seemed to have suffered no ill effects from hanging around her neck for days.

The hot tea made her feel warm and drowsy, and Jael took off her clothes and slipped under the covers, pouring the last of the tea into a cup at her bedside. She carefully tucked the pendant into the box hidden in the frame of her bed, where she stored Shadow's puzzle.

Jael dreamed she lay in a great stone hand, gently cupped and sheltered, safe and surrounded. Above her she could see the lines of another stone hand arching over her. The stone under her was cold, hard but somehow comforting in its solidity. The world was still, the world was stone, peaceful and unchanging.

Gradually Jael became aware that the stone beneath her had somehow changed. Now the hand on which she lay was flesh, warm and softer. Jael felt somehow afraid, not knowing why until she realized that the hand above her was no longer so far away, but was slowly closing over her, descending to crush her, to smother her. She could almost feel the great weight pressing down upon her—

Jael bolted upright in her bed, pushing the covers off her face. For a moment she shivered in the dark room, her arms clasping her knees tightly against her chest. She slid out of bed and pushed another log onto the fire, then crawled shivering back into bed. She pulled the pouch containing Shadow's puzzle from its hiding place and clasped it like a talisman.

When she slept, this time there were no dreams.

V

● "This one looks much better," Jael admitted.

"I think you're right." Urien smiled as he gazed around the empty room. He stepped to the window and looked out. "The neighborhood appears much superior to the southern house we looked at." He glanced upward. "But that gargoyle—"

"Well, you could have it taken down," Jael grinned.

"It's so hideous, I may just keep it there," Urien said, smiling back. "That way, when I invite guests to the house, I can ask them how they like it and watch them squirm for an answer."

Jael chuckled at the image, wondering if Numan had perhaps had the same idea. Grandmother Celene was fond of just such tricks.

"Are you ready for some dinner?" Urien suggested. "I hope this time we can dine on something more appealing than boiled greens."

"Today I can eat whatever I want," Jael said. "And I could eat anything in Allanmere *except* boiled potherbs."

Urien took her to the Basilisk's Eye, an almost decadently luxurious inn in the Noble District. Jael wondered if Urien knew that the small private supper alcoves were a notorious trysting place for nobles wanting to avoid public scrutiny of their liaisons. Thinking about it, Jael decided that Urien probably knew—and probably knew that *she* knew.

Because most nobles dining at the Eye wanted privacy in the alcoves, their meal was served all at once, rather than in courses, so that the servers wouldn't be ducking in and out. Jael was a little intimidated by the sheer quantity of dishes, and even more so when she realized what they were being served: golden blacktail roe; a delicate soup of sawback fin; simmered and seasoned roundshells, together with their liquor; bite-size morsels of daggertooth, stewed in a spicy sauce; pincer-claws baked in butter, and much more—the list was dizzying, and Jael found herself calculating the probable cost preservation-spelling these delicacies and ferrying them *up* the Brightwater. Jael shuddered to herself and thought that she did *not* want to know what Urien was paying for this dinner.

Although wine had, of course, been brought with the meal, Urien did not press any on Jael, for which Jael was duly grateful. Instead he gave the servant a small cake of the Calidwyn black tea to brew, joining Jael in a cup of the fragrant liquid.

"I see you are growing to share my addiction to Calidwyn's tea," he smiled. "Perhaps I will have to send for some to trade in Allanmere after all."

He scooped up a small spoonful of blacktail roe on a thin sliver of toasted bread and fed it to Jael.

"Do you like it?"

Jael nodded and swallowed.

"We don't get seafood too often," she said. "Not much is ferried up the Brightwater this far."

"Did you know," Urien said, taking Jael's hand and smiling, "that many of the fruits of the sea are thought to be aphrodisiacs?"

"I'd heard that, yes," Jael said. She grinned. "I think the sea merchants try to spread that rumor to raise the prices."

"That may be." Still holding Jael's hand, Urien dipped her finger into the bowl of blacktail roe, scooping up some of the tiny golden orbs. Urien's eyes twinkled as he raised Jael's hand and closed his lips around her fingertip, sensuously licking the roe from her skin. He released her hand and smiled. "That doesn't mean it isn't true."

Jael fought down her unease. There were four guards outside the door, two of Urien's and two of hers. Urien was only flirting; there was no harm in that. She was still in control of the situation. The thought relaxed her immediately, and she smiled.

"Then I believe I'll have a little more," Jael said, spooning herself another helping of the daggertooth.

"You like spicy food?" Urien asked, pouring her another cup of tea.

"Sometimes," Jael said smoothly. "In the right company."

Urien pulled a small bottle out of his wallet and set it on the table.

"Did you like the Bluebright?" he asked, his tone gently daring her.

"If my mother finds out you've been giving me this stuff, after she told you to wait until it was tested," Jael told him, "she'd have the City Guard confiscate every drop you've got until it *is* tested. And she'd lock me in my room for twice as long."

Urien raised one eyebrow.

"Are you going to tell her?"

Jael reached across the table and pulled the stopper out of the bottle of Bluebright. This was exciting, the way Shadow must feel when she made a successful theft.

"Not if you'll pour," she said.

Urien took a small pouch from his wallet and removed two lumps of sugar. He carefully dripped a little Bluebright on each lump and took one, raising an eyebrow at Jael. Jael popped the other lump of sugar into her mouth.

This time she was expecting the burst of heat and the following coolness, and the delicious languor that spread through her. She was unprepared, however, when Urien took her hand again and kissed her palm, then the inside of her wrist, for the sudden flush of warmth that followed his touch. His lips slid up her forearm, his tongue touching her skin, and Jael gasped as her skin came alive in flashes of heat and cold.

Urien released her arm then, and Jael shivered, amazed at the unfamiliar, trembling disappointment she felt. Urien leaned closer, but paused long enough for Jael to signal her reluctance if she wished. Jael leaned to meet him halfway.

Jael's heart pounded hard and joyfully, and she could have shouted were it not for Urien's lips on hers. Oh, she'd been so afraid she'd never feel this, this wonderful burning in her blood that stippled her skin with gooseflesh and seemed to melt her bones. She shivered and tangled her fingers in Urien's hair as he nibbled at the side of her neck, and his hand slid under her tunic, cool against the skin of her back. She must have stiffened slightly, however, for Urien released her after a last lingering kiss, his eyes warm.

"I'm sorry," he said gently. "This is better left for another time and place."

Jael could have groaned with disappointment, but a part of her was relieved. She sat up straight, her cheeks hot with embarrassment.

"Perhaps you'd care to go riding with me in a day or two," Urien suggested. "If the weather is pleasant, we could take dinner with us."

"I'd like that," Jael said quickly.

"Then we'll plan for two days from now, midmorning again," Urien said. "In the meantime, the carriage can take us around the market once. The air will clear our heads."

"Or our noses," Jael muttered to herself as they left. Midweek was tanning day at the Leather Guild, and a south wind was blowing.

"This was a poor idea," Urien admitted later as he and Jael wiped tears from their eyes.

"Well, it did clear my head," Jael admitted. "Just as well, too. I really should go to sword practice this afternoon."

Urien ordered the carriage back to the castle, and by the time they arrived, the noxious smell and the late summer breeze together had wiped most of the Bluebright languor from Jael's head. Urien helped Jael out of the carriage, but politely declined Jael's invitation to come in. The guards who had accompanied Jael appeared relieved; riding on the outside of the carriage, they had been more exposed to the tanning odors and seemed more than ready to abandon their posts.

Because Jael had canceled her morning lessons, Larissa was not present, and Rabin was nowhere to be found. Irritated, Jael changed into her old clothes and trudged down to the practice field anyway; at least she could practice her dagger throwing alone, and work on that new kick Larissa had shown her the day before she went to the Heartwood.

To her surprise, Jael found Donya in the practice field, working on a new lunge with one of the wooden practice posts. She stopped, however, as soon as Jael appeared.

"Good afternoon," Donya panted, apparently as surprised as Jael herself. "Rabin isn't here. Since you'd canceled your lesson, I gave him the afternoon free. He said something about seeing to your sword."

"He was commissioning a lighter one," Jael said. "It's probably finished by now."

"Ah." Donya wiped sweat off her brow with the back of her wrist. "I noticed you were wearing that dagger last night at supper." She nodded at the sheath at Jael's hip.

Jael drew the dagger to show Donya the strange light blade.

"Aunt Shadow gave it to me," she said awkwardly. "She said—uh—"

"Farryn gave her that," Donya finished. "Yes, I know. I'm surprised she gave you one, though. She loves those daggers. Then again, she's like that—she'd give you the last copper in her purse at the same time as she was stealing your underthings. Well, come here and have a look. I wanted a last swing with this, and then I was going to leave it in your room."

Donya had laid a long, cloth-wrapped bundle on a bench at the edge of the practice field. Jael watched as Donya unfolded the cloth to reveal an ornately tooled scabbard. Donya drew the sword, and Jael's eyes widened at the sight of the same pale metal from which her dagger was made.

"Did Farryn give you that, too?" Jael asked amazedly. "I've never seen you wear it."

"No, Chyrie gave it to me," Donya said, a little sadly. "It wasn't long after I met Farryn. It belonged to one of his ancestors. I only got to use it once, against the giant daggertooth I told you about. After Farryn left, I put it away for years. I thought if anyone saw it, they'd ask questions, and I didn't want to think about it—well, you understand. Here, try it."

Jael took the sword. The hilt was rather long for her—no wonder, if it had been made for a six-fingered hand—and the blade, too, was a little longer than Rabin had recommended.

As soon as the hilt was in her hand, however, Jael felt the same rightness, the same *aliveness*, that she had felt when she had held the dagger. It felt friendly to her hand, familiar. Even the strange light length of it felt right.

"Go on, take a cut," Donya said, gesturing to the much-hacked practice pole. "But don't cut straight down, edge-on. To take advantage of that slight curve in the blade, come down at an angle and pull *in*—well, like this."

She stood behind Jael and clasped her hands over her daughter's.

"Loosen your grip a little and don't pull the tip down so far. That's right, right shoulder to left hip, down and *in*. No, bend your left elbow up more and don't stiffen your wrist. Got it?"

"I think so," Jael said doubtfully. What Donya had told her was much different from what Rabin had taught her.

"Go on, then," Donya said encouragingly. "But have some respect for that blade; it's sharp enough to shave the fuzz off a butterfly's wing. Don't worry, you can't hurt the sword or the practice pole; just don't chop off your own foot."

Jael took a deep breath and faced the practice pole squarely, focusing the way Rabin had told her. For maximum cut, she'd strike *there*—

"Uh-uh," Donya said, breaking Jael's concentration. "By this time your enemy's cut you in half."

"But Rabin says I've got to calculate—" Jael protested.

"Calculate when someone isn't swinging a sword at your head," Donya said roughly. "Otherwise, get in a good cut *anywhere* to give you time to think. This sword does half the work for you. Now turn back around and cut, don't calculate."

Jael waited only until she was sure that Donya was well out of the way; then she turned. The sword seemed to carry her arm on its own, guiding her through the sweep. She unconsciously braced herself for the jar of the sword against the weather-hardened wood; then she overbalanced and almost fell as the top of the pole fell severed to the ground. Barely, she steadied herself, then dropped the sword as if the hilt burned her.

Donya stepped over and ran her finger over the truncated top of the practice pole.

"Not bad," she admitted. "You didn't pull in enough, but with that sword, I suppose you don't need to. That was a good cut. Now pick up your sword and wipe and sheathe it. You *never* drop your sword, especially on dirt."

Jael picked up the sword and started to wipe it on her tunic; then she thought of the edge of that blade and reconsidered, wiping the blade very carefully with one of the soft leather scraps left in the practice yard for that very purpose. Then the importance of what Donya had said struck her.

"*My* sword?" Jael said in a small voice.

"As I said, I haven't used the thing in years," Donya said, her voice a little rough. "Besides, the damned thing's so light I never had much use for it anyway. No good for my style of swordplay."

"But Chyrie gave it to you," Jael protested.

"Who can say?" Donya shrugged, grinning a little sadly. "She probably meant it for you all along." Donya shook her head firmly. "Practice with it, but I don't think I need to tell you that you never practice against a person with that blade."

"Thank you, Mother," Jael said, awed. "I'll take good care of it."

"I know you won't neglect it," Donya said sternly. "That blade deserves a fine warrior to wield it. I know you'll work hard to become that fine warrior. But don't wear that thing into town."

"Because people would ask questions?" Jael asked.

"That, too," Donya admitted. "But that's not what I meant. There's a lot of duel-happy young lordlings in town, and when they see you wearing a sword, that's something of a challenge to them. So don't wear the sword in town until you're prepared to use it."

"Yes, Mother," Jael said. Just the thought of someone swinging a sword at *her* was terrifying. She glanced at the practice pole, and the severed piece gave her a little jolt of satisfaction. Someday—not now, but someday—she'd give those "duel-happy young lordlings" a reason to show respect for Jaellyn the Cursed.

She took the sword back to her room, dagger practice forgotten. She sat on her bed, admiring the dagger and the sword, plucking hairs from her head one after the other to test and retest the deadly sharp edges. Both blades were amazing in their workmanship; squint as she might, Jael could not make out any trace of the fold lines. Hadn't Mother said something about some of the Kresh molding stone and metal with their minds?

Such as melting a hole in a stone altar?

Or perhaps, drunk on Bluebright, melting a metal drinking mug?

Jael put down the precious dagger and scrabbled in her coin box, pulling out a copper piece. She cupped the coin in her hands, staring intently at it. She willed the copper piece to melt. She stared at the coin, concentrating until her head throbbed and her eyes burned. At last she put the coin down with a sigh of disgust.

Apparently *that* part of her wasn't going to work, either.

As Jael put the blades on the table beside her bed and crawled under the covers, however, she could not feel wholly unhappy. She'd come back from the Heartwood still incomplete, but reaching out to touch the hilt of the sword, she felt that perhaps, just perhaps, today she had found a piece of what was missing.

In the morning Jael presented herself promptly and confidently to Rabin and Larissa. If she had hoped some vestige of the *rightness* and ease she had felt with the Kresh sword might have carried over to her lessons with a wooden practice sword, however, Jael was disappointed. Rabin and Larissa both encouraged her, Larissa complimenting Jael's improvement in unarmed combat. The practice sword, however, felt dead and clumsy in her hands, and the moves Rabin taught her felt awkward and foreign. Jael longed to bring out the Kresh sword, but while Mother might trust Rabin, the same might not be true of Larissa. Jael made a mental note to ask Mother if she could bring the sword to the afternoon lessons when she worked with Rabin alone.

At dinner, however, Mother and Father were distant and preoccupied, and Jael decided not to broach the subject of the sword. An elvan merchant had disappeared somewhere between the Golden Grape tavern and his home above his shop in the Mercantile District, vanished as if by magic. No one knew whether the disappearance in the Mercantile District could be related to the two elves found dead in Rivertown, but Jael knew what Donya and Argent feared—that another round of elvan murders was beginning as it had during the Crimson Plague. No wonder Mother was encouraging her to improve her combat skills, even at the expense of her other studies.

After dinner Rabin presented Jael with the sword he had commissioned. It was a beautiful little sword, shorter than the Kresh blade but not quite as light. The hilt fitted her hand exquisitely, but the sword felt inert and dead in her hand, balanced wrongly, clumsily heavy and straight. As she worked with the sword, she felt Rabin's disappointment—despite the sword he had commissioned and the allowances he tried to make for her size and build, she still moved too slowly and awkwardly. He was also disappointed that she was canceling her lessons for the next day.

"There isn't much I can do until you build more strength in your arms and master the moves I taught you," Rabin said, shaking his head. "Why don't you spend your afternoons practicing on your own until then? And you're never going to improve, Jaellyn, until you commit yourself to regular lessons and regular practice. A day here and a day there won't be enough."

Jael sighed and agreed. She knew Rabin was right—certainly she needed all the practice she could get—but it was much pleasanter to spend her time running through the market with Tanis or riding with Urien than being battered by Rabin and Larissa. A soak in the bathing pools could work some of the knots out of her muscles, but all it did for her bruises was to turn them brilliant shades of yellow and green.

In her room, however, Jael found that Mother or Father had thought ahead of her. A clay pot of ointment awaited her on her bedside table. The stuff had a disagreeable, pungent odor, and it caused a strange tingling, burning sensation on her skin, but it coaxed the last soreness from her muscles and healed her bruises. This was peasant magic at its simplest, so simple that even Jael could not affect it—not even a spell, just the proper combination of herbs and other ingredients.

The next morning, Jael was doubly grateful for the salve's efficacy, although she dared not put any on in the morning because of its strong odor. It had been some time since Jael had gone riding; Argent did not ride, Donya rarely rode for pleasure unless she was hunting, and riding alone had never appealed to Jael.

Today, however, Jael and Urien were favored with a sunny day and a warm breeze, and they ferried across the Brightwater to ride south. The fields of grain were golden and ripe, and farmers were busy in most of them, bringing in the harvest. Wagons were laden with fruits and vegetables bound either back to the farms or directly to the market in Allanmere.

Jael and Urien found a comfortable spot on the banks of one of the many small streams that divided the farmers' lands. The guards spread a blanket and laid out the dinner, then retired to a distance out of sight, but within calling range. Jael noticed how accustomed Urien's guards were to this process, and she wondered uncomfortably how many young ladies of noble birth Urien had invited on similar expeditions.

The dinner Urien had brought was no elaborate meal as their previous supper had been; this was meat pies and roast fowl and fresh bread, a few sausages and some fresh fruit. Jael lounged comfortably on the blanket, enjoying the simple food and the fact that here it didn't matter if her second-best tunic looked rumpled.

"Did you receive my gift?" Urien asked at last, when Jael groaned and shook her head at his offer of another pie.

"Gift?" Jael searched her mind. Surely none of the servants would have misplaced anything he sent, or Mother intercepted—

"The salve," Urien told her. "You mentioned sword practice when we parted two days ago. I remembered my own days of sword training. That ointment used to spare me a good deal of pain after a vigorous lesson."

"The salve!" Jael was instantly relieved. "Oh, you sent that. I thought maybe Father had made it up, being an herbalist. Yes, thank you. It worked wonderfully. It was kind of you to think of it, especially with your eyes watering from tanning fumes."

"Actually, the odors of tanning were what reminded me of the salve," Urien laughed. "It has a rather burning odor of its own."

That made Jael laugh, too, and she was grateful to feel so

comfortable with Urien after the rather awkward incident of two nights before.

"And how do your sword lessons progress?" Urien asked interestedly.

"Not very well," Jael admitted. "I'm clumsy as a newborn calf. All I can seem to do is fall over my own feet."

Urien shook his head sympathetically.

"Then you must apply yourself even more faithfully," he said. "A lovely young lady and a High Lord's daughter must be able to protect herself."

"Especially now," Jael sighed.

"Oh?" Urien frowned. "Have you been threatened? Is there any danger? Jaellyn, remember that my guards and my sword are always at your—"

"Nothing like that," Jael said hurriedly. "But didn't you hear what's happened? Two elves were murdered in Rivertown, and now another elvan merchant has disappeared."

Urien raised both eyebrows.

"Baaros bless us, I hadn't heard," he said worriedly. "What a terrible thing. All elves, did you say? I hope none of Ankaras's teachings at the temple might have inspired whatever rogues committed such a deed."

"I'm sure it's nothing to do with the Temple of Baaros," Jael assured him. "Likely the two aren't even related. The two elves in Rivertown were probably done by some new assassin wanting to make a reputation, and as far as we can say, the elvan merchant sneaked out of town ahead of some angry creditors or got his throat slit in some alleyway for his gold."

Urien sighed, shaking his head.

"Nonetheless, this worries me," he said. "You must be very careful in town, Jaellyn. I would have thought again about this trip if I'd known."

"Oh, wait, now," Jael protested hurriedly. "There's four guards close enough to spit on in a good wind. The city should be safe enough, at least during the day in the good areas."

"Well, it's as well that I didn't buy the house near Rivertown, then," Urien chuckled. "Else they'd likely find *me* lying in some alley. I can hardly thank you enough for your assistance and advice."

"What about Merchant Numan's house?" Jael asked. "Have you bought it already?"

"Tomorrow the scribes will record the transaction," Urien told her. "My servants have already moved my belongings there. In a day or two, when the household is settled and I've hired additional servants, I hope you will do me the honor of supping with me to celebrate."

"I'd enjoy that," Jael said, although her stomach fluttered a little. Supping with a young lord in his home was very different from dining in a public inn with guards just outside the door, or picnicking in an open clearing with her guards only a call away.

They chatted comfortably about nothing of consequence after the dinner. Urien found a tree that grew out over the creek, roots stretching into the bank, and Jael pulled off her boots and dangled her feet into the cold water, throwing scraps of bread into the creek for the ducks and laughing when tiny fish swam up to nibble at her toes. Urien picked blue and purple rush flowers and braided them into a circlet for Jael's hair.

"Your eyes are just the color of new bronze," Urien said, laying the circlet gently on her head. "The way they turn gives you an exotic beauty, like some shy forest creature."

Jael smiled shyly. Apparently Urien did not know enough about the local elves to realize what "forest creatures" they truly were. She had never thought of herself as having any kind of beauty, exotic or otherwise; the only description she had ever heard applied to her appearance was "strange." It was Urien who looked wonderfully exotic with his delicately angular features, his feathery black hair and pale skin. He looked, Jael realized, like some magical person out of a poem or a legend.

"Are you a mage?" Jael asked suddenly, boldly.

Urien raised his eyebrows at the sudden change of subject.

"I have some magical ability," he said. "But in the Temple of Baaros it's customary that we place our magic in service to the temple, using it only for rituals and within the confines of the temple itself. I've never learned much secular magic, if that's what you mean."

Jael stifled a sigh of relief. At least he wouldn't be casting any spells for her to ruin.

They rode back to the castle at midafternoon, Urien

apologizing that he had business at the temple. Jael ran back to her room, changed into her old clothes, and grabbed the sword her mother had given her; she had the rest of the afternoon free and the practice field to herself, an ideal opportunity to put a few more nicks in the practice poles.

A straw-stuffed dummy had been set up for the twins' practice; Jael drew her dagger and practiced some of the simpler turns, kicks, and lunges Larissa had shown her. In *this*, at least, Jael felt she was improving; perhaps she was not quite so clumsy and slow as before.

Then again, how badly could she fare against a straw dummy?

When she was moving easily, her muscles loosened, Jael put away the dagger and drew her sword. Since she had already "decapitated" one of the practice poles, she supposed there was no harm in damaging it further.

Once again, however, Jael found that the style Rabin had taught her felt foreign and wrong, her limbs seeming to rebel against them, her feet becoming clumsy and her hands slow. The lightness of her sword made her overbalance every time she turned or struck, although she managed to "behead" the practice pole twice more. Experimenting, Jael found her own rhythm, her own form, that seemed easier and more natural to her—neither Donya's strength and blunt ferocity, Rabin's calculated and deliberate precision, nor Mist's birdlike grace. At first she was doubtful—she knew nothing about swordplay, no doubt of that, and who was she to scorn the advice of everyone who'd taught her? But as she moved, she could feel a pattern growing in her movements, a smooth liquidity that flowed from sword tip to feet and back again. As her confidence grew, Jael found that it took only a small adjustment to wield the sword in one hand, although the long hilt left ample room for two; Jael believed that when her wrists and forearms were stronger, she could be equally effective either way.

At last, almost regretfully, Jael paused to take a swallow of water from one of the jugs left on the practice field. To her surprise, her mother was sitting on the wall, a sort of puzzled pride in her expression.

"That was good, but Rabin didn't teach you that, nor did I," Donya said, handing Jael the jug. "Is that Mist's style?"

"No," Jael said abashedly. "The things Mist showed me don't seem to work very well. I keep tripping."

"Mmmm." Donya slid off the wall and took the sword from Jael's hand, eyeing it thoughtfully. "No, I see your problem. This blade's too light for Rabin's style and mine, and too long for Mist's, not to mention the curve of the blade and its sharpness. I had some difficulty with this sword myself. It asked me to unlearn everything I'd been taught and had used for years; that's why I soon went back to my own sword."

"It asked—" Jael hesitated. "It's not a magical sword, is it, Mother?"

"No, no," Donya said, laughing. "Warriors and their swords. Sometimes on the road or in battle I'd talk to mine. I've caught other warriors doing the same. Some sing to their blades. Shadow used to tease me that at night, when I'd taken out my sword to oil and polish it, I held it like a lover. That's not as far afield as she thought. When you come to know a blade, all the secrets it tells you, all the special, personal techniques it shows you in time, it becomes something of a friend. When it's saved your life a couple of dozen times, it's hard to think of your sword as just a piece of metal. You make it part of you. That's what you were doing just now—listening to your sword, letting it teach you, getting to know it. That's the only real way to learn."

"But how can I really learn if I can't use it against a person in practice?" Jael asked, frustrated. "The practice swords are made differently, and they're heavier, and they feel wrong."

"Hmmm." Donya squinted critically at the sword again. "I'd offer to don my mail and have a go with you, but an unlucky hit by either of us wouldn't do the other much good, would it? Well, we'll just have to have a good metal guard made to cover the edge, but light enough that it won't hurt the balance. The guard's a good idea in any wise, so we don't have to continually replace the practice pole."

"But do you want me showing the sword to Rabin?" Jael asked hesitantly. "He's sure to be curious about it."

Donya gave Jael a look of surprise.

"That was sharp of you," the High Lady said, smiling slowly. "And kind, too. No, Rabin's trustworthy. Just tell him that Shadow gave you the sword when she gave you the dagger, that she got them somewhere on her travels. If that's the sword you practice with, though, that's the sword you'll one day have to use." Donya shook her head. "As I said, don't carry it in town until you're ready to use it—and I don't just mean training, Jaellyn. Don't carry that sword until you can live with seeing somebody's head lying on the ground instead of a chunk of wood. When that time comes, I'll leave it to your judgment what you tell the curious."

Jael was shocked to her core by the trust implicit in what Donya said. For a moment she had no idea how to react; then, suddenly, she knew exactly what to say.

"Mother," she said slowly, "would you try again to teach me the sword, instead of Rabin?"

Donya abruptly turned away, and when she spoke, her voice was hoarse and shook slightly.

"All right," she said. "I suppose I can make the time if you can. At least it will let me out of afternoon audiences."

Jael grinned to herself. Despite her mother's curt answer, she knew the High Lady was very pleased indeed.

Donya swiped her wrist across her eyes and turned back around.

"If you'll leave the sword with me, I'll have the guard made today," she said. "Go through the equipment racks and find some padding you can use. I don't pull my hits the way Rabin does."

"I remember," Jael said ruefully. Then she added hastily, "But *you* use a practice sword, right?"

Donya chuckled, reaching out to tousle Jael's hair.

"That's right," she said. "*I* use a practice sword. Now come in and wash up before supper. You smell like a stable."

By the time Jael reached the dining hall, the twins had already heard the news, and they were far from pleased.

"Why is Mother teaching *you* instead of us?" Mera asked resentfully.

"We're *much* better than you," Markus added. "She's wasting her time teaching you."

"And she gave *you* her sword," Mera said, utterly disgusted.

"Well, if it bothers you that much," Jael said sourly, "think of it like this—I'm so bad that I need every advantage I can get."

"That's true," Markus agreed, Mera nodding.

"I expect both of you to support and encourage your sister, not tease her," Donya told the twins sternly. "When I've worked with Jaellyn a few more times, I think it would be a good idea for the two of you to practice with her also."

The twins both grinned mischievously at Donya's suggestion, and Jael groaned inwardly. There was no doubt that Markus and Mera were indeed far better with their swords than she, nor that they'd be delighted to give her the bruises and cuts to prove it.

The prospect was so depressing that rather than returning to her room after supper, Jael hurried back out to the practice field to work on some of the techniques Larissa had shown her, despite the waning daylight. She had no more than begun, however, when Tanis peered over the practice field wall.

"Too busy?" he asked sympathetically.

"No," Jael said quickly, sheathing her dagger. "Just wasting time. Want to see if the jugglers are still working the market?"

"All right."

Tanis had to wait, however, while Jael ran back to her quarters to scrabble some of her pocket money out of the box where she kept it and into her purse. When she met Tanis outside the castle wall, she insisted on reimbursing him for the money he had spent on their previous trip.

The jugglers had left, either for the day or permanently, but they had been replaced by a troupe of elvan dancers. Jael found them of interest, for these were not local elves living either in the city or the Heartwood; these were strangers who had traveled from one of the eastern coastal cities. They were very different from the elves of the Heartwood, having none of the extremes in appearance visible in some of Allanmere's forest elves—unusual tallness or shortness, skin translucently fair or nut-brown, large eyes, elongated and sometimes mobile ears, the occasional extra digit on hands or feet, the exotic and often feral cast of features. These foreign elves lacked even the long braid that denoted age and status among Allanmere's elves. To Jael's eyes, they seemed almost more human than elvan in their moderate height and build, their sandy gold hair and blue eyes, their skin not pale but no browner than the sun would make it, their small and delicately pointed ears and somehow too soft features. Their dance was skillful and interesting, but it lacked either the exquisite delicacy of most of the forest dances or the exciting energy of a sword dance. All in all, Jael found the foreign elves largely disappointing.

Tanis, however, enjoyed the spectacle immensely.

"These elves are like the elves in Loroval," he said, tossing some coins to the dancers. "My father used to deal with them before the trouble started between the elvan and human merchants. I was even delivered by an elvan midwife. You know, when I came here and saw all the elves, I couldn't understand why they looked so dif—" He paused, then grinned apologetically. "Sorry, Jael. I didn't mean that."

Jael shook her head.

"There's nothing to be sorry for," she said. "They—we *do* look different. I suppose those elves are thinking 'How strange they look here.' "

"Speaking of elves," Tanis said, tactfully changing the subject, "did you hear about those two elves in Rivertown? And the merchant?"

"Mother and Father told us about it," Jael said, nodding. "How did you find out?"

"I overheard High Priest Urien telling his lesser priests this afternoon," Tanis admitted. "One of the lesser priests said another elf had been found this morning, this time with her throat cut."

"I didn't know about that one," Jael said, surprised. "Where was the woman found?"

"Floating in the Brightwater, snagged on one of the pilings at the Docks," Tanis told her. "She'd been dead for a day or two, probably before the elves in Rivertown were killed. The Docks are just west of Rivertown, though. I wonder if the incidents are linked together somehow."

"I don't see why they should be," Jael said slowly. "If someone cut the hearts out of two elves and left them lying around Rivertown, they must have meant for the bodies to be found. The merchant hasn't been found; there isn't even any proof that he's been killed. The woman, that looks more like someone killed her, then tried to get rid of the corpse. The three incidents sound too different to be related."

"Why would anyone kill two elves and *want* the bodies to be found?" Tanis asked, grimacing.

"Sometimes assassins leave the bodies to be found," Jael mused, "to build a reputation and to let their employer know the contract's been carried out. Sometimes bodies are left as a warning, too—in this case maybe a warning to other merchants, or other elves, or families and friends."

"What if the killer was a worshipper at the Temple of Baaros when Ankaras was High Priest?" Tanis asked slowly. "What if he's one of those who left when High Priest Urien changed the doctrine, and he left the bodies so that High Priest Urien—or maybe the High Lord and High Lady of Allanmere—would know that changing the temple's policy wouldn't change the beliefs of Ankaras's followers?"

Jael glanced around her, then drew Tanis into the closest alley and hunkered down against the wall.

"You don't think any of them would do that, do you?" Jael asked, horrified. "I mean, just as a kind of warning? I know Mother and Father are thinking about twenty years ago during the Crimson Plague, when some of the people in the city were killing elves, but—well, those were mobs of people frightened half to death, shut in the city, most of them sick and crazy. Most of them blamed the elves for the plague. It wasn't a good reason to kill people, but at least it was *some* reason."

"I told you that High Priest Urien doesn't have much use for Ankaras and the rest of us now," Tanis said hesitantly. "Sometimes he relieves us of duty entirely. He doesn't even let us serve at the private rituals anymore. Ankaras has been furious. I think—I think he's been talking to some of the worshippers who left the temple when Urien took the robe. Maybe he's thinking of leaving the temple and setting up a temple of his own in secret, if enough worshippers hate the elves and will follow him instead of Urien. Or maybe—maybe he thinks that if he can muster enough followers, they could even throw Urien out of the temple and place him back as High Priest. I don't know. Ankaras and High Priest Urien both frighten me these days. Mostly I just try to stay out of the way."

"Mother and Father didn't say anything about the elvan woman at the Docks," Jael said thoughtfully. "I don't know whether they didn't want to frighten us, or whether they don't even know about it yet." The thought that she might know something that even the High Lord and Lady of Allanmere did not was strangely exciting, and an idea occurred to her. "Do you know who Ankaras might be talking to? Is there a leader, I mean, of these worshippers who left?"

"I don't know," Tanis said after a moment's thought. "But I could find out who he's talking to. It wouldn't be difficult to follow him when he goes out." Tanis frowned warily. "Why? Are you going to tell the guard or your parents? I don't think Ankaras has done anything illegal himself, after all."

"No, I have another idea," Jael said quickly. "What if we could find out if these murders—and maybe the disappearance, too—are related, and why, and who? What if we could solve this all by ourselves? That way, if Ankaras isn't involved, we could prove that he's innocent, and Ankaras and Urien both would be very pleased with you for saving the temple from official suspicion. And if Ankaras *is* involved somehow, if we could prove *that*, we could also prove that he was working secretly against Urien, and Urien would be very pleased with you then, too. And we might have saved the lives of every elf in Allanmere."

"But it would be dangerous, wouldn't it?" Tanis said doubtfully. "And why do you think we could find out anything that the City Guard can't?"

"Because Ankaras's followers will talk to *you*," Jael said patiently. "You're his acolyte, after all. I can find out everything the City Guard knows from Mother and Father, and Aubry at the Thieves' Guild will talk to me, too. True?"

"I suppose so," Tanis said reluctantly.

"It can't do any harm to try, at least," Jael continued, "and if there's trouble, we can always tell Mother and Father or the City Guard what we've learned, and then at least we've helped a little. True?"

"True," Tanis said cautiously. "I suppose there isn't any harm in finding out what we can. But if it becomes dangerous, we'll go to the City Guard. Agreed?"

"Of course," Jael said impatiently.

"Then we'll have to be careful not to be recognized together," Tanis said with a sigh. "None of Ankaras's followers are going to talk to me if it's known that I'm friends with the High Lord and Lady's mostly elvan daughter. I suppose it's back to the caps and the dirt."

"So first," Jael said slowly, "I'll find out if Mother and Father know about the woman at the Docks, and I'll see if I can learn the details about the merchant and the two elves in Rivertown, and I'll see if Aubry knows anything else, too. You?"

"There isn't much I can do until I can learn who Ankaras is talking to," Tanis said unhappily. "I'll follow him. Shall we meet back here in three days? Maybe I'll know something by then."

By now it was quite dark, and talking about corpses in a dark alley was making Jael feel distinctly shivery.

"We'd better go back now," Tanis said, as if reading Jael's thoughts. "I'll see you back home."

"There's no need," Jael protested. "Then you'll have to walk most of the way back across town again."

"Yes, but I'd sit up all night worrying about you if I didn't," Tanis said wryly. "Jael, in the time it will take me to talk you into letting me walk with you, I could do it and be home twice. Spare me the argument and I'll buy you some honey pastries for the walk back."

Jael stood, her knees crackling as she did so, and started out of the alley; then she gasped and backed up, colliding with Tanis. Lord Urien was there, not three man-heights away, fingering the wares at a clothier's stall.

"Forget the honey pastries," Jael whispered urgently. "Lord Urien's there. Better take the back way home."

They darted down the dark alley, Jael taking Tanis's hand and leading with her keen elvan sight. Tanis cursed and stumbled behind her as his toes caught every roughness in the stone alley.

"Where does this alley come out?" Tanis panted.

"It goes into Rivertown," Jael said, trying to remember the complicated tangle of alleys around the market. "But there's another alley that turns north ahead, and from there we can cut back to the north end of the market, just south of the Noble District."

"Rivertown?" Tanis said, pulling Jael to a stop. "We shouldn't be going near Rivertown, especially at night."

"We aren't going into Rivertown," Jael said patiently. She pulled Tanis to a trot again. "I said the *alley* goes into

Rivertown. We're turning north. See, the alley's just ahead there."

"No, I don't see," Tanis said crossly. "And I don't see how *you* can see. And I don't like being in an alley that goes into Rivertown. Especially in the dark. Can't we just go back and wait until High Priest Urien goes away?"

"This way's faster," Jael said, pulling Tanis around the corner. "Just turn h—"

Her words were cut off as she stumbled over something large. Jael grunted as her teeth clicked abruptly shut on her tongue, and she stumbled sideways. Her head smacked the side of the building forming the east wall of the alley, and for a moment the world went very dark; then Tanis was shaking her, smacking her cheeks lightly.

"Are you all right?" he asked worriedly. His hands were shaking; so was his voice.

"Sorry," Jael mumbled, shaking her throbbing head to clear it. "I guess it doesn't help much to be able to see in the dark if I don't look around the corners first. If you see half my tongue on the ground, would you pick it up for me?"

"Jael—" Tanis's voice was very quiet. "What we tripped over—I think—I think maybe it's a dead person. I can smell blood."

"A dead person?" Jael tried to keep her voice from squeaking. Now that she looked, the few rays of moonlight were enough to illuminate a crumpled bundle of what looked like cloth. She, too, could smell a faint coppery odor of blood on the night breeze.

Jael tottered to her feet, still a little dizzy, the bump on her head throbbing hotly, and stumbled back toward the still form.

Tanis caught at her arm.

"We should get the City Guard right now," he said urgently. "We shouldn't go near . . . it."

"Are you joking?" Jael turned back to Tanis. "If we get the City Guard, at the very least *you*'ll be arrested where you stand and dragged back to the city prisons for questioning. Come on. It may not even be a corpse at all. Won't you feel like a fool if it turns out to be an old rug that somebody butchered a deer on?"

Tanis scowled but said nothing further as Jael tiptoed cautiously closer to the dark form. Now that she was closer, she could see that it was indeed a large rolled rug, but it obviously contained something of some bulk. Very carefully, Jael nudged the edge of the heavy fabric aside with the toe of her boot. A pale face came into view and Jael gasped, turning quickly away. Tanis immediately folded her into warm arms.

"What?" Tanis asked in a whisper. "Who is it?"

"Her name's Evriel," Jael said, remembering how often she had seen that pale face flushed and alive in the marketplace. "She's—she was a fur trader. The really fine stuff."

"An elf?" Tanis asked quietly, and Jael nodded. "How did she die? Can you tell?"

"I don't know," Jael admitted. "I couldn't look."

"Then I'll look." Tanis squeezed her reassuringly, but he was shaking. "Don't turn around. I'll—I'll just be a moment."

Jael stood shivering while Tanis stepped around behind her. There was a long pause, and Jael could hardly keep herself from looking, though she emphatically *did not* want to see. There seemed to be a million tiny noises in the alley, and Jael wondered uncomfortably if there might be anyone else lurking in the darkness. Tanis would never be able to see them.

"Well?" Jael said when she could wait no longer. "How did they—well, you know."

"It looks like she's been—ah—gutted," Tanis said, his voice thick. Jael could tell he had his hand over his mouth. "She's all open down the front and there's—there's nothing left inside her. There's no blood, either, except some on the rug." Jael could hear Tanis standing, and then he was back beside her, clasping her hand, shaking as hard as she was. "Let's go now, Jael, right now. What if whoever did this comes back?"

"You're right," Jael said quickly. "But we'll have to go right past it."

Tanis grimaced and put his hand over his mouth again.

"Squish over against the other wall," he said. "We'll just close our eyes and feel our way past to the intersection, and then turn back toward the market without looking. If I look at it again I think I'll drop my supper. One way or the other."

Despite her nausea, her headache, and the growing fear that someone might come, Jael found this tremendously funny, and she had to stifle helpless giggles as she followed Tanis's advice. His clammy hand clasped hers in a grip of steel as they edged down the alley, faces pressed fervently to the cold, rough stone of the wall. At last the wall ended; Jael took a deep breath, reluctant to abandon the security of the touch of stone. She forced herself to turn around toward the east, toward the market. A smell wafted down the alley.

Honey pastries, Jael thought, and then she was retching even as she turned and dragged Tanis at a run, away from the darkness, toward the lights of the market.

Away from death, toward life.

VI

"You're very quiet this morning," Larissa commented.

"Don't be discouraged, little heirling. You're getting better all the time."

"Yes, your unarmed combat skills have improved visibly, even in the short time Larissa's been working with you," Rabin agreed. "I'm rather jealous, especially as your mother's going to take over your sword training, or so she tells me."

"I suppose she doesn't think you whack me hard enough," Jael said ruefully. She resisted the urge to touch the hot lump on the side of her head. "Being my mother and the High Lady, she won't get in trouble if she breaks my head open."

"Well, if she thinks Rabin's being too kind with you, I'll have to leave you with twice as many bruises to compensate," Larissa said merrily. "Now, let's try again, and a little concentration this time, if you please." She drew both wooden daggers and took a defensive stance.

Jael sighed and grimly adopted the attack posture Larissa had told her, but even the prospect of Larissa's merciless speed and skill could not make her settle into her lesson this morning. All she could think of was Evriel's still, pale face, the smell of blood, the taste of bile in her mouth, the long silent run back to the castle. Gods, she'd *never* be able to eat another honey pastry in her life.

Jael had been so terrified for Tanis's safety that it had taken a long argument before she agreed that sending guardsmen home with Tanis, or making him ride home in one of the castle carriages, would cause more trouble than benefit. Jael had no way of even knowing if he had safely reached the inn where the acolytes boarded, and the worry hopelessly distracted her.

She had agonized most of the night over telling her parents or the City Guard about the body without implicating Tanis. But if the guard investigated, they'd find Tanis's tracks in the dirt and know that Jael had had a companion. Tanis would be brought in for questioning, and at the very least, he'd lose his station at the temple. No, doubtless someone would find this body without her help, just as the others had been found. It was too near the market to go undiscovered for long.

Jael *whoof*ed out her air as Larissa's wooden dagger slammed under her ribs, thankfully knuckles first. Jael fell to her knees, unable even to gasp for breath because of the fierce pain in her midriff.

"Pray to whatever god you like that your next opponent gives you an opening like that," Larissa said unsympathetically. "Now get up and try again, and *watch* me this time."

Jael tried hard to concentrate, and the remainder of the lesson went a little more productively. By midday, Jael had even managed to throw Larissa to the ground once, and thought that perhaps she had left Rabin with a bruise or two in uncomfortable places.

Jael was so sore that the prospect of washing up and going to dinner was intolerable; instead, she retired to the bathing pool and had dinner sent up there. A bath, a pot of Calidwyn black tea, and some of Urien's ointment later, she had regained enough strength to pull on her dirty clothes once more and hurry down to the practice yard to meet her mother. Donya, dressed for practice in old, stained padded leather, had indeed had a guard made for Jael's sword, a sturdy fold of thin metal that tied with leather thongs over the sharp blade.

"I tried this on the practice pole just to be certain," Donya said ruefully. "We tried a leather guard first, but the sword just cut right through it. Try the weight of it."

Jael obeyed. Even though she'd practiced with the Kresh blade only a few times, she could feel the slight difference in the blade's weight, but it was only a small change.

"I can work with this," Jael said. "If you're sure it's safe, that is."

"If I can't cut through the guard against a hard practice pole with my strength, you can't do it against my body with yours," Donya said sensibly. "There's some practice leather for you by the wall. Put it on, and the helmet, too."

Jael hurriedly donned the protective garments. Her mother's practice sword was modeled from Donya's own real blade, which was almost as tall as Jael; Jael imagined that with a blade that heavy and sharp, with Donya's strength behind it, the High Lady of Allanmere could likely cut a charging bull in half lengthwise if she wanted to. Jael wanted as much protection between Donya's wooden practice sword and her ribs as she could get.

"Just a short session today," Donya said, taking position in the yard. "Argent and I have to meet with some of our advisers this afternoon. Get ready; we'll start slow."

Jael soon found herself very glad of the padding indeed; although she was sure that Donya was not putting full strength behind her cuts, the tall warrior was far stronger than Larissa and more skilled even than Rabin. By the time Donya raised her hand to signal a break, Jael knew that she'd ache from head to toe that evening.

"All right," Donya said, and Jael was glad to see that her mother was sweaty and winded. "You've got a good start, I see. I should've thought of the sword years ago." Donya shook her head, and Jael could see pain in her eyes. "No matter. You've got some things to unlearn, I see. Much of what Rabin and Mist have taught you—and what I've taught you, too, I admit—isn't applicable to that sword and the style you're going to have to use with it. But I think you've made a start toward finding that style. When you can stop thinking and start *doing*, I won't get past your guard so often."

Jael tried to smile at what, for her mother, was high praise, but she ached too much. She gingerly peeled the sweaty padding from her body, wincing at the sore places.

"Thank you, Mother," she said. "But if you and Father don't mind, I think I'll take supper in my room tonight." She grinned apologetically. "I'm not certain I'll be able to sit, anyway."

"Sup in your room if you want," Donya said, "but after supper, Nubric wants to see you in his laboratory. Help me with these buckles, will you?"

Jael's own sore fingers fumbled with the buckles at Donya's left shoulder, which Jael knew was often stiff and painful from an old battle wound.

"What does Nubric want?" Jael asked.

"He's going to try a few tests of your quirk of bending magic," Donya said, sighing as she rubbed her shoulder. "If we can't find out how to stop it, perhaps we can prevent the incidents before they occur, or at least understand how they happen. Nubric promises not to paint any green runes on your back."

"He wouldn't be able to read them over the bruises," Jael grumbled, but she smiled to herself. Apparently her mother had taken her promise very seriously.

"One other thing." Donya laid a hand on Jael's arm as they were about to walk through the practice field's gate. "Lord Urien sent a messenger over, asking our permission for you to join him tomorrow for supper." Donya grimaced. "I told the messenger that you had our permission to go—*with* a few guards as escort there and back—but you'd send your own answer this evening."

"Uh, thank you." Jael felt suddenly awkward, realizing that all the while they'd been practicing, her mother had been thinking about that message, perhaps wondering how to deliver it—or even whether to deliver it. "I'll send the message before I go upstairs."

Donya nodded and walked beside Jael to the castle, but to Jael's surprise her mother did not ask what answer she would send.

"If I remember your wardrobe," Donya said slowly, "most of your tunics are getting a little threadbare in the elbows. Since the cleaning maids had some of your clothing anyway, I told the seamstresses to make you a few new tunics and trousers—some for everyday, and maybe a few for best. Something might be done by tomorrow evening."

Jael stared at her mother in amazement, and Donya grinned a little uncomfortably.

"Seems you've got that young lord all moon-eyed over you," Donya said, chuckling weakly. "I can't say I like it much, but as Shadow reminded me, it's true that I've had fancy boots beside my bedroll a time or two, and it's never done me any great harm. Except, of course, the time the youngest son of Duke Eoran forgot to take his boots off and slashed my ankle open with his spur."

"With his *boots* on?" Jael said incredulously.

"With his boots on," Donya said ruefully. "And I've still got the scar to prove it. Shadow liked to tease me about the one wound she tended that *wasn't* a battle injury—in the traditional sense, at least. It was her revenge, I suppose, for having to come stitch my ankle in the middle of the night." Donya sighed. "If you never have anything worse to recall your assignations than a blush, a laugh, and a scar on your ankle, Jaellyn, you haven't fared too poorly. Remember that."

"Mother—" Jael hesitated. Her instinct had been to reassure Donya, to tell her that Jael had never had any desire to seduce Urien or let him seduce her, but that was too embarrassing to say—and it wasn't exactly true anymore, was it?

"What?" Donya said, turning to glance at Jael again.

"Thank you," Jael said lamely. She slipped her hand into Donya's, squeezing it. "I'll remember, I promise."

Donya grinned and slapped Jael's shoulder jovially, knocking Jael somewhat off her stride.

"Go soak in the bathing pool and see Nubric," Donya told her. "He may find something to your benefit. And I'll cancel all your lessons for tomorrow. You may want to practice a little alone, but you look like you lost this match, and the next three, too."

"Mother, what are you and Father meeting about tonight?" Jael asked boldly. "Is it about the elves who were killed? Has anything else happened?"

Donya was silent for a long moment, but when she answered, she met Jael's eyes squarely.

"We still haven't found out what became of the merchant who disappeared," she said slowly. "But there have been three more murders."

"Three?" Jael repeated, not having to feign shock. She only knew of two. "Were they all elves? What happened?"

"Two were elves," Donya told her. "An elvan woman was

found at the Docks with her throat slit, and another in an alley north of Rivertown. She'd been disemboweled. The third was a human, an old one-armed beggar named Nessle, found in another alley to the south of the disemboweled elf. His throat had been slit, we think by the murderers of the elvan woman as they fled south."

"Do you think the murders of the elves are related?" Jael asked. "I mean, they were all killed in different ways, except for the first two elves in Rivertown."

"I wouldn't think so," Donya admitted. "But I saw the bodies of the woman from the Docks and the beggar. Both their throats were cut with a serrated blade, very thin. It's unusual enough to be recognizable. Some of my sages are studying the other—well—the corpses, and Jermyn is going to try a few of the more specific divinations to see if he can find anything that way, but I don't have much hope of him learning anything useful. Hindsight never seems to work well with dead elves. Their past seems to fade right out of them not long after death, or so I'm told by our seers."

Donya shook her head.

"There's no need to concern yourself with this, Jaellyn," she said. "Just be careful in town and there's nothing for you to fear. Now go and send your message, and don't forget to report to Nubric after supper."

Jael was so sore that after finding a messenger to tell Lord Urien she would be honored to sup with him, she could hardly bear to crawl out of her clothes and into the hot bathing pool for her second soak of the day. It was surprising, she mused to herself, how much one could hurt from strikes that didn't even break the skin. In the hot water, great blue and purple splotches bloomed over her skin, and Jael knew there would be twice as many tomorrow morning. Still, she had Urien's salve; this would be a good chance to see just how potent it was.

A long soak restored Jael's appetite enough that she could swallow a little supper. A pot of hot tea and a generous application of Urien's ointment later, Jael was a little more comfortable as she donned a clean tunic and trousers.

Jermyn and Nubric, the castle mages, both had their workrooms on the third floor of the castle, but while Jermyn preferred his workshop near the stairs for convenience, Nubric hid his cluttered laboratory in the most remote corner of the floor. Jael found that all Nubric wished of her was to sit quietly in a chair while he cast this spell or that at varying distances from her, look at this, touch that. Jael did not find the process too tedious, however, since a good many of the mage's spells failed in spectacular ways, occasionally sending both Nubric and Jael scampering under Nubric's workbench for shelter. By the time Nubric paused, there were several charred circles on the floor, and the laboratory stank of scattered potions and powders.

"Isn't there a safer way to do this?" Jael pleaded, groaning as she crawled out from under the table.

"I was trying to establish the radius of your disruption effect," Nubric explained, brushing ash out of his sandy blond beard. "There's definitely an increase in the effect when you are in actual contact with the magic. I believe it's not as simple as direct proximity, however, nor does the type of magic appear to matter. I thought complex spells would be more vulnerable, but that's proved untrue. The only variable I can see is attention."

"Attention?" Jael repeated. "You mean if you aren't concentrating when you cast the spell—"

"No, your attention," Nubric corrected. He scratched his head, then raised his eyebrows and picked a long splinter out of his hair. "When you started to become disinterested and your attention drifted from my magic, my spells worked without interference. When you actually concentrated on my spells, they invariably failed, often dramatically. I believe your—well—talent functions primarily when you focus your attention on magic, pulling nearby magical energies toward you. That's why you could safely pass through the Gate so long as you were asleep. I believe that if you don't come in physical contact with the magic, and you don't actually focus your attention on it, there should be no difficulty. If anything happens to prove me wrong, I'll appreciate you telling me, of course. Magic isn't an exact science."

"But I've gone through the Gate awake before," Jael argued. "Just last summer I did it twice."

"I never studied this phenomenon before, so I can't be certain," Nubric said hesitantly, "but given what your parents have told me about soul-sickness, I would speculate that the problem has become more severe as you age and, well, develop physically. As to the Gate specifically, it might be a factor of how you had your attention focused at the time—were you thinking of the Gate itself, or were you eager to pass through, to be in the forest or to come home?"

Thinking back, Jael had to admit that there was sense in what he said. In the spring she was always excited about joining Mist in the forest and preoccupied with plans for her summer; when she came back later in the year, she was usually exhausted and thinking only of returning to her family, a comfortable bed, and a hot bath.

"So the light globes in the dining hall exploded because I was focusing on them?" Jael asked, thinking furiously. She'd been paying sharp attention to the illusion in the market, true, and she must have actually brushed against Urien's jug of tea. Mist's soupstone might have been either; she'd placed it in the stew herself, and, hungry, she'd fumed over the stewpot while it cooked. She'd been watching Nubric when the water elemental had gotten out of control—

"I imagine so," Nubric said, breaking into her thoughts and startling her; she'd forgotten asking the question. "Look here. Perhaps this will help you understand."

Nubric laid a large piece of lodestone on the table and rolled a small iron ball across the tabletop parallel to the stone, first quickly, then more slowly. On the first trial, the ball veered off its course; on the second, it rolled directly to the stone.

"Sometimes you simply draw magical energies away from their intended pattern, altering the spell's result," Nubric told her. "Other times you may draw it directly to you, making a spell fail entirely. And when you come in direct contact—" He touched the small ball to the lodestone, where it adhered firmly.

"Will it happen every time I even notice magic?" Jael asked worriedly. "Grandmother Celene cast two sleep spells on me, and they worked perfectly."

"Of course," Nubric said mildly. He pulled the iron ball away from the lodestone and then rolled it directly toward the rock. The ball rolled unerringly to its target. "You attract these energies. A spell cast directly upon you—not a potion, for example—should function normally. But magic is not an exact science, as I said, and there's no way I know of to be certain. Do you understand?"

"I suppose so," Jael said, sighing. It explained a great deal, and worse, it made sense. She wanted to ask Nubric how his theory related to the missing part of her soul and her own inability to use magic, but doubting that Donya had told Nubric the details of Jael's parentage, it seemed wiser not to ask.

Nubric was eager to tell Donya and Argent the results of his tests, but Jael had no desire to hear the rather discouraging news again; in addition, her frequent dives under Nubric's worktable hadn't helped her bruises and sore muscles. Well, another coating of salve and a pot of tea would do her some good, and what that didn't cure, a good night's rest and another hot bath in the morning likely would.

In the morning, Jael was amazed to see that most of her bruises had healed, and the rest had faded; she *had* to get the formula for that salve from Urien! She felt well enough to take her sword to the practice yard and work alone for a little while.

When Markus and Mera arrived for their lesson with Rabin, she stayed to watch, interested now that she had learned a little more about the different styles of swordplay. Tall Mera used the human style, where her strength and longer reach gave her an advantage, and Markus fought elvan style, relying on speed and agility. Each had progressed far enough that they could work together with metal swords, although the edges of the blades had been filed dull and the points blunted. Jael knew that the twins sometimes used protective padding, but on this occasion Rabin let them practice with only the helms, and Jael was gratified to see that Markus and Mera would have their own share of bruises in the morning. Jael considered sharing Urien's wonderful salve with them, but when she remembered how they'd sat on the wall and taunted her, she grinned and kept her silence.

To Jael's delight, the seamstresses had finished a dark red tunic with matching trousers, in which Jael looked a little less rumpled than usual. The neck of the tunic was cut low, and Jael realized happily that if she moved the clasp of the chain Urien had given her just a few links, the dark red fabric would frame the pendant beautifully. Jael quickly adjusted the chain, then tucked the pendant into her pocket to put on when she was safely out of sight of home.

"Jael's dressing fancy," Markus laughed, making Jael realize that she had left her bedroom door open.

"Maybe *she's* sitting in audience this afternoon, instead of Mother," Mera giggled.

"No, she's looking to Lord Urien," Markus said slyly. "Everybody knows it."

"But he won't be interested in her," Mera said mischievously. "He's handsome and wealthy. He'll be courting real ladies, beautiful ladies who wear gowns and have breasts."

Jael scowled and slammed her door shut, grinning with satisfaction as the heavy wood caught a booted toe and Markus yelped.

The afternoon crept by with painful slowness. Jael sat in her window looking out as she had a thousand times before, but today she could not sit calmly to dream away the hours. Apprehension and eagerness warred in Jael's mind while she imagined all the possible scenarios that might occur at supper. Urien was a gentleman, but his invitation to sup privately at his home carried certain implications, and her acceptance of his invitation carried certain *other* implications, and she was far from sure in her own mind that she should go to this supper. On the other hand, if she *didn't* go, that would deliver a message of its own, and that message was clear and unequivocal, with the probable result that Jael would receive no further invitations.

At last, unable to sit for another moment, Jael wandered up to her parents' quarters, hoping that perhaps her mother or father had left some notes about the murders. There were no notes, but there were markings on a map of the city with a few terse comments penned beside the markings, including the names of the victims and who had found them. Two of the latter names Jael knew—Solly, one of Aubry's senior thieves who worked in the area around the Docks, and Teva, a City Guard who patrolled the Mercantile District. Jael read the map again carefully, then hurried back to her room to pen a quick copy of her own. At least she'd have *something* to show Tanis tomorrow.

Jael glanced out the window and realized that it was late enough in the afternoon that she had best collect her guards and her carriage and start out for Urien's house. She was relieved to find that the "escort" Mother had arranged was only four guards, plus the carriage driver; then Jael realized that her mother was trying to tell her something—either that she trusted her daughter's judgment, and more guards were unnecessary, or that she knew her daughter was making a stupid mistake, and more guards would be useless. Jael sighed, far from certain that *she* knew which she was doing.

Jael had to admit that Urien had made a good job of Numan's house. The soiled stone had been cleaned, the gargoyle removed, and the blue glass windows had been restored. Servants were waiting to meet the carriage, but Urien was there to take her hand the moment Jael stepped to the ground.

"I am *so* glad you came," Urien smiled, kissing her hand. "Supper isn't quite ready, I'm told, but that leaves me time to show you the house you helped me find."

Jael was relieved that Urien placed no special emphasis on any parts of the tour—bedrooms, for example. To Jael's surprise, she learned that the lesser priests and acolytes Urien had brought from Calidwyn would also live in the house, but Urien added that they were still living at an inn until restoration of the house was complete.

"I see you took the gargoyle down," Jael chuckled. "I suppose you decided not to use it to tease your guests."

"On the contrary." Urien steered Jael into a luxurious sitting room, where Jael laughed to see the stone gargoyle mounted beside the fireplace. "I merely moved him to a suitable place of honor."

A chime sounded, and Urien laid Jael's hand on his arm and escorted her to the dining hall. The hall was elegant and more than a little intimidating, but a smaller table placed close to the fireplace made the room seem comfortable and intimate.

They were served an abundant and tasty supper, and to Jael's surprise, Urien served no wine at all, drinking tea with Jael instead. Jael was relieved and just a bit disappointed that Urien offered her no Bluebright, either.

Urien kept the conversation very light over supper, but afterward, in the warm sitting room, he was interested in Jael's news of the new murders. He shivered when Jael told him of the elvan merchant murdered near the market, omitting her own presence in the area.

"That's terrible," Urien frowned. "Do you know, I was in almost the same area that night. But for Baaros's protection, it might well have been me."

"I doubt that," Jael said comfortingly. "You're not an elf. Except for the beggar, all the victims have been elves."

"They've all been merchants, too," Urien reminded her. "Their work is as likely the cause of their death as their race."

Jael frowned. Had all the victims been merchants? She couldn't recall having heard that, and told Urien so.

"You are of elvan blood, and that's of concern to your parents, and naturally so," Urien said patiently. "They, of course, are the ones from whom you hear these things. I, on the other hand, am a merchant and a priest of a mercantile sect. The news *I* hear is from other merchants. It was some of our worshippers who told me that all the unfortunate persons were merchants. Excepting the beggar, of course, and this last murder, and you told me that yourself."

"But what would elvan merchants be doing in Rivertown?" Jael asked puzzledly. "All our elvan merchants come from the Heartwood. They don't bring in goods from the river, and nothing from the forest is traded out of town, either. Wealthy merchants don't go into Rivertown without a good reason."

"I'm sure the guards have thought of that," Urien said thoughtfully. "Certainly they'll be investigating the reason why the elves came to Rivertown. You can be certain it's an area *I'll* avoid, and I'll be much happier if you do, too. My heart would break if any harm came to you," he added almost shyly.

"I'm in no great hurry to find out which of the temples in Allanmere is right about the afterworld," Jael admitted, then grimaced apologetically. "Sorry. Sometimes I forget you're a priest."

"I'm glad," Urien said gallantly, taking Jael's hand and kissing it gently. "Sometimes I like to forget it myself. Don't you occasionally wish to forget that you're the High Lord and Lady's firstborn?"

"Most of the time," Jael said wryly. "But isn't it a little different, being a priest?" She flushed a little, but continued boldly. "I mean, does your sect allow you to have young women over to supper and go on picnics and—"

Urien laughed.

"And?" he teased gently. "We're not one of those strange new celibate sects, if that's what you are asking, nor one of the ascetic sects that forbid its priests comfort and pleasure. I believe I told you already that many priests have wealth of their own, which they may retain for their own comfort. The only restriction, as I have said, is that temple funds must not be used for more than the simplest needs of the priests if they have no other means. Baaros expects His priests in active leadership of a temple to devote themselves to His worship, of course, but for those of His servants who serve in an administrative role, as I did—and will again soon," Urien added quickly, "many of these priests have Houses and families of their own. I assure you that I'll take an active role as a priest in this temple not a day longer than necessary."

"But Ankaras doesn't agree with the changes you've made," Jael said worriedly. "What if you can't let him resume his position?"

"Then I will train one of the lesser priests to take his place," Urien said practically, "or the temple in Loroval will send another priest to take a permanent post here." He laughed. "I wanted to forget my priesthood for a few hours, but it seems you won't let me."

"I'm sorry," Jael said contritely. Talking about the Temple of Baaros made her uneasy, anyway—she didn't know what Urien might make of her friendship with Tanis, much less of her surreptitious excursions into the temple via the cellar. "Why don't you tell me about Calidwyn instead, and your House?"

"That's all far behind me right now," Urien said smoothly. "Why don't you tell me about Allanmere instead, and more importantly about you?"

Jael found, to her surprise, that Urien was as good a listener as Aunt Shadow, as interested in the small details of her life as he was in the larger stories of Allanmere, although Jael had already decided that there was no chance she'd tell this polished lord some of the more embarrassing details about herself. He sympathized with her sword lesson woes, recalling nights he'd been too sore to sleep.

"It's worth it, though," he assured her. "There's no substitute for knowing that you can protect yourself when necessary. Of course, you never really know until it *is* necessary." He kissed her fingertips. "You have lovely, strong hands. You'll make a wonderful swordswoman in time." He kissed the inside of her wrist, making Jael shiver.

He lowered her hand then, gazing warmly into Jael's eyes. "But do you really want to talk about swordsmanship?" he asked softly.

Jael felt her cheeks flush, and she shook her head.

"Good." Urien leaned forward and brushed his lips very lightly over Jael's, then again, more firmly. Jael steeled herself, then slid her arms around Urien's neck, pulling him close, although she could have ground her teeth with frustration. Nothing! She might as well have been embracing a tree. Gods, did she have to be half-drunk on Bluebright to feel anything for a man?

Urien stroked her hair and pulled back a little to look at her.

"What's the matter?" he asked gently.

"Nothing," Jael said quickly. "I mean—"

Urien nodded, his eyes narrowing thoughtfully.

"You're a maiden, aren't you?" he asked.

Jael's face flamed.

"Well—uh—elvan women don't have—I mean—but—"

"That sounds like a 'yes.' " Urien smiled understandingly, reaching out to stroke her hair again. "I thought as much. This isn't really what you want, is it, Jaellyn?"

"Well—" Jael sighed miserably. "I don't know what's wrong with me, but most of me's never wanted much of anything, if you understand what I mean."

"Ah." Urien smiled again, then pulled Jael close, cradling her head on his shoulder. Jael was grateful that she didn't have to face him. "It was different at the Basilisk's Eye, wasn't it? But that was likely the Bluebright. It sometimes has that effect on people."

"Is that why you gave it to me?" Jael asked daringly.

"No." Urien's voice was gently reproving. "Jaellyn, do you think I have to resort to drugging young ladies with Bluebright to make them want me? Or that I'd even wish to?"

"No, oh, no," Jael said hurriedly. "I didn't mean it to sound that way. I'm sorry." She buried her face in his tunic. "I'm just embarrassed, I suppose, and a little disappointed."

"There's no need for either," Urien said firmly, tightening his arms around her warmly. "My feelings for you aren't dependent on whether I can coax you into my bed tonight. When you want me, Jaellyn, then I'll teach you every pleasure I know. But there's no need to be impatient."

Jael sighed explosively, relieved and dismayed at the same time.

"You're as patient and reasonable as my father," she said wryly. "It's almost irritating."

"Oh, really?" Urien laughed. "Would you prefer that I drug you, seduce you, or just ravish you, then? Hmmm, seducing you seems unlikely, and ravishing you would get me thrown in the castle dungeons. Wait here, I'll fetch the Bluebright."

"All right, all right," Jael growled. "I don't recall asking for salt for my wounds, thank you."

"I'm sorry." Urien nuzzled Jael's short curls, stroking her back gently. "This must be exasperating for you. But I assure you that I'm not disappointed. At least not *too* disappointed."

Jael hid her grimace in Urien's shoulder. Gods, what she wouldn't pay for an hour of feeling like a normal twenty-year-old woman—elf or human, either one.

Urien was kind and understanding and tried to coax Jael back into a better mood with tea and pastries, but for Jael the evening was ruined, and Urien wisely did not protest when she left rather earlier than planned.

Jael wished regretfully that Aunt Shadow hadn't left town—she would have been the perfect person to talk to—but Aunt Shadow *was* gone, and that meant there was only one person she could ask for help.

It was late enough that Donya and Argent were in their quarters, and Jael found them poring over the rough map she'd seen earlier. Donya hurriedly pushed the map aside when Jael entered, but Jael excused herself, saying she'd only come to talk to her father. Argent, very surprised, quickly rose and walked back with Jael to her room.

"What kind of problem could you possibly have," Argent asked her, "that you couldn't ask in your mother's presence?"

"It's rather embarrassing, actually," Jael admitted. "Can I

ask you something as an elf and an herbalist instead of as High Lord and my—my father?"

Argent raised both eyebrows and settled himself on Jael's bed. He poured himself a cup of water from the jug beside the bed before answering.

"I can't promise anything but my best attempt," he said at last. "But go ahead."

"Back when you were working as an herbalist," Jael said slowly, "what would you have given an elf who was—well—soul-sick, for example, and when she was with an attractive person under the—uh—proper conditions, couldn't—well—"

"—enjoy his attentions?" Argent prompted. He shook his head, frowning. "Jaellyn, are you asking me for a potion to make you feel a desire your body isn't ready for?"

"It's not my body that isn't working," Jael protested. "It's because I only have two parts of three of my soul, and I may *never* have the rest of it! Am I supposed to wait forever?"

"I see." Argent looked down at his hands for a long moment. "Jaellyn, are you utterly certain that that is what you want, or are you prepared to listen to an herbalist's advice?"

"I'll listen," Jael said reluctantly.

"Do you remember what Mist told us, that certain potions can temporarily heal soul-sickness?" Argent asked her. "The dreaming potion you took in the forest was apparently such a potion. Remember that magical energies are closely linked with the body's sexual energies as well, and think about what happened when you took that potion. You had a hint of the kind of power within you. If I make a potion which sets that power free before you are capable of handling it, what do you think could happen? Is it worth the possible price, to have a night's passion now instead of later?"

Jael sighed exasperatedly. It was much easier to shout and argue with her mother than to refute Father's gentle, inexorable logic. A night's tumble seemed a small gain when compared to the damage that might be done by a power strong enough to melt stone.

"All right," Jael said reluctantly. "I'll wait. For a while, at least."

"You *are* growing," Argent said comfortingly, "inside as well as outwardly. And with the elvan blood in you, there's no need for impatience."

When Argent was gone, Jael realized that he had had even more potent arguments that he had, perhaps through kindness, chosen not to use. Seemingly casual liaisons often had long-term consequences, Jael herself being a good example. Even though she had never yet ripened, and might indeed be barren, there were plenty of other, less tangible risks. Urien could lose the support of more of his worshippers—possibly even of his priests—were it known that he was engaged in a liaison with the High Lord and Lady's apparently elvan daughter. Such a rumor could do as much harm to Urien as it could benefit Ankaras's cause. The anti-elvan faction in Allanmere, especially those worshippers who had left the Temple of Baaros, could even suggest that the High Lord and Lady had used their daughter as a tool to sway Urien and the Temple of Baaros.

That last was a sobering thought. Jael had never thought that there might be city-wide repercussions to her actions. She could now appreciate the discretion Urien had shown so far. He had met Jael only under very private conditions, or under scrupulous chaperoning. If even Tanis didn't realize that Urien had been meeting with Jael, it was unlikely that anyone else did.

Jael grimaced and shook her head, remembering Urien asking her if she never wished to forget for a short time that she was the daughter of the High Lord and Lady of Allanmere. If being High Priest of the Temple of Baaros caused this much trouble, little wonder Ankaras was such a walking briar patch!

Or that her mother sometimes acted like an overzealous mother wolf trying to defend her only pup. Gods, could Donya even *spit* without it being told from one end of Allanmere to the other? And this would be Jael's lot if she was declared Heir.

Jael carried that disturbing thought into an uneasy sleep.

The next day Jael was almost grateful for her lessons, since at least they passed the uneasy time until evening, when she could go to the market to meet Tanis. She did, however, have time between her afternoon lesson and sunset for an errand or two. She thrust her copy of her mother's map into her tunic and hurried south and east to the Noble District.

Teva was on guard patrol there, and it took only a few inquiries to find the burly guardswoman. Teva had already been

questioned numerous times about Merchant Daral's disappearance, and did not appear overly surprised that the High Lord's
daughter would come to question her again. Daral had left the
Golden Grape early, shortly after moonrise. He had had a little wine at the Grape—what elf would not?—but was still
fairly steady when he left, according to the friends who had
been drinking with him. It was his friends' impression that he
was going directly back to his home, and his usual route was
a busy street, well lit and well traveled at that hour. Daral had
a little money in his purse, but not more than a handful of
Moons; like most elves, he was not clever with money and it
was commonly known that his small wood-carving shop did
not keep him in luxury. He had no known enemies, but many
friends; it was his lover, waiting at his home, who reported to
the guard that he was missing. Beyond that, Teva knew nothing more.

Solly would be more difficult to contact, since Jael had no
intention of walking into Rivertown alone to try to find a
thief; nor could she simply ask about him on the street as she
had Teva. There were a few other options, but Jael chose to
walk south to the Thieves' Guild herself. She could leave a
message for Solly there, and at the same time she could talk
to Aubry.

The few thieves standing idly at the front of the Guildhouse
called cheerily to Jael or waved; Jael was a frequent visitor,
in Shadow's company or alone. Jael found Estar, Aubry's assistant and treasurer, sipping an ale and poring over the Guild
accounts book.

"Good afternoon, Jael," Estar said, closing the book with a
grin of relief. "I don't suppose you've come looking for an
apprenticeship? I hope not. We're fresh out of apprentice to-
kens until next week, when the new lot are done."

"I don't think my parents would really like me to become
a thief," Jael said regretfully. "It would be awfully embarrassing for them if the City Guard caught me, wouldn't it?"

"I suppose it would," Estar admitted, chuckling. "What can
I do for you, then?"

"I'd like to talk to Aubry," Jael said. "And I'd like to leave
a message for another Guild member, if I can."

"Aubry's upstairs, and the message will cost you ten coppers," Estar said, opening the accounts book again with a sigh. "Which Guild member?"

"Solly," Jael told her. "He's the one who found those two elves in Rivertown, isn't he?"

Estar grimaced.

"Yes, he is. That's a nasty bit of work, isn't it? And now these others. Some of our members think it's too much like during the Crimson Plague twenty years ago. Of course, you weren't even born then, but for our elvan members, it's like yesterday. But what do you want Solly for? Never mind, it's none of my affair, is it? What's the message?"

"Tell him I want to talk to him," Jael said. "Ask him to send a message to me at the castle, and I'll meet him anywhere he likes—but not in Rivertown. If he'll meet me, I'll treat for ale and pay him, too, for his time. I promise it's nothing that will make any trouble for him."

"Well, I suppose he'll talk to you," Estar said, grinning. "He's the one who used to steal you sweets, wasn't he, when you were so little Shadow could carry you here on her shoulders?"

Jael chuckled at the memory.

"Half the Guild used to steal me sweets," she said ruefully. "Mother used to scold Shadow for bringing me here. I'd always come back sick-bellied from all the candy. May I go on up to see Aubry?"

"Yes, go on," Estar told her. "He's just looking at his maps. Here, take this wine up with you."

It didn't seem odd to Jael that the Guildmaster's assistant might expect the High Lord's daughter to ferry wine upstairs for her. When she'd been younger, Jael had loved to spend her time at the Guild, running errands for the members in exchange for pocket money she didn't need, or just for the enjoyment of being part of the Guild for a little while. Shadow or Aubry always kept watch over her at first, but their caution soon became unnecessary, as the fumble-footed, bright-eyed child quickly became the pet of the Guild. After her childhood it always amused Jael to remember scarred, vicious-looking thieves carrying her on their shoulders or tossing her, shrieking with laughter, back and forth between them, or dignified elves tickling her with their braid tips, or Guildmaster Aubry sprawled on the dusty floor teaching her ten-stone.

Aubry was in the small back room he used as an office; as Estar said, he was poring over his maps, as much ink on his fingers and cheek as on the parchment, drawing and scratching out new territories. The entire room was cloudy with the malodorous smoke from Aubry's pipe.

"There you are, Estar," he said grumpily, not looking up. "Did you bring my wine?"

"Estar sent it up with me," Jael said. "Fair evening, Uncle Aubry." She coughed.

"Jael!" Aubry put down his pen and reached out for her, then looked at his ink-smeared hands and stopped with a grimace. "Sorry, I don't want to stain your tunic. Sit down and pour a cup for yourself. You haven't had much time to spend with us lately, little sapling. What can I do for you?"

"These elves that have been killed—" Jael shrugged. "Mother and Father won't tell me much. They don't want to frighten me, but I think it's my concern, too, as long as I'm not barricaded in the castle. I hoped you could tell me more."

"You're right that it's every city elf's concern," Aubry said, nodding. "I'd advise you to avoid Rivertown, but you've known that much for years. Let's look at my map."

Aubry pushed the territory charts aside and pulled out another map. Jael was not surprised to see that he had marked the incidents just as Donya had. This was larger than Donya's rough map, however, and more detailed.

"The first two elves, Garric and Crow, were found here," Aubry said, pointing to an alley marked on the map behind the Fin and Flagon. "Solly found them propped sitting against the wall. He thought they were drunk at first and was going to lift their purses."

"Well, nobody would sit quietly against a tavern wall while somebody cut their hearts out," Jael said slowly.

"No. They were obviously carried there after they were killed, or the alley would have been covered with blood, and there wasn't any, just a little on the corpses," Aubry said. He tapped the map where the Docks were marked. "The woman in the river was Aliss, brought in wine from the forest to sell through the local merchants."

"Elvan wine in Rivertown?" Jael asked, surprised.

"No chance of that," Aubry said, shaking his head. "She didn't sell direct to the taverns. She had no business in

Rivertown, and you can imagine she didn't go there for pleasure. She wasn't killed on the Docks, either. She was bled almost dry *before* she was dumped in the river, and that takes some time, even with her throat slit. The guards in Rivertown have seen enough corpses to know, believe it."

"What about Daral, the merchant who vanished?" Jael asked.

Aubry scowled.

" 'Vanished' is a good word," he said. "If he'd gone back to the forest for some reason, I would have heard by now. All my people knew his shop didn't make enough money to make it worth the trouble to rob. Someone might have cut his purse, but he certainly never carried enough to make it worthwhile to kill him or carry him off. He was an easy mark, too— careless in a crowd. Any two-copper pickpocket could've had all he carried without much trouble, surely without having to harm him to get it."

"Evriel didn't deal in the marketplace, either, did she?" Jael asked. "She sold through that furrier in the Mercantile District—Lasic, isn't it?"

Aubry nodded.

"She spent her free time in the market, though," he said. "But again, she wasn't killed in that alley where she was found." He tapped the spot on the map. "Nessle worked Rivertown, but after dark he usually wandered up toward the market. I think her killers were surprised by old Nessle in the process of getting rid of the body. Nessle's old, but he's fast—has to be, to work Rivertown; they had to stop what they were doing to chase him down, and then by that time it was too risky to go back and finish.

"They were so preoccupied with Nessle that they left the rug they carried Evriel in," Aubry continued. "That was sloppy, but they were lucky. The rug was a plain rag weave like you might find anywhere in town, hard to trace, not very old. It was awfully moldy, though. Not much blood on it, either."

"Moldy?" Jael repeated. "Not dirty?"

"According to Zoran, the guard who found Evriel, moldy," Aubry said, nodding. "So either the rug had been stored unrolled for a long time—"

"—or it was in a moldy room," Jael finished.

"Very good," Aubry told her. "Then the one last night—"

"Wait, now," Jael said quickly. "There was another murder?"

"Najel, a local jeweler," Aubrey told her. "I think he was thrown over the wall in the Noble District, because he washed up just north of the Docks—his head did, anyway."

"Why would anyone carry a head through the Noble District to get rid of it?" Jael asked, grimacing. "It'd be much easier to go north and drop it in the swamp. Nobody'd ever find it then."

"I don't know," Aubry said, shrugging. "And what did they do with the body? Maybe they threw it over, too, and it simply sank in the river."

"But there's no way to tell how Najel died?" Jael asked.

"From a head?" Aubry shook his head. "I'm sure the investigating mages have tried everything on all of the bodies short of nescromancy, and nobody but the High Lord or Lady can authorize that."

"*Are* there any necromancers in Allanmere anymore?" Jael asked, surprised. "I thought they were outlawed decades ago."

"And assassins have been outlawed in Allanmere since the Compact was signed," Aubry said patiently. "And thievery is illegal, too."

"All right, all right," Jael conceded. "But if only the High Lord or Lady can authorize necromancy, and the guard have all the—ah—evidence, then what good would any necromancers in Allanmere do anyway?"

Aubry reached across the table and patted Jael's hand.

"Assume for the sake of our conversation that there were necromancers in Allanmere, living in the shadows as the assassins do," he said. "Assume that such necromancers, by solving a series of murders, might save the lives of many elves, most of whom have kin or friends in the Guild of Thieves, but not without the permission and assistance of the High Lord and Lady. Assume also that the Guild might know of such necromancers, but that neither the necromancers nor the Guild could come forward with that information because necromancy, and dealing with necromancers, is outlawed in Allanmere. What might the Guild do in such a case?"

"It sounds to me like the Guildmaster might ask the poor daughter of the High Lord and Lady to broach the subject to her parents," Jael said wryly. "And the poor daughter that I just mentioned might remind the Guildmaster that the High Lord and Lady are having enough trouble with some humans in the city without it being rumored around town that they're trafficking with necromancers in order to solve the murders of a few elves."

"Hmmm. True enough," Aubry admitted. "I suppose the High Lord and Lady couldn't be known to be trafficking with necromancers under the best of conditions. I suppose any such dealings would have to be very discreet indeed."

"That's not exactly what I mean," Jael told him. "What if the necromancers thought to gain something later by threatening to reveal the High Lord and Lady's involvement?" *Gods, Jael, how devious you're getting,* Jael thought.

"I see the difficulty," Aubry said slowly. "What do you suggest?"

"What do the necromancers need?" Jael asked him.

"My understanding is that some part of the corpse is required," Aubry told her. "Even a lock of hair will suffice, so long as it's removed after death."

There was no window to look out at the sun, but Jael knew that she would surely be late for her meeting with Tanis.

"I'll see what I can do," Jael promised. "But I have to go now. I'm meeting a friend at the market."

"I'm glad you won't be out alone this evening," Aubry said, relieved. "But I'm certain a few Guild members will be on their way to the market. I'd be less worried if you'd go there with them."

That suited Jael well enough, as the two apprentices who walked with her to the market were eager to start their evening's work and not inclined to follow Jael around. Jael was relieved to see Tanis at the arranged meeting place, and he looked equally relieved to see her.

"There you are!" he said, lines of worry smoothing from his forehead. "I've been here for almost an hour."

"Well, you deserve it," Jael returned. "At least you knew I got back to the castle safely that night. You could have sent a message over, or left a note in my window, or something. I've been worried about you all this time."

"I'm sorry," Tanis said with a sigh. "But I had to stay close to Ankaras to see if he talked to anybody."

"Did he?" Jael asked eagerly.

Tanis nodded.

"Yes," he said. "But let's find a quiet place to talk before someone sees us."

That made good sense, and this time Jael made Tanis find an alley while *she* purchased their supper, but found this endeavor more complicated than she'd expected. The first two vendors simply ignored her, and the third growled, "Take your coin elsewhere, elf." At last, disgusted, Jael had to give Tanis the money to buy their supper—spiced cubes of meat skewered on sticks and fried in hot oil; sweet, juicy melons still dewed from the chilling spell; and starchy tubers, baked, broken open, and liberally drizzled with rich gravy.

"It's been confused at the temple since the first sign—the burning water in the market," Tanis said. "High Priest Urien set Ankaras the task of trying to convince some of the worshippers to return. Since the signs appeared even after High Priest Urien has assumed leadership of the temple, the High Priest says it's proof from Baaros that the temple still has His favor, despite the change in doctrine, so the worshippers should return."

"What do you think?" Jael asked him.

"I've seen the scrolls of Baaros's teachings," Tanis shrugged. "Truth to tell, I never found anything about elves in the temple's records until around the time that Ankaras took the robe as High Priest. I don't think Baaros would forbid us to deal with elves, or to allow elves into the temple. Frankly I don't think Baaros minds whether we—ah—breed with them, either." Tanis flushed. "He's a god of profitable trade. I imagine that involves elves as much as humans, at least here in Allanmere."

"But who did Ankaras talk to?" Jael asked quickly. "Anyone important?"

"I don't know who's important," Tanis said patiently. "But he spoke to Merchant Gilmar, Merchant Sheesa, Merchant Cherrig, and—"

"Sheesa," Jael interrupted. "Isn't she the daughter of Jannafar, head of the Dyers' Guild?"

"I think so," Tanis said after a moment's thought. "Yes, I think I've heard that. But what of it?"

"A few days ago, when Aunt Shadow first arrived in

town," Jael said slowly, "I heard Mother telling Aunt Shadow
that the Dyers' Guild was involved somehow with the anti-
elvan factions in Allanmere. I can't remember exactly what
she said, though."

"A good number of our worshippers are from the Dyers'
Guild," Tanis told her. "Many of them left when High Priest
Urien announced the changes in the temple's policy. Perhaps
Ankaras is looking to the Dyers' Guild for support, if they
have an interest in maintaining the prejudice against elves."

"I wish I could remember what Mother said," Jael said,
scowling. Was it something about the elves from the Heartwood bringing gold into the city? Well, that, at least, she
could ask her mother outright, the next time they—

"But you haven't told me what you heard about the murders," Tanis said, interrupting her thoughts.

Jael pulled out her map and showed it to Tanis, explaining
what she had learned. She had no pen and ink to add the new
information Aubry had given her, but Tanis raided one of the
many fires in the market and brought her a charred stick so
she could mark the map at least temporarily. Tanis had heard
nothing of the head found on the banks of the Brightwater
and was horrified by the thought.

"To the best we know, the two elves in Rivertown were the
first ones found, but likely Aliss was killed first," Tanis
mused, touching the appropriate marking on the map. "Her
throat was cut and she was bled. Then the two elves in
Rivertown with their hearts cut out."

"Merchant Daral disappeared then," Jael said, moving her
finger to the Mercantile District. "But we don't know what
happened to him."

"Then there was Evriel, gutted, and found between here
and Rivertown," Tanis said, tapping the spot. "Then Merchant
Najel, found north of the Docks, just his head."

"From a slit throat to nothing left but the head," Jael said.
"If the murders are linked, the killers are—uh—keeping
more."

"All of the bodies have been found in or around
Rivertown," Tanis commented.

"Except Merchant Daral," Jael pointed out.

"But he wasn't found at all. That might not even be related
to these killings."

"And we know the others were killed somewhere else, too," Jael said patiently. "Rivertown is just a good place for getting rid of bodies."

"But why would anyone do all those things, if the killings are related?" Tanis protested. "An assassin might possibly slit someone's throat and throw the body in the Brightwater, if they weren't clever enough to realize it'd just foul up on the pilings or they didn't care if it was found, but what about the others? Most assassins have their own particular method of killing. If an assassin killed by slitting throats and trying to hide the bodies, then why kill two more by cutting out their hearts and then leave the bodies to be found in Rivertown?"

"Then there's Evriel," Jael said, nodding her agreement. "If that was an assassination, it was an awfully clumsy one. What kind of assassin takes the time to gut the body and roll it into a rug, then has to carry it through every back alley in the city to get to Rivertown? And maybe that spot wasn't even where they meant to take it, since Nessle seems to have surprised them."

"Then Merchant Daral," Tanis said thoughtfully. "Anyone throwing a head into the Brightwater likely meant to be rid of it entirely, but as you say, the swamp would've been even better."

"It's hard to think of the incidents as related," Jael sighed. "But who uses a thin, serrated blade? And all the victims elves and merchants—except for Nessle—and all within the last few days. They *must* be related somehow, even if the same person didn't kill them all."

"All merchants, all elves, all in a few days, all left in or near Rivertown," Tanis mused. "Were there any other similarities? Did they all work in the market, perhaps?"

Jael shook her head.

"Daral had his own shop in the Mercantile District, and he wasn't in the market on the night he vanished," she said. "Najel's shop was in the district, too. Evriel sold through Lasic's shop in the Mercantile District, although she spent time in the market. Garric and Crow were minor merchants, probably had stalls in the market. Aliss sold wine through local people in the market."

"Different wares, different types of trading, different locations," Tanis said, sighing frustratedly. "But as you say, they *must* be related somehow."

"What if Ankaras was dealing with a group of elf-haters, as we supposed before," Jael speculated, "and that group was killing elves? Let's start with that."

"All right. Elves, because they hate the elves as Ankaras does," Tanis agreed. "Elvan merchants, because they're competition to our merchant worshippers."

"If the same people did some or all of the killings, that would explain the same blades being used," Jael said slowly, "but not the different methods."

"Perhaps they were trying to disguise the similarity," Tanis suggested. "Or perhaps more than one member of the group had the same type of blades."

"Still, why kill them in such strange ways?" Jael argued.

"Spectacular killings make a better example," Tanis said. "Aliss may have been a hasty killing, or perhaps interrupted."

"You don't drain all the blood out of someone hastily," Jael said, shaking her head. "And it looked like the killers at least tried to get rid of Aliss's body and Najel's. That doesn't fit in with your 'example' idea. And what about Daral? He disappeared entirely."

"I don't know," Tanis sighed, giving in. "I can't think of any way that it makes sense. I suppose you'd better find a way to help Aubry and his necromancers."

"And in the meantime, you can keep following Ankaras," Jael said, "and learn if he's actually conspiring with the Dyers' Guild or anyone else. And I'll find out where they've put the—the bodies."

Tanis settled himself a little more comfortably in the alley, nibbling on another skewer of meat.

"It must be exciting to have friends in the Guild," he said wistfully. "Tell me about it."

The Guild was one thing Jael knew a great deal about, through her own experience and from Shadow's stories, and Tanis was gratifyingly interested in everything she could tell him.

"I used to daydream about joining the Guild," he said shyly. "Of course, it would never have been possible—even if my father hadn't wanted me bound to the temple, he would never have allowed a son of his House to become a thief. But

I used to think about it sometimes. It sounded wonderful, living by your wits with no one telling you what to do or when."

"I don't think it's all that wonderful," Jael said with a chuckle. "At least not for apprentices and new thieves. I mean, Aunt Shadow could walk into the market empty-pursed and walk out with her sleeves so full she couldn't lift her arms, but Aunt Shadow's been in the profession for centuries. Most thieves I know are poor and dirty and have fleas in their clothes. A lot of them are missing fingers or a hand from being caught when they were young and not very good at stealing. Some end up in the dungeons or dead, too."

Tanis shivered but looked undaunted.

"Have you ever wanted to join the Guild?" he asked.

"Only twenty or so times a day most of my life," Jael admitted. "But I suppose I'd talk myself out of it even if I weren't the daughter of the High Lord and Lady. I'm clumsy and unlucky. I wouldn't make a very good thief."

"Well, you're not much of a warrior yet, nor a mage, and I know you don't want to be High Lady," Tanis said thoughtfully. "What *do* you want?"

Jael gaped at Tanis, then chuckled.

"Do you know, nobody ever asks me that?" she said. "I really don't think anybody ever cares what Jael the Unlucky wants."

"I care," Tanis protested. "I just asked, didn't I?"

"I'd like to travel," Jael said shortly. An image appeared in her mind, unbidden, of long sweeping plains, of dark snow-cragged mountains.

"You should've been a merchant, then," Tanis laughed. "They travel all over the world, city to city, always trying to find new trade goods and new markets to trade them in."

"But I don't want to be a merchant, and I don't want to go from city to city," Jael said unhappily. "I want to go to far places, lonely places, places people have never seen."

"That sounds uncomfortable," Tanis said, smiling.

"That's what Aunt Shadow says," Jael sighed. "But it's as unlikely as you becoming a thief. Even if Mother and Father don't declare me Heir, I couldn't go traveling like that. I can't even hunt."

"Then you'll have to take someone with you," Tanis suggested. He took Jael's hand.

Jael laughed.

"Tanis, have you ever dug a firepit or gutted a fish?" she asked. "Or spent a single night sleeping on the ground instead of in a wagon?"

Then Jael stopped laughing, surprised at the hurt in Tanis's eyes.

"No, I haven't," he said quietly. "But then I don't imagine High Priest Urien has, either."

Jael felt her cheeks burning.

"I don't know what Lord Urien has to do with it," she said. "Tanis, I didn't mean to insult you. You're my friend. I just meant—"

"But you don't go on private little carriage rides and picnics and suppers with a *friend*," Tanis said bitterly.

This statement so shocked Jael that she was silent for a long moment, staring blankly at Tanis.

"What's the matter with you, Tan?" Jael asked amazedly. "You know how that sounds? You sound like you're *jealous*."

"Jealous? What in Baaros's name do I have to be jealous of?" Tanis snapped. "I'm just your *friend*. Good night, Jaellyn." Before Jael could recover enough to answer, he was gone, out of the alley and lost among the crowds of the market, leaving Jael gaping after him.

Jael shook her head and stood slowly. Gods, all these months that she and Tanis had been such close friends. How long had she been overlooking his feelings as blindly as her elvan kin had overlooked her soul-sickness? That was almost more embarrassing than his knowledge of her meetings with Urien.

The market was still full, but Jael's memory of Evriel's body lying white and gutted in the alley so close by had changed the market for her. She had always thought it an exciting place, bustling and cheerful despite the many arguments, some quite loud, going on all around her. Every bargain seemed like an old and familiar game with strict but never-stated rules. Even the thieves, skilled or unskilled, or the street urchins, snatching fruit from the carts more openly and vanishing into the crowd, the red-faced merchants shouting after them, seemed a part of the game.

Now it was different somehow. Now the shadows cast by the oil lamps or light globes seemed threatening, the bargains hushed and secretive, the faces furtive and sly. For the first time Jael found herself scrutinizing the people around her, wondering what weapons a fold of the cloak or a too full sleeve might conceal. She felt reluctant to push her way through the crowds of strangers; she remembered the ill-tempered vendors and wondered whether she shouldn't try to find some of Aubry's people and ask them to see her home.

Gods, what a coward she was! Jael shook her head defiantly, touching the dagger at her hip. She was the eldest daughter of the High Lord and Lady of Allanmere, not some frightened fawn. No, by the gods, she was going back through the alleys as she always used to do. That way, she could look at the spot where she and Tanis had found Evriel, and see how far it was from there to the Fin and Flagon, where Garric and Crow had been found.

The alleys, too, were frightening, although there was enough moonlight that Jael could see clearly enough. She proceeded much more cautiously than she had two nights before, peering around corners before she turned, her ears twitching as she strained to listen for any sound that might signal danger.

She easily found the spot where she and Tanis had literally stumbled across Evriel. The mud of the alley was so riddled with tracks, likely left by the guards, that Jael knew she'd learn nothing there. She shivered, fancying she could still smell blood, but that was ridiculous, of course; there'd been hardly any blood, even on the body or the rug.

This time, instead of turning north toward the eastern Noble District, or east, back to the market, Jael hurried westward. Although she didn't know this section of alleys too well, she thought it was possible that she could avoid Rivertown proper, skirting the southernmost edge of the Noble District. From there it was only a short distance to the Fin and Flagon.

As she wandered farther westward, however, Jael found that the maze of alleys led her farther south than she would have liked. Abruptly she turned and emerged onto River Road, and realized where she was; if she had followed the alley just a little longer, she'd have been at the vacant house she and Urien had seen. She'd have to go back east just a lit-

tle, then south to the Fin and Flagon. River Road was full of
unsavory types this time of night; even the alleys were safer.

Back in the alleys again, however, Jael found that none of
the passages seemed to turn in the directions she wanted. After a few wrong turns, she found herself nearly back to River
Road again, and stopped in disgust to unroll her map, peering
worriedly at the parchment in the moonlight.

A slow, deliberate footfall broke the silence. Jael gasped
and glanced around her fearfully, her ears turning to try to locate the sound.

Someone—some*thing*—emerged from a doorway. Jael
froze, her mind insisting desperately that her eyes were lying.

The thing stood twice Jael's height and at least three times
her bulk. It stood upon two legs, and some sort of eyes
gleamed yellowly in its head, but there all resemblance to human or elf ended. Four taloned arms with too many joints
sprang from its heavily muscled shoulders, and its head
seemed all muzzle and dripping teeth. Its scent was the rank,
coppery odor of spilled blood.

Jael shivered, her throat straining to scream, her legs straining to run, but unable to move as the creature shambled toward her. She felt the familiar tingling inside her that signaled
the presence of magic, and a part of her thought bitterly, *Here
I am, paralyzed by magic, and for once I CAN'T break a
spell.*

The clawed hands reached out, and Jael wished desperately
she could close her eyes—would she have to watch while the
thing ate her alive? The thing stopped, its muzzle only inches
away, its breath hot and foul in her face; then suddenly, mi-
raculously, it retreated. Jael, unable to move her head, could
not see where it went, nor did she care; as soon as the paral-
ysis released her limbs, she fled blindly, colliding with the alley walls, tripping over offal and rough spots, falling to her
knees and scrambling forward until she could regain her feet.

Then there were lights ahead, and the market, so sinister
and frightening only a short time before, had never looked so
welcoming and friendly. Jael collapsed beside an empty
wagon, shuddering and panting until she regained some frag-
ment of her composure.

Gods, had she only dreamed the thing? If not, why had it
spared her? No, surely it had been an illusion of some kind

meant to frighten her, or to warn her out of the area. No creature like that could be wandering Allanmere, not even in
Rivertown, without being discovered. The thought reassured
Jael tremendously, and her fear slowly faded. No, she'd been
fooled and fooled well, but nothing more. Still, now she *definitely* would find some of Aubry's thieves to see her home.
She stood and brushed the dirt from her trousers, stepping resolutely into the crowd.

"Jaellyn!" Urien's familiar voice startled Jael just before
she collided with him. Urien steadied her, his hands clutching
her shoulders anxiously. "What in Baaros's name are you
doing here in the market alone at this hour?"

"I—uh—was here with a friend," Jael stammered. Would
Urien be angry if he knew the friend was Tanis? Better not to
say.

"Quite a friend, to leave you here alone at night while elves
are being murdered in this city," Urien said, scowling. "No
matter. I have purchases to make, but my carriage will take
you home and then return for me."

"You don't need to do that," Jael protested. "I'll be safe."
She was lying; his offer relieved her tremendously.

"Indeed you will, in my carriage with my guards outside,"
Urien told her firmly. "I could never forgive myself if any
harm came to you through want of such a small effort on my
part. Go home, Jaellyn, and don't come to the market at night
with friends who will abandon you."

This sounded suspiciously like a dismissal to Jael, and she
settled back into the carriage, fuming. If Urien didn't want her
hanging on his heels as he bargained, he might have said as
much rather than bundle her into his carriage like a naughty
child out too late. Apparently it had never occurred to Lord
Urien that *she* might very well have further business in the
market herself!

Jael ground her teeth and slouched lower on the carriage
seat. Human men! If they weren't treating a woman like an ir-
responsible child as Urien had just done, they were pouting
and mooning like a neglected pup as Tanis had. Guildmaster
Aubry himself treated her like an adult with at least a few
clever thoughts to shake around in her head, and any elvan
fellow worth the points on his ears would've simply said,
"I'm fond of you. Want to rumple the furs?" instead of wait-

ing nearly a year and then getting all prickly and jealous. Not that Jael had any natural desire to rumple the furs, of course, then or now, but still—

The carriage stopped, and Jael bounced out the door before the footman could lower the step or assist her, utterly glad to be home. Whether the illusion she'd seen had been a warning or just a horrible joke, she wanted nothing more than to forget it immediately.

Jael was far too agitated to sleep, so she searched out her parents. She found Donya soaking in one of the bathing pools with a chill-spelled mug of ale in hand, and Jael quickly stripped off her clothes to join her mother. A hot bath and her mother's reassuring presence was just what she needed.

"You did well in your lesson today," Donya said, pouring Jael another mug of the ale. "Much better than I would have expected in such a short time. The sword, and letting you work out your own style—it seems to be working for you." She shook her head. "Maybe we've all gotten too dogmatic, too sure that what we've been taught—and the *way* it's been taught—is best. I already knew that any good warrior develops her own style that's different from any other, an instinctive adjustment—relationship, if you will—between warrior and weapon that evolves its own style. I don't know why we all assume that a new learner can't do that."

"It's not as obvious as that," Jael protested. "I mean, forming a—uh—relationship with your sword is hardly the same as trying to do it with a chunk of wood for practice, just like striking at a big wooden pole is different than practicing with a live opponent. Even the blade guard or the dull edge makes a difference, doesn't it, in your mind?"

"There's that," Donya admitted. "A warrior loses some of her edge when she knows there's no real danger. But still, you're doing well."

"I'm glad," Jael said, sighing relievedly. "I thought I'd spend all of my life dropping swords and stumbling over my own feet. If I could actually learn, really be *good*—"

Jael stopped, not wanting to finish the thought—*I could protect myself when I leave Allanmere.*

"—I'd worry about you a good deal less," Donya finished firmly.

Jael sipped a little ale for politeness' sake, although her

stomach didn't approve, while she tried to think of a good way to ask the question she wanted answered.

"I was wondering," Jael said at last, "whether there'd be a death ritual for Evriel and the others. I mean, I knew Evriel a little. Is the—uh—will she be sent back to the Heartwood?"

Donya patted her hand.

"That's a kind thought, Jael," she said, smiling. "But I'm sure her kin in the Heartwood have already held her ritual. They know I can't send any of the bodies to the Heartwood for return to the earth until I'm certain my mages can learn nothing more from them. When my mages are finished, we'll hold a public ritual here in town before I send the bodies back to the forest."

"What can a mage learn from a dead body?" Jael asked curiously.

"Sometimes a divination spell cast on the death wound will show the weapon used," Donya told her. "Although in this instance the serrated blade could be surmised just from the appearance of the wound; anyone proficient with a knife could have seen it. Sometimes if there's dirt on the clothing, another kind of divination can be performed to show where the dirt came from. Or a blood trace can be done using a little blood from the corpse to scry out the location where death occurred. I was hoping that would work in this case, especially since the heart and entrails were removed. It should have left a good strong trace."

"But it didn't?" Jael asked. "Why not?"

"There are many reasons why these divinations sometimes fail," Donya said, shrugging. "Too much time or distance between death and the divination is one, but that shouldn't be the case here. Elvan corpses are always poor subjects for these spells, though. An elf's spirit leaves their body so soon after death—hurrying back to the Mother Forest, they say. Oftentimes that emptiness makes even simpler traces, such as blood to blood, more difficult, because all the life has fled from the blood."

"What about the beggar, though?" Jael suggested. "He was human."

"He wasn't quite like the others, though," Donya said, sighing. "Nessle was killed and left where he fell, and killed quickly. He likely never even had a clear look at his killers,

he being a human in a dark alley at night, or at best had only
a glimpse. There's little or nothing to be learned from him."

"You mentioned tracing the dirt, though," Jael said. "Even
if everything's gone out of the elf, wouldn't the dirt still be
useful for that kind of divination?"

"It should." Donya glanced around her and found an empty
bowl that had once held soap. She dipped it into the bath and
rinsed it out, then filled it with water and sat it on the edge
of the bathing pool.

"Think of looking into this bowl as scrying," she said. "As
long as the water's clear, you could see pretty much what you
liked. But look now." Donya reached into another bowl,
scooped out a handful of bathing salts, and dropped them into
the water. Instantly the water clouded and foamed. "It doesn't
take much to muddy the image. There are any number of
spells which could do it, all very difficult and time-consuming
to break. Each of the bodies we've found—except the beggar,
of course—has been 'muddied' in just that way. That does tell
us one thing, though—that there's at least one mage involved.
Unfortunately it means we can't learn much else from the
bodies."

"What about a necromancer?" Jael asked boldly. "Can that
kind of spell block necromancy?"

"No." Donya dumped the bowl into the bathing pool,
avoiding Jael's eyes. "No, there's very little that can obstruct
a necromancer. That's a different kind of magic."

"Then why haven't you and Father authorized necromancy?" Jael asked. "I mean, if it might let you find out who
killed them."

"It's not that simple, Jaellyn," Donya said slowly. She
crossed her arms on the edge of the bathing pool and rested
her chin on her crossed wrists. "Necromancy has been outlawed in Allanmere for a long time. I'm sure there are necromancers in the city, but I doubt they're the kind of mages we
can trust for something so important.

"Then the victims are elves. Elves have strong convictions
against necromancy, think it's an abomination to bring an
elf's spirit back, however temporarily, from the Mother Forest. The elves' influence was a large factor in outlawing necromancy in the first place. Elves themselves are rather
resistant to necromancy—perhaps for the same reason—but a

good enough necromancer can drag anyone back, it's said. What concerns me is the effect on the city if Argent and I called in a necromancer. Some elves might think it worth the—well—the offense to the elf and to the Mother Forest, if other murders could be prevented, but others won't. The city's elf-haters will protest, of course, if Argent and I authorize necromancy when it's been proscribed so severely for so many years, especially if we utilize necromancers who have been living and practicing illegally in Allanmere. And it might take weeks to bring in a necromancer from another city."

"That can't be what's holding you back," Jael protested. "I've never known you and Father to worry about what a few angry people would say when something needed to be done. You always used to say 'You can't swing a sword in a crowd without letting a little blood.' And if it would save citizens' lives—"

"That's not exactly the problem," Donya admitted. "Fresh human or elvan blood, hearts, entrails—those are things that necromancers use in some of their darker spells. Argent and I believe that it may be a necromancer doing the killing, or having it done."

Jael was silent. She hadn't thought of that; had Aubry? And that raised an even more complicated problem—should she give any aid to these necromancers at all, or should she be trying to find out who and where they were so that her parents could be told?

"Argent and I have discussed it," Donya said, sighing. "I simply can't see any way to use a local necromancer, even if we could find one. We simply must find other ways of getting information, or perhaps my mages can break the divination shroud on the corpses."

Jael sipped her ale, grimacing as she realized that the chilling spell was gone from the mug. Gods, couldn't she even drink a mug of ale without ruining something? She ground her teeth and pushed the mug away, then froze as an idea occurred to her.

"Mother," Jael said slowly, "what if you had something—someone—who could make spells fail?"

Donya glanced at her daughter; then her eyes widened as she realized what Jael was saying. Water splashed everywhere as the High Lady of Allanmere bolted naked from her bath, snatching a cloth to wrap around herself as she strode to the door.

"Get dressed and meet me in the main hall immediately," Donya told her. "I'll fetch Jermyn and Argent."

Jael knuckled water out of her eyes and scrambled out of the bathing pool. She pulled on her tunic and trousers, snatching up her mother's clothes and her boots and trotting down the hall barefoot.

Jermyn was already in the large hall, and Donya and Argent arrived just as Jael did, Donya still wrapped in the wet cloth. Jael mutely handed her mother her clothes, then sat down on the stone floor to pull on her boots.

"By the Mother Forest, Donya," Argent chuckled, "the poor elves have already been dead for some time. A few moments for you to put your clothing back on wouldn't have made a difference to them."

"No, but it might make a difference to the next elf destined for an alley in Rivertown," Donya returned. She glanced down at the wet cloth clinging translucently to her body and flushed. "Argent, take Jael and Jermyn to the cellar. I'll join you in just a moment."

Argent sighed and led Jael and Jermyn down the cellar stairs. He stopped at the wine cellar first, however, opening the tap of one of the great casks and filling a goblet, then soaking his handkerchief in the wine.

"Hold that over your nose and mouth," he told Jael. "The bodies have been preservation-spelled, of course, but Aliss was in the water for a time before she was discovered, and the smell is unpleasant."

Jael swallowed heavily, squeezing the excess wine out of the cloth and holding it ready. Gods, she hadn't even been able to look at Evriel in that alley, and now—

Argent and Jermyn stopped at one of the small locked cellar rooms, and Jermyn made a brief pass over the lock with a wand before Argent fitted his key into the lock. Jael took a deep breath and held the cloth over her nose and mouth, steadying herself as Argent opened the door.

The smell was not as bad as Jael had feared, being well mixed with the pungency of incense, sulfur, and other magical ingredients from the attempted divinations, and muffled by the wine-soaked cloth. Jael briefly noticed the light globes on the walls and quickly turned her attention away from them. Four still figures lay on tables in the room, mercifully covered with cloth. On a smaller table there was a covered box; that must be Merchant Najel's head.

Jael started violently as Argent laid a gentle hand on her shoulder.

"If you need a little time before you go in," he said understandingly, "we'll wait."

"No, I'm all right." Jael was half lying, but Mother had been right; saving lives was more important than the steadiness of her stomach. Jael took another wine-scented breath and stepped resolutely into the room.

"Can you tell if the spell fails?" Jael asked Jermyn, forcing herself closer to the nearest table. With any luck, maybe if she was close enough, that would do it.

"Not without attempting the actual divination," Jermyn said, running his fingers through his dark brown hair thoughtfully. "And if you'll forgive me, Lady Jaellyn, I'm not certain that—ah—"

"That my being here wouldn't just make your own spell fail, too," Jael finished.

"How will you know, then?"

Donya stood in the door, fully dressed now and with a mug in her hand, and Jael jumped again; for once, her sharp ears hadn't heard her mother's footsteps approaching.

"I'll try the divination later," Jermyn said. "If necessary, I'll simply call Jaellyn back down."

Jael shivered. It had been hard enough to come down here once. Well, she'd just have to be sure it worked the first time.

She tried to remember what she'd done before. She'd only looked at the illusions in the market and the light globes in the dining hall, but she'd seen other magic that hadn't failed. Attention, yes, but more certainly—

Jael took a deep breath and lifted the cloth over the body nearest her, uncovering what she hoped was the feet. Fortunately, nothing more horrible than a pair of water-molded boots confronted her, and Jael was thankful she didn't have to look at Aliss's probably fish-eaten face. Before she could think, Jael reached out and laid her hand on the boots.

"I hope that's done it," she said. "I don't know how to tell."

She stepped from table to table, gingerly lifting the edges of the cloth to expose a foot or a white hand to touch. When she came to the covered bucket, however, Jael hesitated.

"Surely there's no need—" Argent said hesitantly.

"No." Donya laid her hand on Jael's shoulder. "We need to learn everything we can about each murder, and this is the newest corpse." She squeezed Jael's shoulder comfortingly.

Jael's hand shook as she slid the cloth off the bucket. She couldn't just reach blindly in; who knew what she might touch? She tried to tip the bucket slightly, but her shaking hand fumbled and the rough wooden container toppled onto its side, its gory contents rolling out onto the tabletop. Mud-slimed hair rolled over Jael's hand and she stared into empty eye sockets; then she turned away and spewed the remains of three spiced meat sticks, half a melon, and two baked tubers with gravy into the basin that appeared as if by magic in front of her. When she was finished, Donya smiled sympathetically and handed Jael the mug of cold ale.

"Sorry," Jael mumbled, wiping her mouth with the wine-scented cloth.

"No need," Donya said easily, her arm around her daughter's shoulders as she led Jael from the room. "Do you know, the first corpse I ever saw, not only did I belch up my meal, but the next one, too. And *my* first corpse didn't smell, either. We'll let Jermyn do his work, and I think you'd like to go back to your bath, maybe, and I'll fetch you a clean robe."

In the bath, Jael scrubbed herself perhaps harder than necessary, wanting to be sure no trace of the odor remained on her skin. She lathered her short curls with perfumed soap twice after imagining she could smell a faint scent of rot. The only thought that distracted her from her disgust was, *Whatever am I going to do about Tanis?*

Argent peered in the door.

"May I come in?"

"Uh-huh." Jael ducked under the water, scrubbing at her hair to rinse it, and contemplated yet another soaping. She reached for the bowl of bath salts and dumped most of the bowl into the bubbling water.

"I was thinking of joining you," Argent said wryly, "but I believe not." He laid a robe near the bathing pool and set a goblet at the pool's edge. "Tomorrow morning we'll hear what Jermyn has learned, if indeed there is anything he can learn. Here is a clean robe for you, and I brought you a potion to settle your stomach and ease your sleep. Your mother thinks I'm fussing."

"You probably are, but I'm glad," Jael admitted, draining the potion as quickly as she could. "I'm sorry I don't have Mother's steel stomach."

"Well, you certainly have her courage." Argent sat down on the stone edge of the pool, reaching out to stroke Jael's wet hair. "You were very brave, Jaellyn, and that was a difficult task. Donya and I were both proud."

"I wasn't," Jael said, grimacing. "Especially when I threw my supper into a bowl."

Argent sighed and shook his head.

"Jaellyn, sweetling, when I saw Najel's head I nearly did the same, and I've seen corpses enough in my years, the Mother Forest knows. Warrior or High Lady, it never becomes easy to see your friends or kin lying dead. There's no special honor in holding your supper in the face of horrible and gruesome death, and your mother would be the first to say so. The honor, Jaellyn, is in doing what you must even while you empty your stomach. You have every right to be proud."

Jael couldn't quite manage a grin, but his words made her feel better than his potion had.

"I suggested that perhaps it might be best to miss your lessons tomorrow, at least in the morning, but Donya disagreed," Argent said hesitantly. "I suppose I'm fussing again."

"Oh, no, I can't miss my lessons," Jael said hurriedly. "Not when I'm only just beginning to make progress."

Argent laughed.

"I never thought to hear you say such things," he said. "But it makes me glad to see you applying yourself, and I know your mother is reassured. I'm sure she's hoping you'll become a master swordswoman and roam about the land hewing your enemies in half."

Despite his jocular tone, Jael could hear a note of concern

in his voice. The thought of hewing someone in half carried unpleasant overtones of what she'd just seen in the cellar.

"Don't worry," she said honestly. "I'd like to become a good swordswoman, but it doesn't look as if I'm much made to be a warrior. And after seeing those bodies, it sounds even less appealing."

"I'd be deceiving you if I said I was sorry to hear you say that," Argent admitted. "But you mustn't make such decisions when you are so upset. Dry yourself and go to bed, dream sweetly and rest well, and soon tonight will only be another unpleasant memory of this terrible time."

The potion she had drunk was already starting to make her drowsy, and the heat of the bathing pool intensified her languor; Jael thought that Argent's advice was probably sound, and stumbled back to her room in the robe, leaving her clothes where she'd dropped them.

Despite the potion, however, her dreams were troubled. First she dreamed that she was dining with Urien, and he gave her an ornately wrapped box; opening it, however, she was horrified to find that it contained Merchant Najel's severed head, the eyeless sockets staring horribly up at her.

Jael sank into the sheltering refuge of stone, sank through the streets of Allanmere until she found herself in some dark place smelling of dust and mold. For a moment the darkness was almost comforting, quiet and still; then gradually she could hear voices from somewhere overhead, muffled as if far away.

Slowly Jael became aware that she was not alone in the darkness. She could hear breathing, deep and slow, and quiet, strange sounds, as if something huge stirred slightly in the space. She could feel huge, cold hands starting to close around her in the darkness—

Jael bolted upright in the bed, shivering and clutching the bedclothes around her. What had frightened her? Had she dreamed? For a moment, a wisp of memory flashed through her mind—stone, darkness—and then was gone.

Her room was still and dark, lit only slightly by the embers of the fire and what little moonlight could trickle through the clouds. Her keen elvan vision quickly reassured her that nothing was out of place; she was alone and safe in her room as always. Still Jael could not return to sleep, imagining sounds or shadows that moved. *Well, no wonder,* she told herself. *Being chased around alleys by horrible illusions, and then coming home to fondle corpses—excuse enough for a good case of the night shakes.*

At last she gave in and took her sword from its resting place on her table and took it back to bed with her. Finally, clutching the sheathed blade like a talisman, Jael slept.

VII

● Jermyn apparently spoke with Donya or Argent in the night, or very early in the morning, indeed, for it was Donya and Argent who took Jael quietly aside after breakfast to tell her the results of the previous night's divinations.

"I didn't think this was a subject for the table, or for the twins, come to that," Donya said quietly, "and I wanted you to eat your breakfast. Jermyn was able to get a few impressions from some of the bodies, although nothing too helpful—as I told you, elves are poor subjects for hindsight after they've died. Still, it was enough for him to be certain that all five elves were killed by the same group of people. He was certain there were several persons involved, although he couldn't say whether it was one person or many who actually killed. He had an impression of darkness and of chanting coming from somewhere nearby, and believes that the killing was part of a magical ritual of some kind. The only other impression he received was that of some powerful presence nearby in the darkness, or perhaps two such presences."

Jael shivered. Donya's description sounded somehow familiar, uncomfortably so.

"So you think a necromancer might be involved?" Jael asked her.

"Jermyn says it's likely," Donya said, looking far from comfortable herself. "Necromancers often use human blood and—and parts in their summonings."

"But why elves?" Jael pressed. "Wouldn't—uh—parts of elves be less useful for that kind of magic, since you said the life goes out of them so fast?"

"Not if the elf was killed then and there, as a part of the ritual," Donya said quietly. "I think Celene mentioned to you how killing uninitiated mages released a large burst of power. None of the elves killed were mages, but all elves have at least a little magic in their blood, I've heard. The release of that magic may be why elves were killed, or the mage may simply prefer killing elves. I'm afraid the divination didn't give us much help. But I thought you deserved to know, after your assistance."

"Chanting, and several people, and a powerful presence," Jael mused. "It sounds like a mage circle, doesn't it? Do necromancers use mage circles?"

"If other mages do, I don't see why necromancers couldn't," Donya told her. "Assuming that, Jermyn's divination could be of some use to us. Darkness seems to imply a cellar or underground area, but I'd already thought of that. This kind of killing takes time and secrecy and a place where noises won't be heard. Unfortunately the city's more riddled with cellars and tunnels than a termite-eaten log."

"But likely it would be somewhere in Rivertown, wouldn't it?" Jael suggested. "It's a good spot where necromancers could meet in secret, residents aren't nosy, and the bodies don't have to be carried far to be dumped in places where they won't be found too quickly. And reputable mages don't frequent Rivertown, so the magical energies wouldn't be detected."

"I think you're likely right," Donya said, nodding. "The last two bodies were found farther from Rivertown—Najel upriver, and I think whoever was disposing of Evriel's body was interrupted in the effort to carry her away from Rivertown and toward the market. Argent and I think the killers are trying to get the bodies farther away from their meeting place, to draw suspicion and guards away from them."

Jael frowned, thinking of the horrible monster—*illusionary monster*, she reminded herself—she'd encountered in Rivertown. No, that was only an illusion, and the elves had been killed with knives, not teeth or talons. There couldn't be any connection there.

Jael was glad enough for her lessons that morning, and she rejoiced with her teachers when she unexpectedly managed to knock Larissa's feet out from under her and send the tiny human woman sprawling to the ground. For a moment she wondered if Larissa hadn't deliberately left her an opening, but the surprised arch of Larissa's brows told her that her teacher was as amazed as she.

"Very, very good, little heirling," Larissa grinned, accepting a hand up. "I didn't see that on its way. You're starting to move like your arms and your legs are attached to the same body. Pick up those practice daggers and see if you can surprise me again."

Jael was sure that the fall had been nothing but luck, but later that morning she was able to land such a blow to Rabin's ribs with her practice dagger that she was happily certain that the weapons master would have a bruise of his own to nurse that evening.

By the time Jael had eaten her supper, steadfastly ignoring the twins' chatter, she had decided that she'd have to risk another trip to the Temple of Baaros to find Tanis. Once the acolyte got over being angry with her, he might well feel embarrassed, and Jael was not sure he'd come to see her. She needed to find out if Tanis had learned anything new of Ankaras's dealings with the worshippers who had left the Temple of Baaros, and it was only fair to share with him what she'd learned about the killings, and the story of the horrible illusion she'd seen. How to deal with Tanis himself—well, hopefully she'd know what to say when she saw him.

That decision made, Jael threw herself into her sword lesson enthusiastically, surprising her mother with her energy. She even managed to get a strike or two past the High Lady's guard. After the lesson, when Donya reviewed her progress, Jael told her mother about the success of her lesson earlier that day. Donya congratulated her, but seemed unsurprised by the news.

"Fighting with sword, dagger, or unarmed is based on the same principles: balance, speed, and coordination," Donya told her. "Now that you've found a style of swordplay that works with your body instead of against it, and a type of unarmed and dagger fighting that suits you as well, your progress will naturally spread from one to the other. You're learning more during these afternoons than simply how to wield a sword; you're learning to move without thinking, learning to trust your instincts and your sword. That kind of confidence affects everything you do. Just don't neglect your practice for either lesson."

Jael promised, but she was already eager to change her clothes and hurry to the Temple District. She had reached the abandoned temple and was quietly working her way around to the entrance when she collided with Tanis himself. For a moment Jael was too surprised to speak; then Tanis grabbed her arm and hurriedly pulled her around behind the temple.

"Thank Baaros! I was just on my way to the castle," Tanis said relievedly. "I was afraid you'd try to sneak in through the cellar again. One of High Priest Urien's lesser priests found your opening in the cellar wall, and now he's got his acolytes taking turns standing guard all the time, day and night. He's afraid the hole was made by someone from one of the other temples, hoping to profane the temple in some way to cause the Grand Summoning in three days to fail."

"Can you come somewhere to talk now?" Jael asked him. "Somewhere safer than this, I mean."

"All right, but not the market this time," Tanis told her. "Let's go somewhere quieter, with fewer people."

"I know just where to go," Jael told him.

They had to travel back west through the Temple District to reach the castle grounds again, but this gave them the opportunity to buy a few meat pies for their supper. Tanis and Jael left the city through the North Gate, and Jael led Tanis around the north wall of the city to the small hidden entrance to the castle gardens.

"This is a secret entrance that only a few people know about," Jael warned Tanis. "Don't ever tell anyone about it."

"I swear by Baaros's purse that I'll never whisper a word,"

Tanis told her, smiling with pride that she shared the secret with him.

A group of bushes had been deliberately planted just inside the wall to conceal the secret entrance to the castle grounds. Within the bushes, however, was a nicely cleared space, necessary to let the hidden door swing open. Jael sat down in this clearing, and after glancing around curiously, Tanis sat down beside her, avoiding Jael's eyes.

There was an awkward pause.

"I just wanted to tell you—" Tanis began boldly.

"I'm sorry about—" Jael blurted at the same time.

They stared at each other a moment, silently; then Jael chuckled, and Tanis joined in.

"You first," Jael said shyly.

"I had no excuse to speak to you as I did," Tanis said quietly. "Our friendship gives me no right to presume on your affections. And to leave you alone in the market when elves are in danger in the city—I'm so sorry, Jael. That was unforgivable."

"No, it wasn't," Jael sighed. "I suppose I needed to be reminded that other people have troubles, too, and that not everybody in Allanmere is like me."

"Like you?" Tanis still didn't meet her eyes.

Jael reached over and took Tanis's hand and squeezed it reassuringly. Suddenly, wonderfully, she knew what to say.

"I'm going to tell you something," she said quietly. "But you've got to swear to me you'll never tell anyone, not ever."

Tanis frowned, troubled.

"It doesn't concern the Temple of Baaros?" he asked hesitantly.

"Uh-uh." Jael flushed. "It's just—um—kind of personal."

"Oh." Tanis cleared his throat. "May Baaros forever deny me a profit if I ever reveal your secrets."

"Thanks," Jael said, a little awed by his oath. "Actually, it goes back before I was born, right before the Crimson Plague came to Allanmere—"

Tanis listened silently while Jael told the whole story, nibbling quietly at his meat pies as the sun sank and finally disappeared behind the wall. Jael blushed once or twice, but spoke frankly, omitting nothing but the details of her meetings with Urien. She finished by pulling off her boot to show Tanis the small, perfect extra toe on her left foot.

"Baaros bless us all," Tanis murmured when Jael was done. "That's quite a secret to trust me with."

Jael shrugged and grinned.

"If you'd wanted to do me harm, physical or not, you've had chances aplenty," she said practically. "Some of Ankaras's friends might have given a good bit to know where and when the High Lord and Lady's eldest daughter could be found unprotected in a market alley. Anyway, you're my best friend."

Tanis smiled warmly, and this time he reached for Jael's hand.

"So a part of your soul is missing?" he asked. "And that's why magic goes all wrong around you, and why you can't use magic yourself?"

"And likely why I'm not a beast-speaker, too," Jael said, nodding. "And why I don't feel—uh—the normal things a young woman my age might feel with a man."

"Like Urien?" Tanis asked, his eyebrows lifting in realization.

"Like Urien," Jael agreed, not mentioning the Bluebright or the potion she'd asked her father to make. "Or you."

"Oh. Oh!" Tanis grinned ruefully. "Is this forever, or will you outgrow it in a few decades?"

"It'd better not be forever," Jael said disgustedly. "If Aunt Shadow or Mother's mages can't think of a solution within a year, I hope my father's people aren't too awfully hard to find."

"I'd pray for you," Tanis said, chuckling, "but I don't think it's the sort of thing Baaros grants—parts of souls, that is."

Jael grinned back, glad that she hadn't lost Tanis's friendship. Many young men from noble houses would have been far less accepting of a friend who had just admitted bastardy. The elves were far more accepting.

"I just didn't want you to think that I was slighting you," Jael said awkwardly. "You've been a wonderful friend, and I care about you as much as—well—as much as I can care about anyone. But whatever you feel about me, maybe you'd be smart to find another girl to feel that way about. I don't want you sitting around lonely waiting for me, and I don't want to feel guilty about you doing it, either."

"Jael—" Tanis hesitated. "Why *are* you visiting with High Priest Urien, then?"

"Being honest, I don't really know," Jael admitted. "At first I suppose I was flattered that he even noticed me. Mother and Father were glad he came to the city, since it solved their problem with the Temple of Baaros, and when he wanted me to help him find a house, it seemed only courteous to help him."

"I suppose your mother and father have encouraged him," Tanis agreed, sighing. "They must be glad to have a noble-man of his station courting you."

Jael forced herself to shrug noncommittally, deeming it wise not to tell Tanis that he couldn't have been more wrong.

"Did you find out anything new about Ankaras?" Jael asked quickly, eager to change the subject.

"He met with Merchant Sheesa again last night," Tanis told her. "They went into a tavern, but there weren't many other people inside. I knew that if I went in after him, he'd see me. So I just went back to the temple. Did you learn anything?"

"I don't know that I learned so much," Jael said ruefully, "but I certainly have a couple of gruesome stories to tell you, no doubt." She enjoyed the way Tanis's eyes widened and the color drained from his face while she told him about the hor-rible creature she'd seen in the alleys, and her encounter with the corpses the night before.

"And all you did was spew up your supper?" Tanis asked, mustering a sickly grin. "After all that, I think I'd have fainted, or at least soiled my trousers. Yecch. Thank you for waiting until I finished my pies, at least. But I think you must be right that the thing was an illusion. A real monster would have killed you, and as you say, even in Rivertown, some-body else would've seen it by now and called the guards."

"Anyway, I'm starting to wonder if Ankaras could really be involved," Jael told him. "I mean, has Ankaras had the time and opportunity to become involved with necromancers?"

"I don't see how he could," Tanis said, shaking his head. "It's been less than two weeks since High Priest Urien took the robe from him. He might have been dealing secretly with some of the elf-haters in town before that, but he *couldn't* have been dealing with necromancers. There were no murders then—beyond what's expected in a city this size, that is."

"And a few days is hardly enough time for him to get this all started," Jael said thoughtfully. "Unless he isn't the leader of the group, and someone else had already made contact with the necromancers."

"Someone like Sheesa, or maybe the Dyers' Guild?" Tanis suggested. "But then why would they need Ankaras, when they could hire necromancers—or any other way of killing elves they pleased—anytime they liked?"

Jael thought about that for a long moment.

"I can think of a couple of reasons," she said slowly. "First, the Temple of Baaros was growing fast. Maybe the Dyers' Guild looked on it as a good way of persuading other citizens of Allanmere in a plan to maybe push the elves out of the mercantile community. Also, the Council of Churches has never been very favorably inclined toward the elves, not since Aunt Shadow made the Guild of Thieves a respectable voice in Allanmere again—the Guild has a large elvan membership and a lot of elvan support. Dealing through the Temple of Baaros might have been a way to involve the Council of Churches."

"But why hire necromancers?" Tanis asked her. "Yes, it's an ugly way to kill someone, and maybe that makes the murders more impressive, but any hired thug could kill someone that way. Why spend the kind of money it must cost to hire illegal necromancers unless they actually wanted necromancy? And what kind of ritual would a necromancer need all these—well—*things* for?"

"I don't know," Jael admitted. "Who knows much about necromancy except a necromancer? But I'll ask Uncle Aubry and the castle mages. Can you keep watching Ankaras?"

"That won't be difficult, but there won't be much to see," Tanis told her. "The Grand Summoning's in three days. High Priest Urien is going to have all of us busy again with preparations, even Ankaras. I'm glad that you don't want to go prowling in the basements of Rivertown, at least, looking for necromancers."

"Not even if I was *really* good with my sword," Jael said fervently. "I don't want *my* head to finish up in a bucket, and I don't even like to imagine what might happen to the other parts. I don't care to find any more illusions wandering in the alleys, either."

"Maybe we should just tell the City Guard what we've learned already," Tanis suggested. "Or maybe you should just tell the High Lord and Lady."

"Tell them what?" Jael asked him. "Tell them that Ankaras has been talking to a merchant who happens to be the daughter of the Guildmistress of the Dyers' Guild? Maybe I should tell them that we were the ones who found Evriel's body in the alley and didn't tell anyone. Or that I was conspiring with the Thieves' Guild to use necromancers without Mother and Father even knowing."

"While you're confessing, maybe you should tell them that Shadow took you to visit the most notorious assassin in Allanmere," Tanis chuckled, joining the game. "Then at least we'll have some company in the dungeons."

He glanced up at the sky.

"I'd better hurry back to the temple," he said. "We have a ceremony at moonrise, and High Priest Urien may let us assist him." He smiled. "I'm glad we were able to talk, and I'm glad you shared your secret with me."

"So am I." Jael patted his hand. "I didn't want to lose my best friend. But will I see you again before the Grand Summoning, if you're so busy at the temple?"

"Likely not, unless I need to tell you something important," Tanis said regretfully. "But if I can, I'll come to see you here." He sighed. "You probably shouldn't let High Priest Urien see you around the temple."

Jael didn't know what to say to that; impulsively she leaned over and kissed Tanis on the cheek. Before she could back away, however, Tanis folded his arms around her and hugged her fiercely.

"Keep yourself safe, please," he muttered into Jael's ear. "I can be patient as long as it takes." Before Jael could try to push him away, Tanis released her and ducked quickly out through the hidden door.

Jael stared after Tanis for a long moment, then sighed and turned toward the castle. She wasn't quite certain exactly how she did feel about Tanis—the thought was too abruptly new and uncomfortable. For that matter, though, she was far from sure how she felt about Urien, especially after his rather brusque dismissal of her the night before. Despite his apparent sympathy when they'd supped together, was he angry at her because he hadn't succeeded in seducing her? Had her meeting him in the market simply been inconveniently public, even embarrassing to him, or did he not want to be bothered with her when it didn't suit his purposes?

Jael shook her head irritably. Argent's warning when she had asked him for the potion had put some uncomfortable thoughts into her mind. Gods, surely Aunt Shadow didn't have to go through all these doubts every time she thought about having a simple tumble with some fellow, did she?

But, then, was there actually such a thing as a simple tumble for the mixed-blood daughter of the High Lord and Lady of Allanmere? Likely not, especially with a handsome, foreign merchant lord who was also the High Priest of the most talked-about sect in Allanmere. Such ingredients sounded like the makings of a marvelous scandal.

She did not have time to brood, however; as soon as she stepped into the castle, she was ambushed by a bevy of servants, who hurried her to the main hall where Donya sat waiting.

"There you are," Donya said relievedly, rising from her chair. "Jaellyn, can your stomach take another trip to the cellar? There's been another murder, a human this time, and this one was found so quickly that Jermyn is sure he can learn something from it."

Jael's stomach lurched at Donya's words, but she took a deep breath and clasped her hands so they wouldn't shake.

"All right," she said. "I'll go."

"That's my brave daughter." Donya steadied Jael with a muscled arm around her shoulders as they descended the stairs. "Jaellyn, it might be better if you don't look at this one. If you like, I'll tie a cloth over your eyes."

"Really, Mother," Jael protested, her indignation momentarily overcoming her anxiety. "Just because I dropped my supper last night, that doesn't mean I'm a complete coward."

"I didn't mean to say that you are." Donya hesitated at the bottom of the stairs. "He was wearing a Thieves' Guild token. I thought it might be someone you know."

"You don't know who he is?" Jael asked, before she realized the true importance of what Donya had said. Unlike the other victims, this one was no merchant.

"The body's in such a condition that it's difficult to tell," Donya said quietly. "It's different from the others in some ways. It doesn't even look like a murder, more like an animal attack. The only reason I would connect it with the other murders is because of the divination shroud over it, and because the blood's gone." She stopped outside one of the cellar doors, different from the one in which the other bodies had been kept. "If you're sure—"

"I'll be all right." Jael had some doubts of that herself, but this was her chance to compensate for her embarrassing nausea of the night before.

"All right, then." There was apparently no spell on this lock, for Donya opened it herself, preceding Jael into the room.

Jael gasped and hurriedly turned around, for this body had not been covered. For a moment the room seemed to spin under Jael's feet, but she took a deep breath and steadied herself against the wall, forcing herself to turn back to the table.

As her mother had implied, there was little to identify the body on the table other than the Guild token worn as a ring on the left hand. The leather clothing might equally have been that of a noble or beggar, torn and shredded and liberally spattered with gore, gaping open in the front where the body had been seemingly ripped open from throat to belly. The body had not been gutted like Evriel's, although some of the entrails were hanging out of the torn cavity. The skin of the face had been savagely slashed and gouged beyond any recognition, and the eye sockets gaped empty. The scalp had seemingly been ripped away and the skull torn open with such strength that the head was almost split in two.

Animal attack, Jael thought, remembering the creature she'd seen in the alley.

Horrified, yet unable to look away from the ravaged face, Jael stepped up to the table. She reached down and gingerly touched the rigid hand, then gasped again.

"Mother?" To Jael's disgust, the word came out almost as a whimper.

"What is it?" Donya laid a steadying hand on Jael's shoulder, bending over the corpse.

"This." Jael pointed to the sides of the corpse's head. On the left ear hung a thick gold ring set with three green stones. On the right ear, the lobe was missing entirely, the heavy scarring showing that the wound was an old one. Another gold ring hung from this ear, but this time from a hole near the top rim of the ear.

Donya gazed at Jael searchingly.

"Do you know him?"

"It's Solly," Jael whispered. "The thief who found Garric and Crow. He lost the other earlobe in a fight with another thief, but he loved those earrings, so he had another hole cut in his ear."

Donya frowned.

"Where did you hear that?" she demanded. "That he was the one who found Garric and Crow, I mean."

Too late, Jael remembered that she'd read Solly's name on Donya's map.

"Aubry told me," Jael said quickly. "Sometimes I go to the Guild for news. Most of my friends are Guild members."

"That's true." Donya's frown faded slowly. "I'm sorry, Jael. Was Solly one of your friends?"

Jael nodded, unable to force words around the lump in her throat. She stared at the torn face, searching in the ruined features for some trace of the familiar gap-toothed smile, the laughter-wrinkled eyes that had winked at her mischievously while Solly's surprisingly nimble-fingered hands snatched sweets or trinkets for her from a merchant's tray or a noble's pocket.

She touched one of those hands now. It was stiff and still and foreign to her, not the hand of her friend. *Solly* had gone from those hands.

Donya put her arm around Jael's shoulders and squeezed her comfortingly.

"Go back outside," she said. "I'll join you in a moment."

Jael was desperately glad to return to the corridor and lean her back against the comforting solidity of the stone wall. She scooted down the wall until she sat, wrapping her arms around her legs and resting her forehead on her knees. Oddly she felt neither nausea nor grief, only a horrified emptiness that seemed to reach deep into her.

A few moments later Donya stepped into the corridor, closing the door behind her. She held out her hand and Jael took it, a little comforted by her mother's strength as Donya drew her effortlessly to her feet.

"Let's get out of this cellar," Donya said, leading Jael to the stairs. "This place is beginning to give me an eerie feeling." She tucked something into Jael's hand; Jael glanced down and recognized Solly's Guild token and the gold earrings, and a leather purse.

"That's everything of any value he had on him," Donya said gently. "There's some kind of dried fluid on his dagger, so Jermyn took that. Do you want to take the token back to the Guild, or shall I have one of the guards do it?"

"I'll do it," Jael said quickly. Solly had been a friend of Aubry's, too; Jael didn't want some guard telling the Guildmaster how Solly had died, and she needed to speak to Aubry anyway. "Mother, where was Solly found, and how? Aubry will want to know."

"He was found in an alley behind the Fin and Flagon, not far from where he found Garric and Crow," Donya told her. "Since the murders I've had thrice as many guards patrolling those alleys. One of the guards heard a scream. It couldn't have been more than a few moments before he reached the spot and found Solly just as you see him. The heart and some of the entrails are gone, but it's more as though they were, well, eaten. The eyes and brain were ripped out. The blood on his clothes was still fairly fresh. The scream wasn't Solly, though; it was the owner of the Fin and Flagon, who had just discovered the body on his back doorstep."

"How could anyone have the time to mangle him that badly and cast a spell to prevent divination, too," Jael protested, "and still have time to carry the body to the Fin and Flagon?"

"*And* bleed him almost dry," Donya added. "Well, now we know we're looking for a place in Rivertown. There simply wouldn't have been time to carry the body from anywhere farther away."

"I'll tell Aubry, if you don't mind," Jael said. "The Guild has so many people in Rivertown, maybe someone's heard something."

"No." Donya stopped and turned to face Jael. "You can tell him where the body was found and the condition of the body, but nothing else. Aubry's trustworthy enough, and we could surely use the information his people could give us, but there are too many ears at the Guild, most of them as keen as yours. I don't want anyone to know what we know. And you can go to the Guild tomorrow morning. I don't want you going through the city this late at night, and by morning Jermyn may have learned something that you *can* tell Aubry. We'll have to cancel your lesson, at least in the afternoon—I won't have time to work with you now." She sighed. "Meanwhile, there's a message for you from Lord Urien. I put it in your room so the twins wouldn't get into it. I also received a formal invitation from the Temple of Baaros for the family to attend the Grand Summoning day after tomorrow, at sunset. It was signed by High Priest Ankaras, too."

"Ankaras?" Jael's amazement momentarily banished her grief.

"That's what the message said." Donya shook her head. "Maybe you can ask Urien to explain. The Temple of Baaros really doesn't concern me anymore, now that it's stopped stirring up the people. We'll attend, of course—inviting us was an excellent gesture. But the whole thing just doesn't seem very important now. Go on to bed now. Argent knows I was waiting for you, and he's left you a sleeping potion."

Jael found the message on her bedside table, sitting beside a small stoppered flask. Jael broke the seal on the message first.

Dearest Jaellyn, the message read, *I hope that you will forgive my impatience in the market last night. As you well know, had we been seen together under such circumstances, there might have been disastrous consequences for me, but much more importantly, for you. My soul could never be at peace if I thought I had caused the slightest hint of impropriety to stain your good character or that of your family.*

I beg that you will allow me to make amends for my unforgivable behavior. Although our temple is busy at this time in preparations for the Grand Summoning, if you will agree to sup with me tomorrow, I will gladly lay aside my responsibilities for that time. If you will only consent to come, it will be my privilege to send my carriage for you.

Jael rolled up the scroll, smiling with satisfaction. Supper with Lord Urien might carry its own complications, but it was one thing certain to distract her from her worries.

Jael drained the goblet; from the taste, it contained the same potion her father had given her the night before, but perhaps a little more concentrated. She was grateful; tonight she wanted all the help she could get to sleep. She touched the stoppered flask once, smiling in satisfaction, and let the potion's warm strength carry her away.

Aubry rolled the token between his fingers silently. At last he put it down on the table and tipped out the contents of the pouch—a handful of Suns, a dozen Moons, a few coppers. That was all.

"These were his luck," Aubry sighed, poking the gold earrings with his fingertip. "He never had much money—lived too fancy when he had more than a few Suns in his sleeves. But he was smart, lived within his abilities, didn't risk himself on marks that were too dangerous for him. He always had a notion that one day he'd take a boat down the Brightwater to the coast towns. I suppose that's why he always loitered around Rivertown."

"Aubry—" Jael hesitated. "Mother thinks a necromancer is involved with the murders, because of the blood and the other things that were taken. The necromancers that you spoke of, are you certain they couldn't be involved?"

Aubry grimaced.

"How can anyone know for certain without a truth spell?" he said wearily. "I'd have said not. One of them came to me, offering her services and those of her associates. If they'd killed the elves and taken what they wanted from the bodies, why would they come to me and say they needed more? And if they were doing it as a bluff, to turn suspicion away from themselves, why come to me? Why not send a nameless message to the High Lord and Lady and work that way? I'd have sworn on the Forest Altars that the offer was genuine."

"What would a necromancer do with those things?" Jael asked curiously. "All that blood, all the rest."

"I asked." Aubry poured himself a cup of wine and raised his eyebrows at Jael, who shook her head. "Blood's for invocations. That's common enough, even in ordinary magic. Mages often use animal blood, sometimes their own blood, too. There's power in blood. But the blood of a victim who's killed—that's only used by necromantic sorcerers in dark invocations."

"Necromantic *sorcerers*?" Jael asked. "I thought a necromancer was a necromancer."

Aubry shook his head.

"Most necromancers are content with divinations, spirit communion, and the like. The more powerful and less cautious ones may risk a deadwalk—animating corpses. But those are still minor magic in most cases. Necromantic sorcerers use death—parts of corpses, as well as the energy released by violent death—for other kinds of invocations. The blood from one murder, that would be enough for the creation of an homunculus or the summoning of a minor demon. This many victims, more taken each time—it must be some vine-rotting *big* invocation."

"What could they invoke with all that?" Jael pressed. *Demon*, she thought sickly, remembering Solly's corpse. "And if they needed that many victims for something that big, why spread out over days? Why not all at once?"

"I don't know." Aubry shrugged helplessly. "The necromancer I talked to didn't know, either, unless it's some kind of repeated invocation. Why was less left of the body each time? I don't know. Why only elves? I don't know. But now there's Solly. He's no elf, and no merchant."

"And he wasn't killed like the others." Jael hesitated. "Whatever was summoned up, could that have killed Solly?"

"I think that's likely." Aubry sighed. "From the way you described the wounds, it sounds like nothing more than a minor imp or blood demon. Still nothing to wave aside, but hardly an invocation requiring so much death. At least that's what I've been told."

Aubry reached out and took Jael's hand.

"I'm pulling my people out of Rivertown," he told her. "And I don't want you even wandering the west side of the market or Guild Row. If any of my Guild members see you there, they've got orders to bring you away, even if they've got to pick you up and carry you; understand?"

"I won't argue," Jael said, shivering. "I *saw* Solly. You couldn't give me enough Suns to poke a toe into Rivertown now. Even though I've got one to spare."

"Speaking of Suns—" Aubry glanced down at the few items on the table. "You know the custom—belongings to the finder. It's yours."

"I didn't find him." Jael looked at the gold and shivered. "I'll take the earrings. Give the money to his apprentice. I don't need it anyway."

Aubry picked up the token.

"We'll miss him," he said quietly. "Fair journey, Solly."

"Fair journey, Solly," Jael repeated. She picked up the earrings. "My ears aren't pierced. Would you do it?"

A few hours later, Jael donned one of her new tunics, gazed in the mirror, and admired the earrings sparkling in her still-smarting ears. They didn't match the necklace Urien had given her, but the gold looked warm and lovely against her bronze hair, and the green stones twinkled prettily. In her new clothing, her short curls as neatly combed as possible and jewels sparkling at throat and ear, Jael was almost satisfied with her appearance for once. As a final touch, she belted on her sword; there'd be no one to challenge her tonight, and the scabbard at her hip looked impressive. Surely Urien would be impressed, at least.

Jael waited until she was almost out of the castle before she caught one of the servants and told him to tell the High Lord and Lady that Jael would not be at supper. It was entirely possible that given the recent violence in the city, her mother and father might actually forbid her to leave, even in the carriage; better simply not to ask. That meant taking no guards with her, but Urien always sent guards with his carriage, so there should be no danger.

Urien's carriage was waiting for her outside, well guarded, as Jael had expected, but to Jael's surprise, Urien was inside it waiting for her.

"My lesser priests are at my home, purifying themselves in preparation for the Grand Summoning tomorrow," Urien apologized. "If you don't object, we'll go to the Basilisk's Eye for supper again."

"The Eye's fine," Jael smiled, more relieved than disappointed. "Mother and Father received an invitation to the Grand Summoning from Ankaras."

"From High Priest Ankaras," Urien corrected her. "I'm tentatively returning the robe to him for this ceremony. I believe he's beginning to adjust to the change in doctrine, and I think his resentment at being deprived of his station is all that prevents him from again becoming a worthy High Priest of the temple. I've allowed him to conduct most of the preparatory rituals, and I think this gesture of trust will do much to lessen his hostility toward me. The worshippers will prefer the High Priest they are familiar with to conduct the ceremony, and temple tradition discourages different priests from performing the Lesser and Grand Summonings. If all goes well, I may be able to return him to his station permanently."

"So you'll just watch?" Jael asked. "Perhaps you could sit with us and explain the ritual." She wanted to ask Urien what would happen if he was no longer needed to keep Ankaras in line, but she had a suspicion she wouldn't like that answer. Most probably he'd simply return to his home.

Urien shook his head regretfully.

"I fear my presence would be an unwelcome distraction to High Priest Ankaras, and convince him of my distrust," he said. "For the sake of the success of the Grand Summoning, I can't attend. But here's the Basilisk's Eye; let us discuss more pleasant things."

The supper was, if anything, even more sumptuous than the other time Jael had supped there.

"I hope I didn't offend you in the market," Urien apologized as soon as they were comfortably settled at the table. "I was surprised to see you there, and concerned that you had been left alone, and worried that a worshipper from the temple might see us together. I hope you can forgive me."

"If I didn't, I'd hardly be here," Jael said practically. "I was surprised to see you in the market, too."

"I suppose many nobles would simply send their servants to shop for them," Urien chuckled, "but no merchant would pass by the chance to assess the local market."

"Merchant one night, priest the next," Jael said, grinning. If Urien was interested in the market, perhaps that meant he'd stay in Allanmere in some capacity, even if he wasn't needed to run the Temple of Baaros. "Which one am I eating supper with tonight?"

"Neither," Urien said, smiling as he joined the game. "I left the priest at the temple and the merchant in the market, so tonight you're only supping with simple, secular Lord Urien.

But after supper, I thought I'd show you the temple while it's decorated for the Grand Summoning, and while all the priests are gone. I'm certain you've been wondering what the temple looks like."

Jael could hardly tell Urien that she'd already been in the temple several times.

"I'd like that," she said shyly.

Jael was surprised and pleased that Urien made no effort to hurry supper. He flirted with her, but on a comfortably light level, feeding her choice tidbits, blowing in her ear to startle her. Urien tickled Jael until she shrieked with laughter and dropped the leg of roast fowl she was holding, and Urien seized her greasy hand, slipping a bracelet around her wrist. When Jael got her breath back, she stared in amazement at a stunning gold band whorled and gemmed to match the pendant he had given her.

"I realize you mustn't wear this openly," Urien said softly. "But I wanted you to have it, nevertheless."

"It's beautiful," Jael said, tracing the intricate designs with her fingertip. "Thank you so much."

"I didn't bring the matching earrings," Urien apologized. "I thought your ears weren't pierced."

"They weren't," Jael admitted, wiping her hand and touching her earrings self-consciously. "A friend just pierced my ears today so I could wear these earrings."

"Ah, a rival for your affections?" Urien asked, frowning in mock ferocity. "I'll cut the knave in two."

"No, just a friend," Jael said, chuckling at the thought. Gods, Aubry was almost *family*. Then she sobered. "Another friend of ours was killed. These were his earrings, and I wanted to wear them."

"How sweet." Urien ran his finger around the edge of Jael's ear, making her shiver. "Then these are the rings you must wear. But I'll give you the others, and someday you may have occasion to wear them. Are you finished here? There's something at the temple I'm eager to show you."

"Yes, I'm finished," Jael said, pushing her goblet away. What in the world could there be to see at the temple? *And don't touch anything while we're there,* Jael reminded herself sternly. If she did something to ruin the Grand Summoning somehow, Ankaras could likely use that failure against Urien.

Urien seemed quieter on the carriage ride to the temple, his arm affectionately around Jael, stroking her hair as she rested her head on his shoulder. When the carriage reached the temple, however, Urien rose quickly, motioning to Jael to stay where she was.

"Wait here while I make certain none of the other priests are in the temple," he said apologetically. "I'd be giving Ankaras a sharp sword to use against me if he learned I brought an unbeliever into the temple right before the Grand Summoning. I'll only be a moment."

Jael nodded understandingly. It wouldn't do her reputation any good, either, to be seen going into the Temple of Baaros with Lord Urien.

It took Urien longer than Jael had expected to return, long enough that she had begun to worry. At last, however, he opened the door of the carriage, carrying a plain gray cloak with a hood. He handed the cloak to Jael.

"There's no one about in the temple," he said, "but there are plenty of folk in the streets. It might be best if you aren't recognized here."

Touched by his thoughtfulness, although it was as much for his benefit as hers, Jael squeezed his hand warmly and donned the cloak, pulling the hood up around her face. Urien took her hand, helping her down the steps of the carriage, and she took his proffered arm as they walked into the temple. It was rather exciting, Jael mused, to have an illicit moonlight meeting with a priest in his own temple. The carriage moved quickly away, and Jael supposed that Urien must have told the driver to return for them later.

"Come in here," Urien said, leading Jael into the main hall. "Quickly, it's almost moonrise."

The main temple was much as Jael remembered it before the Lesser Summoning, although there were more ornaments and decorations, and the ceremonial runes had not yet been drawn. Jael wondered whether the additional ornamentation was due to the importance of the Grand Summoning or the additional funds Urien had brought to the temple.

Urien led Jael to the altar, then turned her around so that she faced out to the open area where the worshippers would sit. He folded his arms around her from behind.

"What am I supposed to see?" Jael asked confused. The empty hall was silent and still.

"Just wait," Urien told her. "It should only be another moment or two."

Jael leaned back against Urien contentedly, enjoying the warmth of his arms around her. The night had turned unexpectedly chill.

Gradually Jael saw a light growing in the room, and she quickly traced its source. Set on the far wall was a window she hadn't noticed on her previous intrusions because of its small size, a window set with glass cut in facets like a gem. As the moon rose, its light touched the cut glass, then struck it fully. Jael gasped as the light shattered into a million rainbow fragments over the floor of the hall.

"Isn't it beautiful?" Urien murmured into her ear. "I found an account of the window in the early records of the building. The temple which previously occupied this building had the window set in a special way. The light only strikes it so for a short time at moonrise, and then only on certain nights of the year. The previous temple used it to mark some of their holy nights."

"It's wonderful," Jael breathed. Suddenly she had to be out there, among those jewellike lights. She unwound Urien's arms from around her and pulled him with her out of the altar area. They laughed as the lights moved slowly over their skin, marking them with diamonds of silver.

Too soon, far too soon the lights faded and died away, and Urien led her back to the inner chambers of the temple.

"When I came in to check the temple, I lit a fire," he said. "It's cool tonight, and I thought you might like some tea."

"I would," Jael agreed. "That tea that you've brought is addictive."

"As I said before, I'll have to start trading it in Allanmere," Urien chuckled. "Or at least have some brought on a regular basis."

He showed Jael to a small room that had been converted to a study of sorts. Scrolls littered the desk and a worktable, and numerous burnt-down candles were stuck to every clear surface. There were a few chairs, and a cot had been set up in one corner. A good fire was burning, and a kettle of water was already heating on a hook.

Urien motioned Jael to a chair, taking a block of tea from a box and shaving curls into the hot water. Jael craned her neck to see over the piles of scrolls.

"You must forgive the disorder," Urien said, appearing at last with a cup of tea, which he handed to Jael. "It took me some time to familiarize myself with the business of this temple. Ankaras is, at least, an extremely thorough record-keeper. Drink your tea, and I'll pour myself a cup."

Urien had sweetened the tea with honey, and its rich, fragrant taste was just what Jael craved. The hot tea made her feel pleasantly warm and tingly inside, a sensation that quickly faded, leaving Jael thirsty for more. Urien pulled a chair up beside hers, sitting down with his own cup.

"Did you enjoy my secret window?" Urien asked her.

"It was wonderful," Jael sighed. "I'm surprised all your priests weren't here to see it."

"None of them know," Urien said, smiling. "I saved that secret to share only with you."

Jael smiled to herself, feeling the warmth rush to her cheeks.

"I'm flattered," she mumbled.

"I have another secret to share with you when you're ready," Urien said tenderly, taking her hand.

Jael hurriedly gulped down the last sip of her tea, wincing as the hot liquid burned her tongue a little.

"What is it?"

"Finished already?" Urien lifted his eyebrows. "I'll make another cup to take with you. I'm going to take you to the cellar, and it's chill there even when the weather is warm." He disappeared behind the mounds of scrolls again, then reappeared with a steaming mug and lit candle. "Come along, then, and bring the cloak. As I said, it's chill there, and damp, too."

Jael draped the cloak around her shoulders and accepted the mug of tea, taking Urien's arm with her free hand. She already knew the way to the cellar stairs well enough, but let him lead her. She didn't need to feign hesitation at the top of the dark cellar stairs; a damp, dusky, unpleasant odor drifted up that Jael didn't remember being there before. The candle seemed to make no difference in that profound blackness.

"You must excuse the smell," Urien said apologetically. "I

chose to leave some of my goods in the cellars here rather than move them to my house. One of my casks of wine developed a leak and thoroughly wetted a bundle of leathers, and I'm afraid they molded badly. If the smell bothers you too much, we won't go down."

"It's all right," Jael said hurriedly. "I've smelled far worse." Indeed she had, and not long ago, either. Compared to what the castle's cellar held, the temple's cellar, however damp and smelly, must be a delightful place.

"Then be careful on the steps." Urien steadied her all the way down, as if she were made of glass.

Other than the smell, little appeared to have changed about the cellar. There were more boxes, barrels, and the like— Urien's trade goods, Jael assumed—and the thin wooden wall had been replaced with a much more solid wall, but everything else appeared the same. Jael could see, however, that the boxes had been cleared away from the area around the trapdoor set in the floor.

"What's down here?" Jael asked dubiously. "Is it something you brought with you from Calidwyn?"

"In a manner of speaking." Urien glanced at her puzzledly. "Jael, are you feeling well?"

"Hmmm?" Jael gulped down more tea to combat the damp chill of the cellar. "I'm fine. Why do you ask?"

"You seemed a little pale." Urien frowned a little. "I thought perhaps the smell was troubling you too much."

"No, it's not so bad." Jael swallowed the rest of the tea. "What did you want to show me?"

"Hmmm. Come and look." Urien stepped to the trapdoor and pulled up on the ring, lifting the heavy square of wood easily. He gestured at the opening. "See?"

Jael cautiously bent over the opening, squinting down into the darkness. Even with her keen elvan vision, she could see nothing but a steep flight of stairs leading downward, but she could hear something moving, something that seemed too large to be rats.

"I don't see much," Jael said. "But I hear—"

Sudden sharp pain flared at the back of her head, and then she saw nothing at all.

VIII

Jael felt that she was floating gently, warmly, comfortably, as she sometimes floated in the bathing pool.

"Open your eyes now," a familiar voice said. Who? Oh, Urien, of course. Jael opened her eyes. Urien was bending over her, his face drawn with worry.

"Does your head hurt much?" he asked tenderly. "I hope not. You may speak."

"Uh—no." Jael tried to sit up, but her body refused to obey her. There was a soft surface under her, and nothing seemed to be restraining her, but try as she might, she could not so much as twitch a finger. The warm, floating sensation continued, seeming to hold her. "I—I can't move."

"Yes, I know." Urien patted her cheek gently. "I'm sorry. This would have been unnecessary if the spell I placed in your tea had worked. You'd have simply slept quietly through the whole thing. But someone must have placed some elaborate protections on you. I was forced to resort to casting a spell directly while you were unconscious."

The unavoidable stupid questions flashed through Jael's mind—*how, why*—but she suspected she already knew the answers. She looked around as best she could without being able to move her head. The damp smell and cool air told her she was still in the cellar, but in a smaller room—one of the storage rooms, perhaps—and the surface she was lying on felt like a bed. That carried unpleasant suggestions.

"So what are you going to do with me?" Jael asked. "How much of me are they going to find in Rivertown?"

"Nothing." Urien stroked her hair. "Your fate won't be nearly so painful or messy."

"What, the thing in your cellar doesn't like the taste of half-breeds?" Jael asked bitterly.

"That?" Urien chuckled. "It's only a minor demon, not at all choosy. All it needs is a good quantity of blood every few days, although it's delighted with flesh when it can get it. Unfortunately it's not a neat eater."

"It's a greedy eater, if you've had to feed it half a dozen elves in two weeks," Jael told him.

Urien smiled gently.

"You're looking for an explanation," he said. "I don't mind. There's time while we finish the preparations." He began unbuttoning Jael's tunic. "I'm sorry, this must be embarrassing to you. Would you prefer to do it yourself?"

"Of course I'd rather be able to do it myself," Jael said angrily. "But I can't move."

Urien unbuckled Jael's belt and slid it off her, then briefly searched her. He drew her dagger and her sword, frowning over them.

"What curious things you carry," he said. "What sort of blades are these?" He held up the dagger and the sword.

"Gifts from Aunt Shadow, just things she got from distant places," Jael said.

"Good enough." Urien laid them aside. "Sit up, Jael. You may move, in obedience to my directions."

Jael found herself sitting. She shivered, secretly relieved that she was even able to shiver.

"Your bath has been prepared," Urien said, gesturing at a large copper bathing tub steaming nearby. "Remove your clothes and bathe."

Jael found herself obeying, flushing miserably as she dropped her clothing to the floor. She grimaced at the strange, pungent odor of the hot bathwater as she stepped into the tub.

"I hope you like this scent more than I do," she said, picking up the sponge and the soap. "It certainly doesn't put *me* in a romantic mood, any more than being whacked on the head and abducted."

"Unfortunately, you're not being prepared for me, but for my lord Eiloth," Urien said regretfully. "But it may comfort you to know that you needn't fear rape."

"That's who you've been trying to summon up?" Jael asked. "A demon, I suppose."

"Not 'a demon,' but one of the Higher Darklings," Urien corrected her. "And we had no need of summoning Lord Eiloth; in fact, it was he that called to us, brought us here from our hiding places, our waiting places. It was my friend Ankaras who summoned him—by accident, I believe. And he's never known otherwise; my lord Eiloth is a great master of seemings."

Jael scrubbed her face.

"The Lesser Summoning, I suppose."

"So I'm told," Urien agreed. "Of course, I was far away when it happened. Summoning a god is no light matter. A little carelessness can open the door to other summonings, other beings drawn to such potent magic."

Carelessness. Jael winced, doubting that carelessness had had anything to do with the failure of the summoning.

"Seemings," Jael said. "I suppose you're not really a merchant lord, any more than you're a priest of the Temple of Baaros."

"Oh, but I am a merchant lord, or I was," Urien told her. "And from Calidwyn, too, at one time. But you must have realized already that I could never have reached Allanmere from Calidwyn so quickly after the summoning, even if I walked the same slow roads over this world as other men. Lord Eiloth gave me the knowledge I would need, and brought us by another road, a quicker road, to be his eyes and his hands in this city."

"But why?" Jael found herself standing. Urien handed her a cloth, and she dried herself as slowly as she could. "You said he was already summoned."

"Lord Eiloth came through an imperfect door not meant for him," Urien told her. "The full manifestation into flesh of a Higher Darkling is a slow and difficult matter. It takes days of sequential sacrifices—"

"Elves, I suppose," Jael said, dropping the drying cloth. She blushed again, but could not raise her hands to cover herself.

Urien handed her a pot of scented oil.

"Rub this into your skin, and then I'll perfume your hair." He sat back down. "No, the sacrifices could have been elf or human, although it pleased Lord Eiloth that the elves have a little magic in them. He only required certain portions of their flesh, more each time, to build his strength for his passage into this world. It was convenient to choose elves because of the conflict already in the city. There were so many in the city who wished harm to elves—especially elvan merchants—that blame would be hard to place on anyone, especially in a place like Rivertown where death and violence were almost commonplace."

"But how did your people get the bodies there so quickly?" Jael asked as she smoothed the oil into her skin. The oil had a familiar pungent scent; Jael realized wryly that it smelled much like the ointment Urien had given her.

"In the same way that our little pet in the subcellar reached Rivertown, to prowl the alleys and claim our sacrifices," Urien said. "We made a Gate, a very small and limited Gate, between this temple and the empty house you showed me near Rivertown. I bought it the very day we saw it, and we set the Gate the next night, casting the Gate from there so the magic wouldn't be detected here. The Gate's closed now, of course. We don't need it anymore."

"Not since your 'little pet' killed Solly, the thief who found Garric and Crow," Jael said.

"Ah, the human found the bodies?" Urien asked, raising his eyebrows. "That I didn't know. That explains his curiosity, and why he'd trouble to creep into an empty house where there was obviously nothing of value to steal. He even searched the cellar, an unfortunate decision for him, as we were there that night. We didn't need another sacrifice then, so we gave him to the demon."

Urien handed Jael a dark blue robe embroidered with glyphs in silver.

"Put this on and sit down."

When Jael had obeyed, Urien lightly brushed a sweet-scented perfume into her hair.

"If you didn't need another sacrifice, what are you doing with me?" Jael asked, almost shaking with frustration as her body refused to move.

"I said we no longer needed the Gate," Urien corrected her gently. "You're the final sacrifice, the sacrifice that will give Eiloth flesh in this world. For that we needed a very special sacrifice—an uninitiated mage of noble birth and powerful family."

"And a maiden?" Jael guessed.

Urien laughed.

"Dear Jaellyn, Eiloth has no more use for your virginity than you do," he said kindly. "I'm sorry that you will die without ever knowing the pleasures of man and woman. I would gladly have shown them to you, but deflowered maidens often suffer from guilt or remorse afterward, often resulting in confiding in their mothers or fathers, and that might have had serious consequences for me. I was quite disappointed, I can assure you."

"Well, why should it matter that I'm of noble birth, then?" Jael asked, wondering how much longer she could keep Urien talking. Gods, what time of night was it? Surely someone at the castle would discover that Jael was still missing. "There must be plenty of other uninitiated mages in the city, ones whose abduction wouldn't cause such a stir in town."

"But only one who is the Heir to the ruling family of Allanmere," Urien told her. He replaced the pendant he'd given her around her neck and slipped the bracelet back over her wrist. "Hmmm. No, those earrings won't do." He carefully removed Solly's gold rings, replacing them with exquisite drops that matched the pendant.

"Our ritual will be timed carefully with the Grand Summoning Ankaras will be performing," Urien continued almost conversationally. "Sunrise isn't the most propitious time for summoning one of the Greater Darklings, but in this case it works to our advantage. At the moment Lord Eiloth manifests, he will consume you utterly, soul and mind and body together. The magic released by your death at that moment, aided by the residual magic from the summoning above us, will bring Lord Eiloth fully into this world. As I told you, Lord Eiloth is a master of seemings. When he has consumed your memories, your knowledge, he will assume your form, just as he took the seeming of Baaros for his purposes, and Jaellyn, Allanmere's Heir, will return home."

"But I'm not confirmed as the Heir," Jael argued. "In fact, it's likely that Mother and Father will choose one of the twins instead."

"There are many ways to be certain you're chosen," Urien assured her. "Those who protest the choice might die, or simply disappear. Of course, it might be simpler if the twins disappeared instead. Hopefully none of that will be necessary. I'm sure Lord Eiloth will be able to convince the High Lord and Lady that you—he—would be the best choice."

Urien walked around Jael, eyeing her critically.

"Beautiful," he said. He bent to brush her cheek with his lips.

"I wish it didn't have to be you," Urien said with a sigh. "I assure you that my feelings for you are quite genuine. But the final sacrifice must be prepared days in advance with the proper ceremonial herbs for purification, and you were the one chosen for preparation."

Jael grimaced. Of course—the tea and the ointment. Gods, how easily he'd manipulated her! A little flattery and attention, a few gifts, some pretty words, and she'd been his. Or Eiloth's, more accurately.

"But I can see this is disturbing you, as of course it would." Urien sighed again. "I'm sorry. I wanted you to sleep peacefully, die unaware. I didn't want you to suffer fear, although I'm almost certain you'll feel no pain. If you like, I'll try another sleeping potion."

Jael's mind raced. What if she asked him for some Bluebright instead? Grandma Celene had said that some potions could temporarily overcome soul-sickness, as the potion she had taken in the forest had done. If the Bluebright had made her capable of feeling desire, could it make her somehow able to change stone, as she had at the Forest Altars, or when she'd melted the mug in her room? But that had been instinctive, unconscious. She wouldn't know what to do, how to begin.

But there was one thing she *knew* she could do.

"No," she said. "I'm the High Lord and Lady's daughter. I don't want to die sleeping."

Urien smiled.

"Bravely spoken," he said. "As you choose, then. Come, my priests should have finished the preparations for the ceremony." He picked up her belongings. "Lord Eiloth will need these. Follow me, and quietly."

Jael obeyed, shivering at the cold, damp stone against her bare feet. Apparently Lord Eiloth liked his sacrifices' bodies anointed and clean, but he wasn't so particular about their feet.

Urien led her back out into the main storage area of the cellar. Dimly, Jael could hear voices from the top of the stairs—talking, not chanting, so the ritual had not yet started. Ankaras's voice was plain, demanding, and Jael was certain she could hear Tanis's softer replies. Gods, if only she could shout! She tried to concentrate on the magic muffling her voice, binding her limbs, tried to find the warm, buzzing, tickling sensation she associated with magic. Why hadn't she talked with Nubric sooner, learned to somehow *use* this thing inside her?

The trapdoor was up, and again, Jael could hear something moving. Obedient to Urien's commands, now she could not even shiver as she padded silently after him across the open area to the dark opening.

"Don't be afraid," Urien said. "What you hear is my priests preparing for the ritual. The demon is guarding the other end of the subcellar. You won't have to see it."

Sudden light startled Jael's eyes as Urien uncovered a lantern resting on a case of bottles of Bluebright. He picked up the lantern and took Jael's hand, steadying her down the steep, rather narrow stairs that curved gradually around. To Jael's surprise, as they descended the stairs, light grew ahead of them; apparently the stairs curved enough to block the light from below.

When they reached the bottom, Jael would have stopped in surprise if she could. The subcellar was huge, much larger than the cellar above; as she thought about it, Jael realized that the subcellar must extend even beyond the area of the abandoned temple. Only a small portion was lit with torches in wall sconces and tall oil lamps on stands, but the movement of the air and the echoes of every sound told her that this area must be gigantic. Jael's heart sank when she saw the oil lamps; she'd hoped that Urien would light his temple with light globes, as Ankaras did. An exploding light globe at the wrong moment might cause his ritual to fail.

Not far from the bottom of the stairs, an altar had been built of smooth stone deeply incised with runes. Jael wondered at it; had it been here already, or had Urien somehow brought it with him? Had it perhaps been magically created? Dark stains on the stone around the base of the altar made Jael think of the previous rituals that must have been performed here, but a sheet of dark blue velvet stitched with silver designs, similar to those on Jael's robe, now covered most of the altar's top. On a table past the altar, four long knives with thin, toothed blades had been pushed aside.

Urien's three lesser priests were still busy with preparations, meticulously setting out small bowls filled with powders, pastes, or oils, or chalking designs here and there on the stone floor. The acolytes were equally busy assuring that the oil lamps were full, and placing ritual candles of various colors at certain points on the chalked markings as they were completed. As soon as Urien and Jael entered the chamber, however, one of the acolytes bowed to Urien and hurried out of the lighted circle, and the others moved to stand at the opening to the stairs.

Jael had wondered how Urien planned to pace his ritual with the one far above them. She shortly had her answer as the acolyte returned from the darkness with a small crystal sphere, such as was commonly used in scrying, which he placed carefully on a stand near the head of the altar. One of the lesser priests laid his pale hands on the crystal's surface briefly, and suddenly muffled sounds emerged, and a dim, poorly focused image of the summoning nearly ready to begin above. Another of the priests stepped forward, bowing to Urien.

"Everything is prepared," the priest announced, accepting the small bundle of Jael's belongings.

"Excellent," Urien said. "Jaellyn, come here. You two, lift her up. And clean her feet."

Jael raged inwardly as the two acolytes lifted her awkwardly onto the altar, unable to struggle even slightly. The stone of the altar was cold even through the velvet, but its solidity was comforting, and Jael fought desperately to calm herself. Stone was firm and unmoving, alive only if you knew how to look deep within it. She would be stone, strong and solid and enduring. She would be stone, anchored firmly to the bones of the world.

"We begin," Urien said. "Light the candles of invocation."

I am stone, Jael thought firmly. She could not move her head, but that was all right; stone did not need to move. Out of the corner of her eye she could see the movement in the ball of crystal, hear the chanting as Ankaras began his own ritual of summoning. Her heart leaped as she saw Tanis assisting him, but she quickly turned her eyes away from the globe. She might destroy the scrying spell and cause Urien's ritual to end at the wrong time, but that was no assurance that he wouldn't succeed anyway.

Urien had begun to chant. One of the priests approached with a bowl and a brush and painted something on the palms of Jael's hands and the soles of her feet in an ink that smelled suspiciously like blood.

"Light the candles of summoning," Urien said from somewhere near Jael's feet.

Jael realized that the scrying ball had only been necessary, actually, to time the beginning of Urien's ritual. As she had in the hiding place in the main temple hall, she could feel the power of the Grand Summoning gathering even here. A similar power was gathering in this hidden temple, slowly eclipsing the awareness of magic from above, and Jael's heart pounded as she tried to focus her concentration on Urien's spell, listen to each word, to feel the magical energies he was calling to him. She ached with frustration because she could not see him.

Something was beginning to disturb the air over Jael, as if a slight breeze blew there. A priest stepped to the head of the altar and turned Jael's face to the other side, and now she was staring directly into the crystal. Ankaras was standing before the altar, his arms raised as he began the final chant of the summoning, but the image was dim and vague.

Time to try.

Jael stared as intently as she could into the crystal, trying to feel the energy of Ankaras's spell, trying to focus more clearly on him. If she could yank a summoning off course once before, she *could* do it again. Gods, if only there was more light, if only she could see him more clearly! This time she'd yank it so far off course that—

The scrying globe flared with light, then went black. Urien's chant faltered for only a moment, then continued, and Jael could have screamed with despair as the priest quietly turned her head back upright. Now the disturbance above her was more visible, like a cloud of oily smoke, just as she'd seen at the Lesser Summoning, but concentrate as she might, Urien's ritual was proceeding smoothly, the cloud growing more solid. Now she could see something like features in one part of the cloud.

Jael tried to ignore the forming image and focus only on Urien's words, on the ticklish awareness of magic inside her. Gods, why was it that she could ruin every spell when she *didn't* try, and couldn't send one spell awry when she *tried*?

Because maybe I'm trying the wrong way.

She'd never deliberately tried to cause a spell to fail until she'd gone to the cellars with her mother, and then she'd been too queasy to do anything but touch the corpses and hope it would work. Even in Nubric's workroom, she'd hoped that his spells would somehow succeed, that he would find some clue toward solving this problem of hers.

All right, then.

I'm stone, Jael thought again. *I don't want to move. I don't want to speak. I want to lie here perfectly still, like stone, and this spell Urien's cast over me feels warm and nice, like a blanket against the cold. I like it.*

Nothing.

"Light the candles of admission," Urien commanded.

How nice it feels, like floating in the bathing pool, Jael thought firmly. *Soothing, relaxing, making me feel safe and warm and—*

Then the warmth was gone. Jael moved her fingers once experimentally, and a shock of joy ran through her. It was all she could do to keep herself from leaping off the altar and shouting triumphantly.

No sense in that. I couldn't get far enough away, not with the acolytes guarding the way out. Jael forced herself to lie still. The image above her was almost complete now, and she could see a face clearly, beautiful and terrible, and eyes, eyes that drew and yet repelled, eyes that tugged at her soul, made her want to give herself—

"The door is open, Lord," Urien said triumphantly. "Pass through and be whole."

All right, Jael thought grimly, staring into those eyes, letting them draw her. *If you want me, Eiloth, I'm all yours. Body, mind, and soul—and especially soul.*

The figure above her reached for her, and quickly curling to gather her legs under her, Jael leaped as high as she could to meet it. For a moment her fingers clasped something, something not quite as solid as flesh—

—than an unearthly scream shook the world, and another, and another, and Jael felt her hands now grasping nothing but smoke. She fell, and this time stone was not her friend; she crashed awkwardly, striking the edge of the altar with her shoulder, and lay where she landed, all the breath driven out of her lungs and her head spinning. One of the oil lamps crashed over, and there was another terrible scream. A priest in a burning robe ran past.

Jael lifted her head and her vision cleared. Urien had fallen to his knees only a few feet away, his head and shoulders enveloped in the same oily smoke Jael had seen earlier. His body was shaking violently, his scream fading. One priest lay dead on the floor beside him. Jael could not see the other priest, but from the dark area beyond the lamps she could hear the gruesome, wet sounds of something feeding.

Jael forced herself to her knees, glancing frantically around to see where the priest had laid her belongings. There! Using the altar to pull herself to her feet, Jael stumbled over, picking up her sword and sliding it out of its scabbard. She had to use the altar to steady herself as she walked back.

Urien's screams had faded to a whisper now. The oily cloud was gone, but Urien's features were changing, melting like the wax of a candle, re-forming slowly. His eyes snapped open.

Jael hurriedly looked away from those eyes and raised the sword.

Just a practice pole, she thought, and struck. There was a brief resistance; then her sword was free. Hot liquid spattered her legs, and Urien's head thumped wetly to the floor, the melting features becoming still.

Jael felt her gorge rising, but then she remembered—there were still the acolytes. She turned as quickly as her dizzy head would allow, but the acolytes were gone, whether they had dissolved into the air or merely fled up the stairs.

That left only the demon, and Jael, still shaking, had no illusions that she would survive a second encounter with it. Listening to make certain that the ugly feeding sounds still continued, Jael quickly retrieved the rest of her possessions and hurried toward the stairs. She'd just have to retreat back through the temple, block the trapdoor so the demon couldn't get out, and send some of the City Guard to finish here.

Footsteps sounded on the stairs, rapidly approaching. Jael quickly flattened herself against the wall, sword ready, only to slump against the stone in relief as Tanis emerged, followed closely by Donya, Argent, and the twins, all in full regalia.

"There you are!" Donya said angrily, seizing Jael's shoulders. Her anger evaporated instantly as she saw the blood spattering Jael's robe and the dripping blade in Jael's hand. "Are you hurt? What's—" She stared over Jael's shoulder and her eyes went wide; before Jael could react, Donya wrenched the sword from her fingers and threw Jael behind her. Tanis caught Jael before she could knock everyone off their feet.

The demon had obviously finished with the priest. Spattered with gore, it squatted just outside of sword range, its eyes darting from one to the other as if contemplating which might make the choicest morsel.

"All of you, back up the stairs," Donya said, her voice steady. "Markus, Mera, you guard those robed men we caught and send the guards back down, and send for a mage who can perform a banishment. Argent, you guard the trapdoor and be ready to close it if anything tries to come up that isn't me. Jael, you and—whatever your name is—"

"Uh-uh," Jael said, swallowing heavily but not moving. She drew her dagger. "I'm staying with you."

Tanis glanced disgustedly down at his ceremonial robes, looked quickly around, and pulled one of the torches from its sconce.

"Then I'm staying, too," he said, his voice shaking.

"Don't be foolish," Donya snapped, striking at the demon as it stepped forward. The demon batted at the sword, but retreated a pace. "You can't kill a demon with ordinary weapons."

"Then what are you doing with my sword?" Jael panted, wondering if the dagger was too light for a throw. With her skill, she'd probably miss anyway.

The demon darted forward again, and this time Donya struck true; the sword buried itself halfway in the demon's gut and then pulled free. A little bluish ichor trickled out and the demon roared with anger, retreating a few steps, but it seemed otherwise unharmed.

"Keeping it back until we can get a mage down here," Donya replied, advancing and forcing the creature back a little farther. "Which I could do much more effectively, Jaellyn, if you'd do as you were told and leave."

"What about fire?" Tanis suggested, swinging the torch feebly in the direction of the demon.

The demon roared and leaped forward, swatting at the torch and Tanis with all four arms. Tanis screamed and went flying backward, blood flowing freely from five deep gashes in his shoulder. Without thinking, Jael struck, burying the dagger to the hilt in the creature's belly as she leaped away. At the same time, Donya wheeled and brought the sword flashing down, and the demon roared with rage as its severed arm dropped to the stone floor, claws still flexing.

Five guards appeared in the stairway. They froze momentarily at the sight of the demon, but quickly moved forward to stand beside Donya, helping her to keep the demon back from the stairs.

"Jael, take your friend and get out of here!" Donya shouted, forcing the demon back away from the stairs again. "There's nothing you can do!"

But was there?

Jael hurried to Tanis's side and helped him to his feet, supporting most of his weight as they staggered up the stairs. Argent was waiting at the top, and he quickly helped Tanis away from the trapdoor.

"What's happening down there?" he asked anxiously. "Is Donya all right?"

"So far," Jael answered, snatching one of the bottles of Bluebright from the case. "The guards are helping her. I've got to go back down."

"Jaellyn—" Argent reached out to stop her, but Jael ducked under his arm and half fell, half ran down the stairs. As soon as she reached the bottom, she pulled the stopper out of the Bluebright and gulped down two large mouthfuls.

There was no warning, no pleasant drifting; this time the Bluebright hit her like a paving stone in the gut. Jael gasped as her legs went limp under her, huddling on the floor against the wall.

Some potions, Mist had said, could temporarily stop the effects of soul-sickness. The dreaming potion she'd taken in the forest had allowed her to melt a good-sized hole in one of the Forest Altars, but that wasn't the only time she'd done it; after a dose of Bluebright, she'd unconsciously melted her drinking mug into an unrecognizable lump. Could she do it consciously? Jael didn't know, but with Mother and the guards facing a demon, there was nothing to do but try.

Suddenly the battle between her mother, the guards, the demons all seemed very far away, moving with incredible slowness and clarity. Jael marveled at that for a precious moment, then laid both hands flat against the stone of the floor and closed her eyes.

This time stone seemed to welcome her, and she let it draw her down into its cool, sheltering strength. Nothing would pull her back this time. She could feel the feet of her mother, the guards', the demon's, like gentle taps against her skin— her mother's fancy slippers, sliding somewhat on the damp floor; the hard boots of the guards, and—there, the scaly heat of the demon's feet.

Until a mage comes, Jael thought almost gaily, *it's time, as Uncle Mist would say, to put down roots.*

She was stone, and stone opened to accept its prisoner.

Jael sighed with satisfaction and let the Bluebright carry her away to dreams of stone, and peace.

"Jael." Argent was shaking her, and Jael opened her eyes. The High Lord was bending over her, smiling.

Jael rubbed her eyes.

"Is the demon gone?" she asked confusedly.

"Not yet, but Jermyn is on the way," Argent reassured her. "It will do no harm, though, being sunk up to its eyes in the floor."

"Oh, that's good," Jael smiled, utterly relaxed. "And Mother? She's all right?"

"She's well enough, if rather angry," Argent chuckled. "Look." He moved out of her way.

Donya and the guards stood where Jael had last seen them. Donya and one of the guards bore a few scratches, testimony to the demon's ferocity and speed, but appeared otherwise unharmed.

They were behaving, however, in a most unusual fashion, jerking at their legs and cursing. Jael was most impressed at her mother's considerable vocabulary of obscenities.

"Mother?" she called. "What's the matter?"

Donya twisted awkwardly to face her daughter, taking a deep breath to calm herself.

"Whatever you did to make the floor swallow up the demon, I'm impressed," the High Lady of Allanmere said slowly. "But could you please possibly make the floor let go of our feet?"

Jael started to stand, then gasped in surprise. She had sunk into the stone so deeply that it had flowed over the tops of her thighs, trapping her where she was.

"What's the matter?" Donya called. "Are your feet stuck, too?"

"Not exactly," Jael said, blushing.

IX

"I must admit, I've never seen stonemasons find such amusement in their work," Argent chuckled, tying the last bandage into place. "There, Tanis. That should keep you comfortable enough while you mend. It's a pity that demon-inflicted wounds can't be healed more quickly. But you'll stay here at the castle, tended by our healers, until you're completely well."

"Thank you, High Lord," Tanis said, grinning ruefully. "I suppose the soreness will remind me of the idiocy of facing a demon while armed with nothing but a torch."

"Or maybe remind you of the bravery of a true friend," Jael added, hugging him as best she could without causing him pain.

"You were the one who was brave, and clever, too," Tanis protested. "We'd never have known where you were, or what was happening, if you hadn't warned us as you did."

"It wasn't intentional," Jael said, thoroughly embarrassed. "I thought I'd simply broken the scrying spell on the crystal."

"When we received your message and you didn't come home, we thought—" Donya shook her head. "Well, we thought you were with Lord Urien, and we were surprised and worried when we didn't see you in the temple the next morning." She chuckled. "But when every light globe in the temple exploded in the middle of the ritual, we knew you had to be somewhere nearby."

"I guess I can't say I'm sorry I ruined Ankaras's summoning," Jael admitted, "since that was what I was trying to do. But I'm sorry he's decided to close the temple in Allanmere. It wasn't his fault, not really."

"It's best that he leaves," Argent said firmly. "Even though he actually had no involvement with the murders, he was helping Urien, however inadvertently, by his involvement with the anti-elvan factions in Allanmere. Were it not for the conflict within the city which he helped to create, it might have been possible to discover the source of the problem sooner. As it was, his sympathies with the Dyers' Guild and other disruptive factions made it simple for Urien to make him a scapegoat for our suspicions and to confuse our investigations. Jermyn's divinations using Solly's body revealed the location of the Gate in the house near Rivertown, but by then the Gate was closed, and Urien had even purchased the house in Ankaras's name, although we didn't learn that until afterward."

"Tanis and I made the same mistake," Jael admitted, sighing. "If I hadn't been so ready to believe Ankaras was behind all of it, I might not have been so eager to believe everything Urien told me."

"We all believed him," Tanis said disgustedly. "Even Ankaras. And now that rumors are linking the Temple of Baaros with the murders, I don't think even bringing in another High Priest could save it."

"What will you do?" Jael asked unhappily. "Go back to Loroval?"

Tanis grinned and shook his head.

"I believe the priesthood's too dangerous for me," he said. "I think I'll go see if the Thieves' Guild has room for another apprentice. If they'll leave me enough free time for my other lessons, that is. After all this, my family shouldn't complain too loudly."

"I think the Guildmaster will take you, if I ask him nicely," Jael grinned back. "But what other lessons?"

"Oh, things like digging firepits and gutting fish," Tanis

said casually. "If I can find someone to teach me, that is. I may not have too many months to learn."

"You can't learn thievery in a few months," Donya told him. "It takes time and patience."

"I'm a patient fellow," Tanis said, but his smile was meant for Jael.

"And you." Donya rounded on Jael. "Next time you're feeling inquisitive about something going on in Allanmere, Jaellyn, you remember who the law is in this city, and it isn't you. And after your involvement in this business is rumored from one end of the city to the other, it's never likely to be you, either. I imagine even the elves are going to start looking favorably at Markus over someone who gets into this much trouble. I'd half believe you did it on purpose."

"Yes, Mother," Jael said humbly, but she chuckled to herself.

"Oh, don't smile, young woman," Donya said sternly. "I'm half of a mind to set you to shoveling in the stables for a week, just in revenge for putting me up against a demon wearing slippers and finery and that damned light sword."

"But you were wonderful," Jael said quickly. "Even in slippers and finery and my sword that's 'too damned light.' "

"Well." Donya's mouth twitched at the corners. "Perhaps I'll just beat you head to foot at our next sword lesson, then. Or lock you in a room full of light globes."

Jael cowered in mock fear.

"Not that! Please, not that!"

"Enough," Argent said mildly. "Donya, shall we leave the city's newest apprentice thief to his rest?"

Donya glanced from Jael to Tanis and sighed.

"All right," she said, shaking her head. "Priests and thieves," she muttered as she followed Argent out of the room.

"Your mother is right, though," Tanis said more seriously when Donya and Argent were gone. "Even if your parents declare Markus as Heir, that won't make some of the folk feel any more kindly toward 'Jael the Unlucky.' "

Jael shrugged resignedly, removing the gold drops from her ears and slipping Solly's gold rings back in.

"When you walk the dagger's edge, you've got to have good balance," she said, gazing down at the earrings in her hand. "I'm not the only one in the city who slips sometimes. And then you likely end up with—"

"A broken heart?" Tanis said gently, squeezing Jael's hand.

"No, nothing so serious as that," Jael said, sighing. She dropped the earrings into her pocket, then turned back to Tanis and smiled.

"Just sore feet."

Shadow Novels from
ANNE LOGSTON

Shadow is a master thief as elusive as her name. Only her dagger is as sharp as her eyes and wits. Where there's a rich merchant to rob, good food and wine to be had, or a lusty fellow to kiss...there's Shadow.

"Spiced with magic and intrigue..."—Simon R. Green
"A highly entertaining fantasy."—*Locus*

__SHADOW	0-441-75989-0/$3.99
__SHADOW DANCE	0-441-75990-4/$4.99
__SHADOW HUNT	0-441-30273-4/$4.50
__DAGGER'S EDGE	0-441-00036-3/$4.99

And don't miss other Anne Logston adventures...

__GREENDAUGHTER	0-441-30273-4/$4.50

Deep within the Mother Forest, Chyrie, an elf with the gift of animal-speaking, must embrace the human world to fend off barbarian invaders,...and save both worlds.

Payable in U.S. funds. No cash orders accepted. Postage & handling: $1.75 for one book, 75¢ for each additional. Maximum postage $5.50. Prices, postage and handling charges may change without notice. Visa, Amex, MasterCard call 1-800-788-6262, ext. 1, refer to ad # 463

Or, check above books and send this order form to:	Bill my: ☐ Visa ☐ MasterCard ☐ Amex	
The Berkley Publishing Group	Card#_____	(expires)
390 Murray Hill Pkwy., Dept. B		
East Rutherford, NJ 07073	Signature_____	($15 minimum)
Please allow 6 weeks for delivery.	Or enclosed is my: ☐ check ☐ money order	
Name_____	Book Total $_____	
Address_____	Postage & Handling $_____	
City_____	Applicable Sales Tax $_____ (NY, NJ, PA, CA, GST Can.)	
State/ZIP_____	Total Amount Due $_____	

"Redwall is both a credible and
ingratiating place, one to which readers
will doubtless cheerfully return."
—New York Times Book Review

BRIAN JACQUES

SALAMANDASTRON
—— A Novel of Redwall ——

"The Assassin waved his claws in the air. In a trice
the rocks were bristling with armed vermin behind him.
They flooded onto the sands of the shore and stood like
a pestilence of evil weeds sprung there by magic: line
upon line of ferrets, stoats, weasels, rats and foxes.
Banners of blood red and standards decorated their
skins, hanks of beast hair and skulls swayed in the light
breeze.
    The battle for Salamandastron was under way...."
—excerpted from Salamandastron

0-441-00031-2/$4.99

Payable in U.S. funds. No cash orders accepted. Postage & handling: $1.75 for one book, 75¢
for each additional. Maximum postage $5.50. Prices, postage and handling charges may
change without notice. Visa, Amex, MasterCard call 1-800-788-6262, ext. 1, refer to ad # 484

Or, check above books   Bill my: ☐ Visa   ☐ MasterCard ☐ Amex
and send this order form to: (expires)
The Berkley Publishing Group   Card#_____
390 Murray Hill Pkwy., Dept. B   ($15 minimum)
East Rutherford, NJ 07073   Signature_____
Please allow 6 weeks for delivery.   Or enclosed is my: ☐ check ☐ money order

Name_____   Book Total $_____

Address_____   Postage & Handling $_____

City_____   Applicable Sales Tax $_____
                                   (NY, NJ, PA, CA, GST Can.)
State/ZIP_____   Total Amount Due $_____

<u>NEW YORK TIMES</u> BESTSELLING AUTHOR

___ ANNE McCAFFREY ___

__THE ROWAN   0-441-73576-2/$5.99

"A reason for rejoicing!" —<u>WASHINGTON TIMES</u>

As a little girl, the Rowan was one of the strongest Talents ever born. When her family's home was suddenly destroyed she was completely alone without family, friends-or love. Her omnipotence could not bring her happiness...but things change when she hears strange telepathic messages from an unknown Talent named Jeff Raven.

__DAMIA   0-441-13556-0/$5.99

Damia is unquestionably the most brilliant of the Rowan's children, with power equaling—if not surpassing—her mother's. As she embarks on her quest, she's stung by a vision of an impending alien invasion—an invasion of such strength that even the Rowan can't prevent it. Now, Damia must somehow use her powers to save a planet under seige.

__DAMIA'S CHILDREN 0-441-00007-X/$5.99

They inherited remarkable powers of telepathy, and their combined abilities are even greater than those of their legendary mother. But Damia's children will need more than psionic Talent to face the enemy's children—an alien race more insect than human.

Payable in U.S. funds. No cash orders accepted. Postage & handling: $1.75 for one book, 75¢ for each additional. Maximum postage $5.50. Prices, postage and handling charges may change without notice. Visa, Amex, MasterCard call 1-800-788-6262, ext. 1, refer to ad # 363

Or, check above books Bill my: ☐ Visa ☐ MasterCard ☐ Amex	
and send this order form to:	(expires)
The Berkley Publishing Group	Card#_____
390 Murray Hill Pkwy., Dept. B	($15 minimum)
East Rutherford, NJ 07073	Signature_____
Please allow 6 weeks for delivery.	Or enclosed is my: ☐ check ☐ money order
Name_____	Book Total $_____
Address_____	Postage & Handling $_____
City_____	Applicable Sales Tax $_____ (NY, NJ, PA, CA, GST Can.)
State/ZIP_____	Total Amount Due $_____

Captivating Fantasy by

ROBIN McKINLEY

Newbery Award-winning Author
"McKinley knows her geography of fantasy . . . the
atmosphere of magic." —Washington Post

__ **THE OUTLAWS OF SHERWOOD** 0-441-64451-1/$4.99
"In the tradition of T.H. White's reincarnation of King Arthur,
a novel that brings Robin Hood delightfully to life!" —Kirkus

__ **THE HERO AND THE CROWN** 0-441-32809-1/$4.99
"Transports the reader into the beguiling realm of
pageantry and ritual where the supernatural is never far
below the surface of the ordinary."
—New York Times Book Review

__ **THE BLUE SWORD** 0-441-06880-4/$4.99
The beginning of the story of the Kingdom of Damar
which is continued in The Hero and the Crown, when the
girl-warrior Aerin first learned the powers that would make
her a legend for all time.

__ **THE DOOR IN THE HEDGE** 0-441-15315-1/$4.99
Walk through the door in the hedge and into the lands
of faerie—a world more beautiful, and far more
dangerous, than the fairy tales of childhood.

Payable in U.S. funds. No cash orders accepted. Postage & handling: $1.75 for one book, 75¢
for each additional. Maximum postage $5.50. Prices, postage and handling charges may
change without notice. Visa, Amex, MasterCard call 1-800-788-6262, ext. 1, refer to ad # 258

| Or, check above books | Bill my: | ☐ Visa | ☐ MasterCard | ☐ Amex | |
| and send this order form to: | | | | | (expires) |

The Berkley Publishing Group   Card#_____

390 Murray Hill Pkwy., Dept. B   ($15 minimum)

East Rutherford, NJ 07073   Signature_____

Please allow 6 weeks for delivery.   Or enclosed is my: ☐ check   ☐ money order

Name_____   Book Total $_____

Address_____   Postage & Handling $_____

City_____   Applicable Sales Tax $_____
                                                                (NY, NJ, PA, CA, GST Can.)
State/ZIP_____   Total Amount Due $_____